Praise for *Maybe Meant to Be* (formerly titled *If We Were Us*)

"Gripping… Entertainingly depicts mature views on life, friendship, and romance."

— *Kirkus Reviews*

"An excellent choice for most YA collections, this will be welcomed by fans of Becky Albertalli's *Simon vs. the Homo Sapiens Agenda* and Molly Backes's *The Princesses of Iowa*."

— *School Library Journal*

Praise for *The Summer of Broken Rules*

"[It's] a rose-tinted romance that readers will want to toss into a beach tote for some relaxing, enjoyable fun."

— *The Bulletin of the Center for Children's Books*

"The mix of budding romance, competitive hijinks, a close-knit circle, as well as dealing with loss, make for a satisfying read."

— *Kirkus Reviews*

"[A]n engaging read… Recommended for larger collections with dedicated romance readers."

— *School Library Journal*

"[I]deally suited for those who enjoy contemporary romance…a perfect summer or beach read!"

— Andrea Reid, *The Nerd Daily*

"Seamlessly weaves in the importance of family, and by the end, I felt like I had joined the Fox family and their traditions…a quick and easy read recommended for anyone who is looking for a lighthearted book sprinkled with elements of reality."

— Sachi Sharma, *Manhattan Book Review*

Praise for *What Happens After Midnight*

"A complete delight! This is a swoony second chance love story intertwined with a comedy of errors, performed by a lovable, vivid ensemble."

— Samantha Markum, author of *This May End Badly*

~ What ~
HAPPENS
~ After ~
MIDNIGHT

Also by K. L. Walther

Maybe Meant to Be (formerly titled *If We Were Us*)
The Summer of Broken Rules

What HAPPENS After MIDNIGHT

K. L. WALTHER

Published by Sourcebooks Fire, an imprint of Sourcebooks
P.O. Box 4410, Naperville, Illinois 60567–4410
(630) 961-3900
sourcebooks.com

Cataloging-in-Publication data is on file with the Library of Congress.

Printed and bound in the United States of America.
VP 12 11

Tibble Twins:
How many times did he tell us this story?
How many times did we laugh?
This one's for us.

BEFORE

ONE

Fears are meant to be faced. I just didn't expect to be facing one of mine this early in the morning. Perhaps later in the day, but before 8:00 a.m.? I could barely keep my eyes open as I yawned my way down the stairs and found my mom in the kitchen. She was eyeing the far corner cautiously, as if in a standoff with the espresso machine that sat on the soapstone countertop. "It's time." She glanced at me. Her mouth was almost a straight line, but one corner had tugged up with optimism. "We have to try."

"No, we don't," I quickly said. "We don't have to *try* anything."

My mom turned and held up the Tupperware of biscotti Mrs. DeLuca had gifted us yesterday. Our neighbor was the one who'd passed down the espresso machine in the first place; she'd bought a bigger one but hadn't wanted to get rid of the original. It was still in perfect working condition—supposedly. We'd never used it. "Lily, we must," she said. "Mrs. DeLuca specifically said that the biscotti is best when dipped in a cappuccino."

I considered the golden-brown almond biscuits. Truthfully,

they did look magnifico…and I *was* hungry. "Ah, okay," I conceded. "Let's give it a go."

Grinning, my mom hugged the Tupperware and pointed to our stainless-steel Starbucks situation. "I think the directions are somewhere in the lower cabinet."

That was my cue. My mom's strengths included storing leftovers inside the refrigerator, using the microwave, and switching on the teakettle. We'd both agreed it was best if she stuck with those. This was *my* kitchen, so naturally the cappuccinos were to be my area of expertise.

I found the car manual-sized instructions and the unopened bag of coffee beans before moving to the machinery. *A cappuccino is two-thirds milk*, I reminded myself, examining the steam wand. *A shot of espresso and then steamed milk with a frothy finish.*

Barely coffee!

Because the thing was, my mom and I didn't like coffee. We didn't like it *at all*.

My mom had disappeared upstairs to change out of her pajamas but was back by the time I had finished grinding the beans. The kitchen had been engulfed by the smell of espresso, and I gestured at her outfit through the pungent smog. "It'll never be fair that you get to wear that."

While I was stuck in a sundress and my school blazer, she sported purple camo leggings and a breezy lilac shirt. The perfect model for Lululemon, especially when she dramatically jutted out her hip. "Well, you know I'm hopping on my Peloton after first period," she teased and gave her long hair a nice fluff. I absentmindedly did the same to mine, only it was wavy and shockingly red instead of curly blond. You could spot me from a mile away. My guess was I'd gotten it from my father, but I'd never asked. He had no idea I existed, which was fine by me. He wasn't *missing* from my life; he just wasn't a part of it. And I didn't imagine I would ever need him to be. I had my mom.

"Nice nail polish," I added dryly. My mom's flip-flops showed off ten periwinkle-painted toes. Why students had a firm dress code but faculty did not was something I would never understand. "Where'd you get it?"

"Oh, from my favorite little boutique," she replied with a wink and a smile. "It's not very far from here. Just upstairs, actually..."

I rolled my eyes but maintained my barista bravado. The espresso brewed without incident, and after grabbing the milk from the fridge, I successfully steamed it into a puffy white cloud.

"Do we dunk first?" she asked after I'd poured the cappuccinos into two mugs. "Or sip?"

We decided to sip.

"Pinkies up," my mom said, and on an unspoken count of three, we raised the mugs to our lips.

"Coffee..." I soon rasped with a burnt tongue. "It's *still* coffee!"

Nose wrinkled, my mom dumped her cappuccino in the sink and waved me over to do the same. "Tea," she finally said. "We'll make tea tonight and soak the biscotti in that?"

"Deal." I nodded. "Now how about an *actual* breakfast?" I crossed the kitchen and opened the refrigerator, where two mason jars sat front and center. "I made overnight oats for us last night," I said. "I think my maple syrup-peanut butter-banana slice ratio is really coming along, and I added chia seeds this time too."

My mother considered. "I'm more in the mood for a short stack today," she admitted. "May I take those for a snack later?"

I sighed and shook my head as I handed her a jar but smirked when I raced upstairs to grab my backpack. If she wanted pancakes, we had to hurry.

Half a minute later, we hustled out the door, both weighed down by schoolwork. The sound of the sea said good morning, and I couldn't help but close my eyes and inhale the briny scent. Our house—a white clapboard cottage with dark-green shutters—might've been on the very edge of the faculty neighborhood, but it had its perks. My backyard being a beach was one of them. I had been falling asleep to the Atlantic Ocean's rolling waves for sixteen years now, ever since I was two. I'd practically lived my whole life on the Rhode Island coast. Or more specifically, I had always lived *here*, at the Ames School.

"Hello, Hopper ladies!" someone called as we speed walked through the neighborhood, my mom's flip-flops slapping against the pavement and my ballet flats warning me my day would end with blisters. "Beautiful morning, isn't it?"

"Gorgeous!" my mom called back to Penny Bickford,

who was walking toward the main campus in one of her chic power suits. I caught her assessing my mother's athleisure wear, but Ames's head of school said nothing. She never did because my mom was the most beloved teacher in the English department—maybe even the whole school since the yearbook's superlatives did not lie. Favorite teacher? That title wasn't up for grabs. Ames's Almanacs hadn't come out yet, but with only twelve days left before graduation, they would soon and everyone knew Leda Hopper was a lock.

And as her daughter, I was fortunate to be a student here. If tuition wasn't free for faculty members' children—or "fac brats" as most people called us—we never could've afforded a prep school like Ames.

"Congratulations again, Lily," my headmaster said with a proud smile. She'd known me so long that she treated me like a granddaughter. "I'm sure your speech will be marvelous."

"Thank you." I smiled back but felt my cheeks warm. Last week at our all-school meeting, I had been announced as this year's salutatorian. It was an honor, but I was also dreading it. Because while the valedictorian had the main stage at graduation, the salutatorian spoke at the senior class dinner the night before and was supposed to give a humorous address instead of a serious speech. The goal was to make your fellow alumni-to-be *laugh*.

I wasn't exactly known for my stand-up comedy routines.

"Okay, be cool, be cool," my mom stage-whispered once

we'd crossed the covered bridge that led to campus. We slowed our pace to a casual walk. Beautiful brick, clapboard, and cedar-shingled academic buildings and dormitories rose in front of us, and students were everywhere. Some were on their morning runs while others had clearly just rolled out of bed to drag themselves over to the dining hall for breakfast. I overheard a group of girls giggling about their upcoming freshman formal.

"Yeah, Ross asked me last night," one girl said. "It was super sweet. He asked for help on our math homework, and under the final question, he wrote 'Will you go to formal with me?'"

"Good for you, Ross," my mom murmured, smiling. Her students didn't just talk to her about grammar and *The Great Gatsby*. She had a way with them, a way that encouraged them to truly open up to her. Insisting they call her by her first name instead of "Ms. Hopper" was always an effective first step. She was a beyond-tough grader, but they adored her.

The freshmen soon noticed us. "Leda, guess what?!" they shrieked, and while she got all the exciting details, I pretended to listen along but really thought back to my own freshman formal. He'd called me, introduced himself as if we weren't already acquainted, and then asked if I wanted to go with him in a nervous rush of words. "Yes, that would be nice," I'd replied, and several weeks later, my gold dress had been splashed with salt water and sand by the end of the night. While walking me home, he'd raced me barefoot along the beach and I'd kissed him as soon as he'd caught me up in his arms. His lips had been warm despite the wind. "Tag," I remembered whispering afterward, my smile so wide. Both of us were breathless.

"You're it," he finished for me, then laughed before I kissed him again and took off into the darkness, hoping he would follow.

I wish we could go back, I thought, the words a murmur in my mind. *I wish we could go back to the very first night…*

"Lily?" I blinked to see my mom looking at me. The freshmen were gone; they must've migrated toward the dining hall, but we hadn't strayed from our route to the historic Hubbard Hall. My mom held the door open and ruffled my hair as I walked through it.

With soaring white columns, distinguished brick chimneys, and innumerable windows, Hubbard Hall looked like a mansion that once belonged to the last great American dynasty. It had a rooftop balcony and housed the Alumni Relations, Financial Aid, and College Counseling departments on the upper floors, but Ames's student center ruled the ground floor. Leather couches and wing-backed armchairs and an array of Persian rugs created a lounge-like lobby, and every time you looked at the cream walls, you noticed something new. There was a rotating gallery of student artwork and Ames memorabilia from the library's archives: old newspaper articles, photographs, and even antique school flags.

Beyond the lounge, the hall's huge limestone fireplace was flanked by built-in bookcases and study nooks. To the left were the newspaper and yearbook offices and the mail room, and to the right was what everyone simply called "the Hub." The little restaurant was the student center's main attraction. Vintage nautical lanterns hung over each booth, and the white beadboard walls held an impressive collection of black-and-white photos featuring generations of fishermen showing off their catches.

Oh, and the mouthwatering diner food. Everyone was always trying to squeeze in a quick bite between classes or during their free periods.

But only seniors and faculty were allowed to eat breakfast here. We pushed through the door to find the place packed. "Well, it's a good thing I made special arrangements," my mom said, leading me to a table in the back. I'd wager it was only empty because of a folded piece of paper that read, RESERVED!

My mother plucked it off the warm wooden table and slipped it in her tote bag, but the Hub's head honcho was on us the second we got comfortable in our teak chairs. "Reservations are not allowed," Josh said, all deadpan with a pencil tucked behind his ear.

"I will have cinnamon roll pancakes," my mother replied brightly. "Please do not skimp on the vanilla frosting."

Josh gave her a look. "Leda."

She tilted her head and smiled. "Josh."

I glanced around the Hub, not interested in listening to my mother and her boyfriend flirt today. It would sound like bickering to anyone else, but Leda was the ray of sunshine to

Josh's seriousness. Any true romantic would agree that they were a perfect match.

Half the boys' lacrosse team had jammed themselves into a booth and were rehashing their recent playoff loss, cradling invisible balls in their invisible sticks. At the next table over, Zoe Wright caught my eye and threw up her arms. *You lost!* she mouthed. *Get over it!*

I smiled and shook my head, then spotted Tag Swell and Alex Nguyen sitting together at the counter. Alex was talking a mile a minute and taking colossal bites of his waffles while Tag strategically squirted ketchup all over his scrambled eggs.

Gross, I thought but continued to watch him with a pang in my stomach. He liked putting ketchup on everything.

"But like, are you *sure*?" Alex said. "Because…"

I rolled my eyes. They were most likely talking about Tag's latest breakup. He and Blair Greenberg had gotten together last year, and their relationship had been a feast for the hypothetical tabloids. One second, they were stupidly in love, and the next, they were a hot mess, shouting at each other during Saturday night dances. The student body had been pretty much over the whole song and dance until Tag broke things off with Blair yesterday. "Who cares anymore?" we'd mumbled to ourselves, but the truth was, everyone cared. We all wanted to know what went down between them. Would this be the last time? The final time they went their separate ways? Or would they get back together in a couple days?

Because again, it was the tail end of Ames's "senior spring." With less than two weeks left in the term, we upperclassmen cared about approximately three things.

The prom was one of them.

And Tag Swell had dumped his girlfriend right beforehand, with no apparent rhyme or reason. "Yes, I'm sure," he told Alex now. "I want to go with someone else."

Who? I wondered at the same time as Alex said, "Who?"

Tag finally put down the ketchup bottle. "Well, isn't it obvious?" He smirked at his best friend. "You, Alexander."

Alex didn't miss a beat; he raised his water glass in a toast. "It'd be my pleasure, Taggart. How do you feel about matching boutonnieres?"

A small lump formed in my throat. Tag and Alex's bromance was one for the books; they were so close that sometimes they seemed like the same person. "We met in freshman algebra and just *knew*," Alex once told me. "Whoever marries him is marrying me too."

I'd punched him in the arm. "And she shall be the *unluck-iest* of ladies!"

God, that had been ages ago.

Soon, I heard Josh sigh in defeat. My mom had worn him down for the morning. "Okay, Lily," he said to me. "What would you like for breakfast? Your mom"—he looked at her with revulsion—"is having cinnamon roll pancakes."

"I'll take an orange juice, please," I said as I unzipped my backpack and began digging around inside. "With a spoon on the side." I emerged victorious with my jar of overnight oats. "I brought my own today."

"Yes!" Josh snapped his fingers. It was ironic he ran the Hub because he was really a health nut. "This is what I'm talking about, Lil. I love to see it." He faced my mom. "You should try eating something off your daughter's menu."

My mom folded her hands on the table. "For your information, she made a lovely chicken stir-fry last night. I helped with the prep work."

Josh turned to me for confirmation, and I nodded. "But cinnamon roll pancakes *do* sound amazing," I added. "May I get a fork with my spoon? That way, I can steal some bites?"

We laughed when Josh groaned. "Exasperating," he said. "You two are endlessly *exasperating*. First, reservations. And now this?" He shook his head.

"Excuse me, but endlessly exasperating?" my mom said once her boyfriend had disappeared into the kitchen. "I'd say he finds us endlessly *fascinating*."

"Yes," I agreed. I loved these breakfasts with her. "Endlessly fascinating, for sure."

～

"I don't know if you noticed, Lily, but Blair was eyeing you like a dartboard during calc today," my friend Pravika commented.

She and I were spending our free period with Zoe in the Crescent, a rounded seashell-encrusted terrace overlooking the ocean and an extension of the greenspace aptly named "the Circle." It was Ames's beating heart, the place to be before, between, and after classes. White Adirondack chairs and hammocks dotted the lawn, and if one was free, you wanted to be sitting in it.

"Really? Am I bleeding?" I deadpanned. The three of us were sunning ourselves on the Crescent's wall. "She should work on her aim."

"Who was sitting next to you in class?" Zoe asked.

I didn't respond. Truthfully, Blair had hit the bull's-eye.

"Lily..." my friends singsonged.

"He was late," I explained. "There weren't any other open spots."

They laughed, and I tried not to think of Tag's eyes. They had been gray instead of glinting green today, their light dimmed. "Do you mind if I sit here?" he'd whispered, and it had taken almost everything to stop myself from running my fingers through his dark brown hair and gently rubbing the back of his neck. It had been over a year since we'd been this close; we had a way of dancing around each other on campus, a dance I thought had been expertly choreographed, right down to us only exchanging a few words during class. But today Tag had missed a step and we'd had to sit together, which made me stumble as well. It ached not to feel his hand on my knee under the table. Or for him not to kiss the inside of my wrist before threading his fingers through mine...

Why? I asked myself for the millionth time. *Why did you do it?*

"I wonder who he'll go to prom with now," Zoe mused.

"No idea," Pravika said. "Some sophomore, probably. All the jocks—"

"Can we chill on all the prom speculation?" I grumbled. "Who cares? We'll find out soon enough."

Zoe and Pravika were silent, because earlier this week, Daniel Rivera, our student council president, had promposed to me after classes with a beautiful bouquet of lilies. It hadn't mattered that I was allergic to them; I could feel people's eyes on us, so I summoned a smile and hugged them to my chest. *Don't think about any impending doom*, I'd thought, knowing full-blown hives were on the horizon. *You're excited! Show everyone how excited you are!*

I sighed. "I'm sorry. I don't know what that was."

My friends nodded slowly, like they *did* know what it was. I felt my neck flush. "It's not too late to change your mind," Zoe had said the other day. "I know you haven't broken a promise in, like, your entire life, but prom with Daniel isn't a real promise—you didn't pinkie swear or anything. If you aren't excited to go with him, why *actually* go with him?"

Because I accepted the flowers, I'd almost said. *I accepted the flowers, and I threw them in the trash as soon as I got home, so I can't give them back.*

And even if I could, I wouldn't. A promposal might not exactly be a promise, but it *was* a commitment. I didn't break my commitments.

Some clouds shrouded the sunlight. "Okay, so new topic…" Pravika ventured. "The guys in bio this morning would not shut up about the senior prank." She cleared her throat. "I mean, about how it looks like there *isn't* one this year."

"Ooh, yes," Zoe murmured. "I've been doubtful too. The Jester has been quiet."

"Try mouth-taped-shut *silent*," I said. The senior prank was another year-end tradition, but an underground one. Students were obsessed with it because the whole thing was very cloak-and-dagger. Not just any upperclassman could brainstorm a prank and put it into motion…only "the Jester" could do that. Their identity was always anonymous; only the previous Jester knew who the next Jester was, passing the "hat" off to them. And if the prank master required a crew to pull off their plan, several others were let in on the secret.

But they never told a soul.

Zoe was right; it didn't look like there was going to be a prank this year. The order always went prank, prom, graduation. And prom was beckoning! Girls had their dresses hung in their closets and hair and makeup appointments scheduled.

"Who do you think it is?" Pravika asked. She pointed across the Circle, where Blair Greenberg held court in an Adirondack chair. "My money's on her."

I wrinkled my nose. "Seriously, Veeks?"

"Yeah." Pravika nodded. "She's more than devious enough."

Truly in a league of her own, I thought before biting my pinkie nail. The farther I stayed away from Blair Greenberg, the better.

"Personally, I hope it's Alex." Zoe swayed us away from Blair. "He was my vote for the Class Clown superlative."

"Zoe, he was *everyone's* vote," Pravika said while I failed at battling back a grin. Alex Nguyen would be the perfect Jester. He'd been devising pranks for forever.

"He will *not* stop," I remembered Tag saying sophomore year. We'd been doing homework together in the library, legs entwined under our study table. "Becoming the Jester is the Alexander Nguyen equivalent of winning an Oscar."

"But you would help," I'd said. "If he was chosen as Jester and tapped you to help, you wouldn't even hesitate."

We stared at each other for a moment before Tag's lips curled up in a mischievous smile. "No," he replied, eyes evergreen. "I wouldn't."

"I'd love to see what Alex does," Pravika giggled. "You'd *know* it'd be a major production, so he'd need a team." She raised an eyebrow. "Would you guys do it?"

Zoe groaned. "Girl, don't get my hopes up!"

Pravika turned to me. "Lily?"

"No," I said without any hesitation.

"Why not?"

I shrugged. "For a million reasons. The first being that I would never make it out of my house undercover. You know what a night owl my mom is. She grades papers until 2:00 a.m." I waved my hand. "Recruiting me would yield zero results."

"Wait, so is *that* why there's been no prank?" Zoe joked. "Because you can't sneak out?" She lowered her voice. "Are *you* the Jester?"

I flipped her the bird.

My friends laughed.

"No, no, we know." Pravika smiled. "It would never be you, Lily."

"Yeah, never me." I smiled back, hoping neither of them noticed it was forced. There was no chance I'd be the Jester, let alone ever joke with the Jester, because the Ames student body couldn't be too sure where my loyalties lay. With them? Or with the teachers who had raised me?

As a fac brat, I was caught in the middle.

⁓

Josh was coming over to make dinner tonight, so knowing my mom would be safe from a takeout menu, I stayed on campus and ate in the dining hall with my friends. Tonight's enchiladas made us sweat, but we persevered through their spice before sharing a slice of chocolate cake and going our separate ways. Zoe and Pravika headed back to their dorm while I made one last stop: the mail room. Students checked their mail often at Ames, and not just because of Amazon Prime's two-day shipping. Teachers returned homework assignments, lab reports, essays, and exams through the mail instead of spending class time distributing them. Administration notices also appeared in our boxes. Tonight, I unlocked my box to find a Latin paper from Mr. Hill—the *A* in his signature meandering handwriting—along with a reminder from the dean of students' office that a draft of my salutatorian speech was due three days before graduation for approval. Mrs. Epstein-Fox had only given me a B-plus on my physics lab report, but before I could read her feedback, I noticed a strange piece of paper. It was a black envelope with **LiLY HØPPER** spelled out in colorful cutout magazine letters.

Creepy ransom note-style.

My stomach began stirring as I quickly ripped open the flap and pulled out a piece of cardstock. Again, no handwriting—only the magazine letters. It said:

> *The game is almost afoot.*
> *It's happening in forty-eight and you*
> *have twenty-four to decide.*
> *Will you join my band of fools?*
> *Email TheJesterXXIII@gmail.com with your answer.*
> *If yes, be ready for further instructions.*

"Oh, Alex," I whispered to myself, staring at the card so hard that the words blurred together. It was him; I was sure it was him. The note *sounded* like him! "Why me?"

TWO

I tried to remain cool, calm, and collected while walking home, but I failed miserably. Thank goodness most of the boarders had retired to their dorms for the night and that Campus Safety—or "Campo"—simply smiled and waved to me from their patrol Priuses, because my stilted, stupefied, *paranoid* gait suggested I was campus's newest whispered-about dealer. Pot or coke, which would you prefer? No, I don't do Venmo. Cash only.

Before fleeing the mail room, I'd stuffed the Jester's invitation into the deep depths of my backpack. You would have to dig through all my heavy textbooks and spiral notebooks to find it. *Just get to the covered bridge*, I told myself, lungs sucked in tight. *Once you get over the covered bridge—*

"Hey, Lily," someone said, and I turned to see Anthony DeLuca falling into step with me. He was the only other current fac brat on campus, a junior and Daniel's sailing partner. He'd taken Tag's place after Tag had dropped sailing to swim on a local club team.

I willed my heart to slow down. Everything was fine. "Hey, Anthony," I said casually. "Good day?"

"*Long* day," he replied as we crossed the bridge together. "Finals are gonna be a total nightmare." He groaned. "You're so lucky you're a senior."

I laughed. Seniors didn't have spring exams at Ames. We'd already gotten into college, so what was the point? The last two weeks of school were simply a formality; we still had assignments to complete but didn't do much in class. My "Reinventing Shakespeare" elective now spent each period watching various movie adaptations. We'd finished Baz Luhrmann's *Romeo + Juliet* today.

Anthony and I walked through the neighborhood together until we reached his house. It had a sprawling porch and was much bigger than mine since his father was the Dean of Students. The windows were open, so I could hear wisps of whatever Disney show his younger sisters were watching. "Do you have Vaseline?" he asked by way of a goodbye.

"Uh, yeah, at home." My eyebrows knitted together. "Why?"

He gestured to my ballet flats. "You've been walking all weird. If you have blisters, Vaseline does the trick. Or helps, at least."

"Okay, thanks." I swallowed, realizing that my heels *were* screaming in pain. I'd just been a little too preoccupied to notice. "Night, Anthony."

"Night, Lily."

All the cottage's lights had been turned on, a lighthouse to guide me in the dark. Josh's Ford Explorer sat in the driveway, and I grinned, happy he was still here. In addition to running the Hub and coaching swimming, he was the freshmen boys' housemaster and lived in an apartment in their dorm.

He must not be on study hall duty tonight, I thought. Otherwise, he'd have left hours ago to go supervise his young charges.

"Hi!" I called as I banged through the front door. "I'm home!"

"Lily!" a chorus of voices responded. Not just my mom and Josh.

I closed my eyes and stood in the doorway for a moment. Would I trade living at Ames for anything? No, absolutely not. But was it difficult that my teachers were also my neighbors and friends? Yes, sometimes. I could never truly *leave* school.

One, two, three, I counted, then walked into the family room smiling sunnily. "Mmm, something smells yummy," I said. "What was for dinner?"

"Carrot-ginger soup and garlic bread." Josh jumped up from the couch. "Do you want me to heat up a bowl? We saved you some." He smirked. "Your mother loved it."

"I did as well," Bunker Hill, my Latin teacher, remarked from the purple velvet armchair near the bookcase. "At first I thought it sounded a bit too autumnal for late May, but Mr. Bauer here proved me wrong." He toasted Josh with his whiskey-filled tumbler before focusing on my mother. "Leda," he said, "I've always been a Scotch man, but this bourbon is quite smooth."

"Thank you," she replied. "The brand is Bulleit. Bulleit Bourbon."

"Well, I must say you might've made me a convert tonight."

My mom laughed. "I'll get you a bottle," she said. "Or my guy will take care of it."

"You mean me?" Josh called from the kitchen.

"That depends!" my mom called back. "You know I have a lot of guys!"

Bunker Hill was one of them, her mentor. He had been teaching at Ames for who knew how long and was my mom's de facto father, grandfather, and eccentric uncle all rolled into one. Some people said he'd been here two decades, others said half a century. Maybe as long as the Circle's massive maple tree had been alive?

I always kept my lips zipped when pressed by my classmates, not wanting to spoil campus lore for them. The old man deserved to remain an enigma. "Just tell us his *actual* name!" Tag and Alex used to plead. "Because Bunker cannot be his real one. It's way too cool!"

The family room was pretty crowded for a Monday night. Several other faculty members and their significant others had turned my mom and Josh's casual dinner for two into a party. My mom always let neighbors wander into our cottage. She was one of those people who left the door unlocked.

I socialized for a while, but once I'd finished my soup and

hunk of garlic bread, I rose from my spot at the driftwood coffee table. My mom must've cleaned it because there was no clutter. Our old issues of *Vogue, Cosmopolitan,* and *People* were gone. "This was delicious," I told Josh, holding up the empty bowl. "I'd give it a VFG."

We always rated Josh's recipes. VFG, or "very fucking good," was the top honor.

Then I said a grand farewell to everyone, announcing that I had to start on homework. Josh followed me into the kitchen. "Take me with you," he whispered as I loaded my bowl and water glass into the dishwasher. "Please."

"Only if you do my homework," I replied.

Josh let out a deep sigh. "I am so ready for summer vacation."

Most of the faculty vacated Ames for long breaks. Housing on campus was free, so a lot of teachers owned homes elsewhere. Josh had an amazing cabin in Montana.

"Twelve days," I emphasized before winking and disappearing upstairs to my room. It was small with peach-pink walls, the color I'd chosen when I was little. And all these years later, the room was even more of a statement thanks to all the photos and my collection of National Park posters. My mom and I had vowed to visit each and every one before I started college. This summer, we were concluding our tour in Alaska.

I flicked on my fairy lights and lit a floral-scented candle before changing into a pair of sweats and a Georgetown T-shirt. Then I wove my hair into a messy braid and went to work on my blisters after grabbing Vaseline and Band-Aids from the bathroom. Even my pinkie toes were swollen. "Much better," I said to myself after a couple minutes. A nurse I was not, but I had confidence I would survive.

Now, self-imposed study hall. I let a moan loose, unzipping and unloading my backpack. Laptop, books, and overstuffed pencil case. Ugh. I really wasn't in the mood for homework tonight, even senior spring homework. Some students at Ames never studied at night; instead, they woke up absurdly early to study. "You're nuts," I'd told Pravika after she'd started routinely waking up at 4:00 a.m. "I'd rather stay *up* until 4:00 a.m."

My brows furrowed as I rustled around in the bottom of my bag. *Okay, where's my gum?* I thought. Because whether I was at home or in the library, Orbit Sweet Mint was forever a necessity. It helped me focus.

Once I finally located the squashed pack of gum, my heart leapt...but it plunged to the floor when I also found something else.

The Jester's bid. With half the neighborhood over for dinner, I'd managed to forget about it, but it hadn't forgotten about me. I bit my pinkie nail and read Alex's note again.

Will you join my band of fools? it asked, and I swore I heard a clock ticking. Less than twenty-four hours—I had less than twenty-four hours to decide whether to join the fun.

Would it be fun? part of me wondered, but the other part quickly nipped the thought in the bud. *No, it would be risky.*

Too risky. What if we got caught?

My mother would *murder* me.

I tore the envelope in half and buried it in my wastebasket, then popped in some gum and opened my textbook to start on physics.

But before I finished, I'd dug out the invitation and carefully taped its pieces back together.

Maybe, I thought as I climbed into bed later. *Just maybe.*

I would talk to Alex tomorrow.

THREE

Approaching Alex was not as easy as I'd imagined. Instead of going to the Hub for breakfast the next morning, I made egg white omelets that my mom and I wolfed down before driving to campus. It was a gray rainy day. "I better play some music in class so no one nods off," she said while maneuvering our car into her faculty parking spot outside the English building. "It's perfect sleeping weather."

I laugh-yawned in agreement before opening my umbrella and heading off to history. My teacher was a big fan of cold-calling students, so I knew none of my classmates would be falling asleep. They'd come equipped with coffee or energy drinks to save themselves the embarrassment. Pravika was never without a dirty chai latte. Whatever that was.

Later, during midmorning student-teacher consultation, I booked it over to the student center, suspecting Alex would be there. No seniors would be hanging out in the Circle; the rain was too heavy. "Please be here, please be here," I chanted as I pulled open Hubbard Hall's wide front door.

The first floor was unsurprisingly flooded with students, but after taking a slippery lap, there he was: Alex Nguyen chilling on one of the couches with Tag and their other friends.

Shit, I thought. *Tag*.

He too had come in with the rain.

With Alex as the Jester, Tag had one hundred percent been tapped to assist him. How could he not? Alex always had Tag's back and Tag always had Alex's. "Despite these unfortunate circumstances, I still think you're spectacular, Lily," I remembered Alex saying after things between Tag and me had ended. "Seriously." He tried to smile. It was unspoken that we wouldn't be hanging out as much anymore. "I'm sorry."

"Thank you." I'd sort of smiled back. "But it's okay; he's your best friend."

Alex nodded. "Yes, he is."

My heart twisted now. An entire evening with Tag. I couldn't decide if that was a pro or con for the prank. Sitting next to him in class yesterday had been painful but also a wish granted. Because I missed him. I *really* missed him.

I watched as several underclassmen girls confidently sauntered up to their couch, each wearing a Barbour raincoat and a pair of colorful Hunter rain boots. It wasn't difficult to figure out what they wanted. In a nearby club chair, I caught Blair Greenberg roll her eyes and flick her glossy brown hair over her shoulder. Unlike Tag and me, their friend group always weathered the storm whenever Tag and Blair fought or broke up. Everyone could stay cool and act like nothing had happened.

Something curdled in my stomach. Had Alex tapped Blair too? Had he tapped his whole inner circle? And if so, what was the point of asking me?

I needed to know. I had never been a go-with-the-flow type of girl. I needed more information. What was this prank? Who else was involved? I wanted time to study the material.

Alex and I have physics together, I reminded myself, but in typical Alex Nguyen fashion, he strolled into our classroom right when the bell rang. It was as if it were announcing his arrival instead of signaling the start of class.

Mrs. Epstein-Fox spent the hour writing various equations on the whiteboard. Equations that I copied into my notebook but didn't fully comprehend. If I needed help later, I would ask Daniel; we sat next to each other and were study partners for a couple classes. Physics was his best subject, and he took every opportunity to remind everyone of that. His mansplaining always tempted me to dump my water bottle over his head, but at least he answered my questions.

Once class was dismissed for lunch, my muscles tensed—I was about to make a casual mad dash over to Alex—but by the time I made it halfway across the room, he'd already slung his backpack over his shoulder and had his phone pressed against his ear. "Afternoon, Paul!" I heard him say, and then right before he disappeared into the hallway, "Yes, I'll have the usual, please and thanks. Taggart's gonna change things up, though. He's feeling a diablo…"

Provisions, I realized. Alex was ordering lunch from Provisions, a sandwich shop in town. Josh said their food was overrated, but the rest of Ames begged to differ.

I quickly texted Zoe and Pravika that I wouldn't be at the dining hall for lunch. "Where're you headed?" someone asked, and I turned to see Daniel at my side. He tilted his head so he could see my phone screen. "Ah, Provisions?"

"Oh, um…" My spine straightened. This wasn't the first time Daniel had peeked at my messages. "Yeah." I said, pocketing my phone before grabbing my umbrella. "I'm going to brave the rain."

Daniel held up his own umbrella. "I'll brave it with you," he offered.

No, thanks, I thought. *I'm on a mission!*

I also didn't want to have lunch with Daniel. It would make things worse. "Saying yes to prom sends the wrong signal," Pravika had pointed out. "Everyone knows he's liked you forever, and now that you're his *date*…" She shook her head. "You need to be honest about only wanting to be friends."

"Okay, sure," I heard myself say now. "Let's go."

Daniel smiled, and we set off together. But while I kicked my pace into a high-gear speed walk—I couldn't miss this chance with Alex—Daniel moved at a casual clip. "Jesus, what's the rush?" he asked right before we reached Ames's front gates, just as I heard someone call my name. "Lily!"

It was Gabe, who worked in the brick guardhouse.

"Hey, Gabe," I said, reluctantly veering away from the gates. "What's up?"

"Major stuff." He grinned. "The school's finally giving me a shot in the big time."

"The big time?" Daniel looked skeptical.

"Campo is letting me out of the isolation station," Gabe explained, gesturing around the guardhouse. "You know Harvey is retiring, so they're giving me his car and hiring some new guy to work this gig." He held out his hand for a fist bump. "I'm finally joining the patrol squad."

"Congratulations!" I exclaimed. Gabe had always wanted to be out on the "streets" with Campo. "I bet you can't wait for next year."

"Oh, yeah, for sure." He nodded. "My first shift is actually the day after tomorrow. I'm gonna shadow Harvey for the rest of the term."

I shifted from one foot to the other. Mr. Harvey wasn't the head of Campo but definitely had seen the most action in the Ames "underworld." He'd caught students sneaking out of their dorms, having sex on the sports fields, drunkenly serenading the moon after dances, and negotiating tennis court drug deals.

He was perhaps my biggest worry about getting involved with the Jester. Everyone was convinced that the only reason last year's prank had gone off without a hitch was because Mr. Harvey hadn't been on campus that night. He was at home recovering from a knee replacement.

After congratulating Gabe one more time, Daniel and I crossed into town. Provisions, with its yellow siding and dark blue-and-white awning, wasn't too crowded.

But Alex was nowhere to be seen.

"Hello there!" the owner greeted us as I scanned the shop again, even though it was obvious Alex had picked up his food and run. My shoulders sagged. "What'll it be?"

Daniel nudged me. "You ready?" He held up his debit card. "I've got this."

I tried not to wince. I didn't want Daniel to pay for me but worried it would be rude if I straight up said no.

Instead, I voiced a version of it. Something my mom would say: "Yeah, I'll Venmo you." Then I quickly rattled off my sandwich order before he could protest. Five minutes later, we were at a high-top table with turkey and roast beef sandwiches, potato chips, and tall fountain sodas. Salted caramel brownies for dessert too.

Provisions's sandwiches were so massive that you could only eat them in silence, so there was no talking until we took a break. "I have some news," Daniel said as I took a long sip of Pepsi.

My pulse quickened. *News? What news?*

"Good or bad?" I inquired.

"Well, not as *awesome* as Gabe's promotion," he deadpanned, "but I'd still say good news." He smirked. "I swung by the yearbook office this morning, and the Almanacs have *finally* arrived."

I put down my soda, eyebrows furrowed. "What do you mean finally? Haven't they *been* here?" Because Ames's yearbooks were supposed to be handed out Friday after classes...two days from now.

Daniel leaned closer to me. He wasn't on the yearbook staff, but distributing the Almanacs was one of his final duties as student council president. "No, they haven't," he whispered in case of eavesdroppers. "The publisher kept delaying their printing, and after that, the shipping was a total mess. It wasn't until Swell called FedEx last week and ripped them..." He dropped off to roll his eyes. "Well, you know how he can be."

"Mm-hmm," I said lightly. Tag was an Edible Arrangement of many things, and when the situation called for it, "ballsy" and "unyielding" were two of them. He was only the Almanac's assistant photo editor, but naturally he'd been the one to get the whole clusterfuck straightened out.

Daniel kept talking about the yearbooks, about how the editor in chief was so relieved and proposed they crack open a box for a preview, but Daniel said no because...

I didn't realize I was tapping my fingers on the table until Daniel had put his hand over mine. "Hey, what are you thinking about?" he asked.

"The piano," I answered, blinking a few times.

Daniel cocked his head. "I didn't know you play piano."

"A little." I shrugged. "But not very often, and not very well." I wriggled my hand out from under his so I could reach for my brownie. Tag had never stopped my mindless tapping. Instead, his left hand joined my right so that it looked like we were one person playing the invisible keys. "What's the song?" he'd ask, grinning and trying to match my rhythm.

It usually ended with us slowing way down and trying to tap out "Hot Cross Buns" together. "You guys should take that on the road," Alex would say dryly from across the lunch table. "Tickets would sell out in *seconds*."

Then we'd all laugh, and I would tell Tag what was bothering me. I told him everything until last year, because what was bothering me then was *him*.

Him and *them*. All the girls who woke up one day and decided they were madly in love with Taggart Matthew Swell and would stop at nothing to get him, even though he was mine. Instead of having him, I suddenly had to *compete* for him.

Or that was what it had felt like, at least.

I unwrapped the brownie and inelegantly shoved half of it into my mouth. Late-night Leda-style. Daniel circled back to the Almanacs. "But Manik and I *did* end up opening one box and scanning the superlatives," he admitted with a sly smile. "You won a few, FYI."

"Really?" I asked through my brownie, curiosity piqued. "Which ones?"

"Favorite Fac Brat."

I swallowed. "That's because I'm the only senior fac brat. The male fac brat column is blank, right?"

Daniel nodded, then made everything *so much better* by saying, "Teacher's Pet."

"Super," I mumbled.

"I got Teacher's Pet too," Daniel said, obviously thrilled about it. "You're also Everyone's Friend." He chuckled. "Oh, and Best to Bring Home to Your Parents." He gulped some soda. "Quite the roundup."

Yeah, I thought, my blood suddenly burning through my veins. *Quite*.

There was no choice but to devour the other half of my brownie. It was my only option. Favorite Fac Brat? Teacher's Pet? Everyone's Friend? Best to Bring Home to Your Parents?

The theme was really fucking clear here. I was nice, well-liked, respected, and polite.

But I was also a goddamn Goody Two-Shoes.

~

After classes that afternoon, I went straight home. Won't be back until after dinner, my mom had texted earlier. Have a department meeting and then will probably stay to draft some exams.

Meh, I replied.

Bleh, she countered, and understandably so. Writing exams was no fun, but I was relieved to have our house to myself for a while. I'd had a one-track mind since lunch with

Daniel and didn't want anything or anyone to interrupt my racing thoughts. I was so distracted that I'd accidentally left my umbrella behind in the English building and was soaking wet by the time I walked into my bedroom. It was now absolutely pouring outside. The ocean waves were churning like my stomach.

"Okay," I said to myself as I sat down at my desk and fired up my laptop. "Okay, here we go…" I opened a new Chrome window with one hand while using the other to fumble through my desk's top drawer. My pruned fingers tingled when they found my taped-together prank summons. The twenty-four-hour clock was rapidly winding down, and my confidence would soon do the same.

Email TheJesterXXIII@gmail.com with your answer, I read for the hundredth time, noting the Roman numerals. XXIII—or in other words—twenty-three. How formal, how old-fashioned. How Alex. Before dashing off a response, I logged out of LHopper@ames.edu and decided to create another account—just to ensure there wouldn't be an electronic paper trail leading back to me.

Several email creation attempts later, bells_whistles82@gmail.com was born. Alex was our Jester, and I was one of his bells and whistles. Ready and willing to help pull off his master plan, ready and willing to help him *entertain*.

I can't believe I'm doing this, I thought with gritted teeth.

To: TheJesterXXIII@gmail.com

From: bells_whistles82@gmail.com

Subject: Answer to your disturbing ransom note

Hi,

Yes, I'm in...as long as we aren't wearing those stupid
jingly hats.

- Lily

I shut my eyes and hit Send, then opened them and stared
at the screen for a good while. I even clicked to refresh my
empty inbox, although when no response appeared, I admitted
defeat and went to take a hot shower.

It wasn't until I was in dry clothes and about to reheat
leftover chili that my phone lit up with a new email. I'd made
sure to log in to my new account.

To: bells_whistles82@gmail.com

From: TheJesterXXIII@gmail.com

Subject: Re: Answer to your disturbing ransom note

Lily,

Welcome. No, we won't be wearing festive hats (they're

NOT stupid). I thought about it, but unfortunately, they make noise, and we want to avoid noise.

Yours with merriment,

The Jester

PS: Please do not diss your invitation. Each one took a lot of time and patience to make. Crafting skills at their finest, no?

I rolled my eyes. Alex.

Who else is in on this? I asked.

Please not Blair Greenberg, please not Blair Greenberg…

A new email appeared within a minute.

Hard to say, he said. Not every fool has answered yet.

That was surprising. I'd thought for sure I'd be the last to respond. Alright… I typed. What are we doing then?

Oh, that's confidential.

My thumbs flew frustratedly across my screen. But your note said that if we said yes, we should expect further instructions!

Yeah, the Jester wrote. FURTHER instructions. Not IMMEDIATE instructions.

I stirred the chili on the stove top. Same thing.

Are they, though? came his response when the chili had begun to simmer, and I saw that he'd included definitions for "further" and "immediate."

The tips of my ears prickled, suddenly unsteady. The two words weren't synonyms, but of course I'd known that. What was throwing me off was the message itself. It didn't read like Alex. He wasn't…a dork. Or at least a dork who used the dictionary.

Alex isn't the Jester, I realized. It was someone else.

Pulse pounding, I took a few steps back from the stove to lean against the kitchen's small butcher-block island.

I hate you, I wrote to see if my inkling was right. I used to tell Tag I hated him all the time and he always had the same comeback.

I don't believe you, read the next email.

Tears prickled in the corners of my eyes. Why not?

The minute that passed after I pressed Send might as well have taken an entire day.

Twenty-four hours.

My heart lurched when an answer finally appeared.

Because you've got my favorite smile on your face, Tag had written.

Tag. Taggart Swell, this year's Jester.

FOUR

I didn't respond to Tag's last email, and he didn't offer a follow-up message or any sort of "further instructions." The conversation ended, so I went back to stirring my chili, blinking away my stupid tears and annoyed with myself that I'd never considered Tag as a Jester option. His other half was the obvious choice—popular, whimsical, and always up for a good time—and I knew how much Alex wanted the title. I guess I'd wanted that dream to come true for him.

And how did I miss it? I berated myself. His Jester email address's Roman numerals! Tag and I both took Latin; the XXIII should've been an easy tip-off.

Ugh, Tag—oh, I could see it now. He too was popular but perhaps the previous Jester saw a little bit more *edge* in him. While Alex and Tag were both smart, Tag was also clever and calculated. Alex could be too spontaneous, but Tag was his perfect counterpart, a careful planner. Together, no one was funnier than they were. But Alex was a goofball twenty-four seven while Tag could easily dial his humor back and become thoughtful and serious. "That kid is a true leader," I'd once overheard Josh telling my mom during swim season. "He never fucks around on the pool deck; he gives the meet his all. Hell, his pump-up speeches are better than mine."

The Jester knew him, I thought. *Whoever had tapped Tag knew all this.*

I hated that my mind immediately went to the senior girl he'd hung out with last year whenever he and Blair weren't together. She'd been a star on the swim team and absolutely gorgeous and—

Shut up, the now-boiling chili told me. I moved to take the pot off the burner. *You broke up with him, remember? He can date whomever he wants. It's none of your business.*

I didn't like that my fears had come true. With girls flinging themselves at Tag left and right, spiked vines had tangled around my heart—making me worry that he would dump me for one of them, because he hadn't exactly been pushing the attention away. "He's a good guy, Lily. You know he's just being nice," Alex had tried to reassure me, but soon the vines had become too tight. Three weeks after Tag and I broke up, he and Blair had been spotted making out near the basketball court after a dance. From then on, he was attached to her or his swim teammate.

Does he miss me, though? I sometimes wondered. *Even a little bit?*

We'd dated for almost two years. I had been so in love with him, and our memories—even the silly arguments—were like my favorite movie. I replayed them over and over again in my head.

Which, deep down, I knew meant I was in love with him still.

I shook the thought away and ate my dinner alone. My mom didn't burst through the front door until almost eight. "I am putting on pajamas!" she announced while running up the stairs. "And then how about we binge *Criminal Minds*?"

"Capital idea!" I replied. *Criminal Minds* was our comfort show.

"How was your meeting?" I ventured halfway through an episode. We were both snuggled on the couch, my mom now wearing her exploding fireworks PJs.

"Complete chaos," she replied, chili long ago inhaled. "We discussed the freshmen's final exam's structure and content."

"Ah," I said. "Modeled after the classic fifth grade language arts test?"

My mom nodded. "There will be a matching section right out of the gate."

"True or false?"

"Naturally."

"Short answers?"

"No, too difficult," she kidded. "It'll be fill in the blank instead...*with* a word bank."

We both laughed. "So pretty brutal, huh?" I asked, thinking

of my prior English finals. Five very tricky multiple-choice questions, a handful of short answers, and then two essays.

Yikes.

"They'll be fine," my mom said. "Or at least *my* students will be. It was decided that the content should be the same across classes, but..." She sighed. "Mr. Rudnick doesn't like Arthur Miller, so he never spends much time on *Death of a Salesman*."

"And that's the big essay topic," I guessed.

She smirked. "If anyone asks, you know *nothing*."

I nodded solemnly before resting my head on her shoulder. "Don't worry, Mom," I murmured, feeling my eyelids flutter closed. Today had been *a lot*. "I am a vault."

But was I?

The next day—the day of the Jester's mysterious prank—I felt like I was being eaten alive by anxiety. "Do you feel okay, Lily?" Zoe asked me at lunch. "Because no offense, but you seem a little off..."

I said I had a headache, which was true. Last night I'd tossed and turned, unsure whether I wanted to play a part in the prank anymore now that I knew Tag was the Jester. *Do I dare spend a whole night with him?* I wondered.

I only fell asleep for good when I realized the answer was

yes. Because I'd already committed...and because I was curious. Alex had brainstormed so many schemes over the years, so what did Tag have up his sleeve?

Whatever it was, I wanted to watch it come together. Tag Swell had a Midas touch.

That didn't make me any less restless, though. During the day, I avoided Tag and Alex at all costs. Sometimes we crossed paths, but I would crack if I saw them today. *What are you waiting for?* I imagined publicly interrogating Tag. *Where is this promised "further information"?*

There had been no word from his Jester email account, and I knew he wasn't procrastinating or stalling; no, he was *timing*. Tag had this all figured out. If I hadn't gotten a message from him yet, it was for a reason.

That reason revealed itself at 4:00 p.m. while I was trying to draft a salutatorian speech at the huge oak table in my mother's classroom. It was a true marvel, looking like you'd time traveled back to a 1920s Parisian writing salon. Persian rugs covered the floor, and the walls were a deep plum and decorated with more framed oil paintings than possible. I always smiled at the one of dogs playing poker. Books were also everywhere, tucked into tall bookcases and piled on low shelves. A record player sat near one stack, but instead of Cole Porter, Leda Hopper preferred Dave Matthews. "You haven't worked in here in a while," she commented as I typed DRAFT 1 at the top of a blank Word document.

"Well, the underclassmen have all moved into the library," I said. "There isn't one free study carrel, and the upperclassmen..." I trailed off to glance out the classroom's big casement window. The Circle and Crescent looked like a circus with my fellow seniors everywhere. Some were darting around playing Frisbee, others balancing on the slackline set up between trees, and most relaxing in the Adirondack chairs. None of them had a care in the world.

"They look like they're having fun," my mom said, smiling.

"Because they aren't the salutatorian," I mumbled before sighing. "Mom, my speech is seriously going to be a flaming pile of—"

My computer suddenly pinged with an email notification. "Ooh, a love letter from a not-so-secret admirer?" my mom teased. She'd said anyone with eyes knew how Daniel felt about me and that I was putting up a pretty good front about feeling the same way.

She also kept advising me to tell him the truth.

"No, just a reminder that Anthropologie's having a sale," I lied quickly. Anthropologie was always having a sale. Their clothes went from outrageously expensive to reasonably expensive.

"Mmm, let me know if there's anything that must move into our closets..." My mom's voice drifted up to the classroom's ceiling. I looked over to see that she was wrapped up in skimming a book with a highlighter in hand.

So I stole the chance to open the Jester's email, hoping its message wouldn't trigger a fainting spell.

To: bells_whistles82@gmail.com
From: TheJesterXXIII@gmail.com
Subject: Tonight

Dear Lily,

They say good things come in threes, so...
1.   Please be at King's Court by the stroke of midnight.
2.   Please wear all black.
3.   Pretty please with cherries on top bring Leda's keys.
See you in several hours.

Best wishes, warmest regards,
The Jester

Good things come in threes? Well, it felt like I'd just been slapped in the face three times. If I hadn't figured out Tag was the Jester yesterday, this would've been the ultimate giveaway. *Best wishes, warmest regards.* Leave it to him to slip in a *Schitt's Creek* reference.

Midnight. *Okay.* I gritted my teeth. I could pull a Cinderella

running away from the royal ball. Had I worked out the partic-
ulars of *how* I was going to sneak out of my house? No, but I
would. And I had plenty of dark clothes. That was a non-issue.

But bringing along my mom's keys—*stealing* my mom's
keys. My heart rate heightened. It suddenly made crystal clear
sense why Tag had recruited me: This year's senior prank
required the Jester and his fools to sneak into campus buildings.
Before now, all the hijinks had taken place outside, but here Tag
was, wanting to kick it up a notch.

And he needed me to make it happen.

Again, curiosity made my mind spin.

But curiosity also killed the cat, I reminded myself.

I tried to ignore the thought.

Every student had an Ames School ID card that let us
swipe into academic buildings, but we lost access once the sun
went down. Besides the dorms, Ames was locked up tight at
night. Only faculty IDs worked twenty-four hours a day.

Tag had been over to our house a million times. He knew
my mom always tossed her Red Sox lanyard in the kitchen's
catchall when she got home, and he knew that in addition
to her ID, she'd charmed physical metal keys out of various
departments. "Why do you need a key to the Buildings and
Grounds facility?" I'd once asked, to which she airily replied,
"I'm not sure yet."

I wanted to scream. Tag expected me to steal my mother's
keys?!

TELL ME WHAT WE'RE DOING RIGHT NOW, I replied to his email.

No need to yell, Ms. All-Caps, he wrote back. It'll be easy.

Easy? I typed. You think swiping my mom's keys will be easy? When she probably won't even be asleep yet?

YES, I DO, he said. YOU'VE GOT THIS!

I rolled my eyes when "the Jester" went offline. Hopefully to go brainstorm a contingency plan if I showed up tonight without my mom's loaded lanyard.

Guilt squirmed in my stomach when I shut my laptop and looked over at my mother. "Mom…" I whispered but astonishingly went silent before I could add, *I have something to tell you.*

I told my mom everything, absolutely *everything.* From good grades to bad grades to student gossip to my first kiss with Tag. God, I'd even told her about our first time sophomore year. "Mom, Tag and I slept together!" I'd blurted after coming home and finding her in the family room. I hadn't even bothered to take off my heavy winter coat or brush the snowflakes out of my hair. "And it was fine!" I barreled on before she could respond. "Totally fine! We were safe, so you have nothing to worry about! Again, totally fine!"

Then I nearly collapsed, breathless.

"Well, okay." My mom nodded, a look of both bemusement and concern on her face. "I'm glad it was *totally fine.*" Her lips twitched up in a smile. "But now how about you take off your coat and stay a while…" She patted the couch cushion next to her. "Because I take it there's a more romantic version of this event?"

Yes, there was, and I told her that too. Not every little detail, but most of them. That year's winter musical had been *The Sound of Music*, and I'd somehow been cast as Liesl von Trapp. What had Mrs. DeLuca, the head of the theater department, been thinking?

Tag always picked me up after rehearsal, but one day he'd been late because his swim meet had run long. Everyone had left the auditorium's basement lounge by the time he'd finally arrived. "How old are you, *junge Dame?*" he asked cheekily, finding me on the couch still wearing my floaty pink dress with my script. The show opened next week, but I kept butchering some lines. "Sixteen, perchance?"

I glared at him. "Nice try, Herr Swell."

Tag laughed and climbed onto the arm of the couch. This was when he was still all arms and legs, after his first growth spurt but before he started hitting the gym. "Bambi," Alex and I liked to call him back then. I watched as he spread out his arms for balance and began humming "Sixteen Going on Seventeen."

"Okay, stop." I stood up, my skirt swirling. "Seriously."

"Why?" He was now precariously perched on the back of the couch. "This is a pretty good makeshift gazebo bench."

I sighed. "We rehearsed this scene a lot today."

"But not with me."

I shook my head and smirked.

"Come on, Lily." He crouched and kissed my cheek. "We've sung this song together so many times." His green eyes glinted because it was true. Tag had always offered to duet with me when I'd first needed to learn the lyrics. "*Please* give me my time to shine."

My heart swelled. "You're such a dork," I told him but didn't say no. Instead, I queued up the music and shooed him off the couch. "It's *Liesl* who dances on the gazebo benches."

Tag's voice was hoarse from his meet, so he was a terrible singer that day and I couldn't stop laughing. But we could dance together; we were so good at dancing together, even if it wasn't remotely the right choreography. And of course, Liesl and Rolf's scripted kiss was supposed to be light and quick like a butterfly, but instead Tag put one hand on my waist and weaved the other through my hair. I rose up on my tiptoes and wrapped both arms around his neck. "That wasn't meant for the stage," I said when we pulled back a few inches for air. Our breathing was heavy but fully in sync.

"How convenient that we're *backstage*, then," Tag quipped, and before long, we ended up tangled together on the couch. His warm skin smelled like chlorine. "Do you want to?" he whispered after a little while.

"Yes," I whispered back, feeling his hands slipping up my skirt. "I do."

"Me too," he said, nodding as I kissed his neck. "I do too."

So we did, because we loved each other.

I made zero progress on my speech that afternoon, racked with too many nerves. My mom ordered Italian for dinner, but I only pushed around my ravioli, appetite nonexistent. She didn't notice because she was overwhelmingly preoccupied with her plans tonight. Headmaster Bickford was a member of a local wine club, and so was my mother...theoretically. The club met once a month, but my mom had managed to get out of the last eight gatherings. "You know I'm not ageist, Lily," she once said, "but I *am* the youngest member by at least thirty years, and those women..." She huffed. "I have nothing in common with them."

"How would you know?" I goaded her. "You haven't been to a single meeting."

"Because Penny took me to that ladies' luncheon, remember?" She rolled her eyes. "All they talked about was the goings-on at their country club. It was a full-on gossip session. Penny had to keep feeding me information to keep me in the loop."

I made a face. "Penny's a member?"

"Yes, almost every family in town is."

Right. Most of the faculty was from elsewhere, but Penny Bickford was a true Rhode Islander. She had a whole community outside of Ames.

Unfortunately for my mom, there was no getting out of

wine club tonight. It disbanded for the summer, so this was the last meeting until September, and Penny wasn't taking "I'm swamped with schoolwork" or "Josh's family is in town" for an answer. She'd even politely insisted on driving my mom to the hostess's house.

Which, as I later watched the two of them speed off in Penny's jet-black Jaguar, gave me the perfect opportunity to commit tonight's impossible crime. I spotted the Red Sox lanyard lying lazily in the kitchen catchall with the usual assortment of crap. Lip gloss, spare change, hair ties, Post-its, colorful gel pens, and way too many Bed Bath & Beyond coupons. My stomach somersaulted with excitement.

This could work, I thought as I unzipped my backpack's front pocket and pulled out my own red-white-and-navy lanyard. *This just might work...*

Josh had given us the matching lanyards last year, and like my mom, I kept my Ames ID and house key on it. But *unlike* my mom, I didn't have a hundred other keys and kitschy key chains.

Time to get to work.

I needed my mom's ID and master keys, but I also knew this couldn't be an overwhelmingly obvious theft. Sprucing my lanyard up with her key chains and leaving it in my mom's usual place would be a good enough disguise...right?

My fingers fumbled as I unhooked key chains and transferred them to my lanyard, soon finding a rhythm. The only thing that caught me off guard was the Chicago Cubs key chain.

My mom had tried to convert Tag to Boston's sports fandom, but he had remained loyal to his hometown. Once upon a time, that key chain had been a "teacher appreciation gift."

Now it wouldn't budge. I pried as hard as I could, but the Cubs logo was determined to stay linked to the Red Sox.

Leave it, I told myself. *One key chain is not going to make or break this mission!*

I let out a deep breath when I finished. If you didn't check the photo on the ID card, my lanyard was now a dead ringer for my mom's and hers for mine. Now all I had to do was carefully position it in the catchall. My gut told me that she wouldn't touch it once she got home, but the Red Sox logo needed to be visible in case she glanced over in that direction. I made sure to tuck my ID under a coupon. Again, my red hair stuck out like a forest fire.

Then I ran upstairs and hid her keys under my pillow.

Penny's Jaguar pulled back into our driveway at 9:45 p.m. "It was wonderful, no!" I heard my mom say after getting out and shutting the passenger door. "No, you should definitely order a case of the Sancerre. And no, Cynthia's bathroom renovation was stunning. I loved the gilded mirror!"

Oops, too many nos, I thought. *She must've really hated it.*

"Okay, fine, I'm lying," she admitted after Headmaster Bickford called her out on the last part. "That mirror *was* a travesty." She laughed. "Thank you for tonight, Penny!"

Once I heard her heels *click-clack* on the front walk and

then a twist of the doorknob, I assumed my position on the couch: curled up under a blanket with *Pride & Prejudice* on TV.

The 2005 version, of course.

"Hi," I said when my mom walked into the family room. "How was it?"

"Let's see," she said. "Extremely uninteresting with a few moments of mind-numbing boredom."

"Come on," I said as she unbuckled her high heels and tousled her blond curls. She looked gorgeous in her strapless lavender jumpsuit. "Something funny must've happened."

"Mmm…" She pretended to think. "Oh, every woman there asked for my number—"

"I *knew* they would."

"—to pass along to their divorced sons."

"Wait, ew." I wrinkled my nose. "Did you tell them about Josh?"

"No, but they'll find out soon enough."

I gasped. "Mom, you didn't!"

She kicked away her shoes. "Hey, I wasn't going to give them *my* number!"

"Okay, but Josh is going to get all these bizarre texts telling him how *beautiful* he is and how *dazzling* he sounds and then they'll ask if he'd like to grab a drink sometime at their *club*."

"I know." She beamed. "It'll be amazing."

"Did you have anything to drink?" I asked. She didn't seem tipsy. Just loopy.

"I wish," she answered through a gritted-teeth smile. "But apparently you only drink *wine* at a wine club. They hide all the good stuff."

"Huh, how odd," I said dryly. My mom preferred whiskey to wine.

"Please remind me to make a dentist appointment," she continued. "The one glass I had was so sweet that I'm going to need some cavities filled…" She trailed off, noticing Elizabeth Bennet and Mr. Darcy onscreen. "Crap, I missed the hand flex."

I winced. *You idiot,* I thought. *If you hadn't passed the hand flex, you would've had her.*

Pride & Prejudice was my mom's clickbait. If it was on TV, she watched it, obsessed with the scene where Mr. Darcy flexes his hand after helping Lizzy into a carriage. "It shows how moved he is," she'd say reverently, "just from touching her hand…"

If we had the hand flex to look forward to, my mom would've collapsed on the couch and drifted off to the movie instead of popping open a Red Bull before grading her students' assignments.

And I *really* didn't want to sneak out of my house with my mom awake, alert, and highly caffeinated in her study just off the front hallway.

"Well…" she said a few seconds later. "I'm gonna head to bed."

My pulse spiked, a shock to the system. "What?"

"I'm going to bed," she repeated. "Tonight took a lot out of me. I'm going to make a cup of chamomile—"

"Why don't I make it?" I volunteered, heart racing. If I could avoid it, I didn't want her going into the kitchen. "I was going to make some and go up soon too. Do you want honey?"

Ten minutes later, I climbed the stairs with two mugs of hot tea. My mom was in bed with a book. Her phone had been plugged into its charger and rested on her bedside table. "Thank you, sweetheart," she said and gave me a kiss on the forehead. "I love you very much."

"And I love you very, *very* much," I replied, squashing my sudden guiltiness with a sip of tea. "Sleep well."

"You too." She smiled, but before I left her room, she asked if I'd locked the doors and turned out all the lights downstairs. Nights were the only time we truly shut down the cottage.

"Yes," I lied. The lights were off and the front door was locked, but I had cracked open the back door so I could sneak out later. "All good."

She snuggled into her pillows. "Good night, Lily."

I swallowed hard. "Good night, Mom."

FIVE

As I sipped my tea, I realized it wasn't escaping the faculty neighborhood that especially worried me. While boarders had strict nightly curfews and had to stay in their houses until morning, I had more leeway. People might call me a fac brat, but *technically* my file said I was a day student. If I wanted to claim insomnia and go on a late-night run, no one could question me. Campo didn't drive around town to make sure the other Ames day students were tucked into their beds now, did they? Staying away from main campus was a given, but I wouldn't get in trouble if I was caught jogging past Headmaster Bickford's or Dean DeLuca's house.

Around 11:15, I started getting ready. *By the stroke of midnight*, the email had said, but I didn't know how long it would take me to sneak over to campus under these circumstances. I quietly changed into dark clothing—black gym shorts, black T-shirt, and a lightweight black Dri-FIT. The pullover had pockets, so I shoved my mom's keys in one and my phone in the other. I pulled my hair into a low ponytail and then dug through my closet until I found a black baseball cap. It wasn't ideal that CHICAGO MARATHON was stitched across the front, but it was the best I had. Tag and I had trained all summer for that race, and we'd run it together when I'd gone home with him for fall break junior year. The rest of the day had been spent soaking in a hot bath and napping in his heavenly bed.

His parents had no idea because they weren't home. According to Tag, they were almost *never* home. The Swells lived right outside Chicago, but his parents commuted into the city for work. "We own a condo near their law firm," he'd explained, "so they spend a lot of time there."

Tag had an older sister, but she was already moved out and married, so the thought of him alone in his big house bummed me out all over again as I slowly crept down the stairs in only my socks. No wonder he spent half the summer in New York with Alex.

I would've liked to say I snuck out through my bedroom window and shimmied down a tree, but that was a fairy tale. The tree near my window was tall with a tire swing that my mom had hung when I was seven, but it wasn't quite close enough to safely catch hold of a branch. Jump, then fall? Far from ideal.

The back door it was.

After slipping outside, I silently begged its hinges not to squeak when I closed the door behind me. My mom wasn't a heavy sleeper. There was also a chance she was still awake, possibly playing *Wordscapes* on her phone. "I'm on level 2,700!" she'd bragged the other day.

The ocean waves crashed hard tonight, and it was chilly enough that I thought about backtracking to grab a sweatshirt, but it was too dicey. My thin pullover would have to work. "You'll warm up," I whispered to myself, rubbing the goose bumps from my legs before taking off into the night. Even though lights were still on in my neighbors' houses, sprinting through the streets seemed like the smartest thing to do. In the distance, I heard the yips and yaps of a French teacher's toy poodles—they preferred walks after dark—but I didn't slow my pace. Madame Hoffman always wore noise-canceling headphones to listen to her podcasts. She wouldn't hear me.

Only when I reached the covered bridge did I stop, press myself against the side, and take several deep breaths. *In through the nose, out through the mouth.*

Here was where it would get tricky. Eyes were everywhere on campus. Students might be confined to their dormitories, but only the freshmen were required to be in bed by 11:00. I had a feeling the other houses would be lit up like Christmas trees. Ames's avenues and alleys were lined with streetlamps and of course two or three Campo sentinels would be roving around in their Priuses. I thought of veteran Mr. Harvey and Gabe, the new kid on the block. He would be hungry to catch someone.

And to top it off, there was a full moon tonight. Shining bright like a police spotlight. "We couldn't have consulted the moon's cycle?" I muttered, feeling sweat slide down my back.

It had been warm from my run at first but had quickly turned cold.

I shivered.

One would think the "King's Court" the Jester had summoned us to would be the Circle or student center, Ames's top social hotspots…but it was neither. King's Court was right outside the school chapel, where a bronze statue of Ames's founder had been erected. Kingsley John Ames had founded our school in 1803, and the tall bust was quite regal. The pretentiously named Kingsley sat with perfect posture in a throne and held a scepter-like cane. His left foot had been worn down and rubbed shiny; it was a school tradition to give it a brush if you needed some luck. King's Court was the closest thing campus had to holy ground.

On a normal day at a normal clip, it would've taken me ten minutes to reach the chapel. It was the halfway point between the two senior dorms, which were tucked away from Ames's academic village. I had to admit that it wasn't a bad rendezvous point.

But instead of ten minutes, it took me double that to get there. I had to stick to the shadows, avoiding the streetlights' beams and stopping under trees to reassess my surroundings. Overhead lights and bedside lamps *were* still on in dorms, and I had to hide from one Campo car on patrol. If anyone could hear my hammering heartbeat, I would've been burnt toast.

Only one streetlamp sat outside the small, ivy-covered

chapel. Fortunately, it was another memorial to our centuries-old school: an old-fashioned gas lantern that the Buildings and Grounds crew never thought to light. The moon shone faintly through the trees, so I navigated my way across the deserted cobblestone courtyard. It was 11:49; I'd managed to arrive early.

Punctuality, my friends affectionately teased, was one of my core values.

Good evening, your royal highness, I thought as I began circling dear Kingsley's statue, staring up at his slightly scowling facial expression. *Are you ready to have that frown turned upside—*

I stumbled over something. Suddenly stumbled and nearly tumbled…over the Jester's long legs. He was down on the ground, leaning back against the statue's marble base and rocking a green-yellow-and-purple jester's hat. Bells and all, despite his email. "Christ," I breathed. "Thanks for the warning."

Tag scrambled up from the ground, and once the moonlight found him, a lump formed in my throat. He was just so *Tag.* I saw him in class and around campus in his blue blazer and chinos, but I'd always thought him more handsome out of dress code. Tonight, he was wearing a pair of scuffed Blundstone boots, dark jeans, and a black sweatshirt with a Scotch-plaid flannel over top. My lips quirked. Who did that? Wore a shirt over a sweatshirt?

He was so tall too. When we'd met at freshmen orientation, we were the same height, but after two growth spurts, he was now six foot three to my five foot six. He was this magnetic force who kept dropping times in the pool and adding muscle in the weight room. First Josh and the athletic department noticed, and then Ames's administration, colleges, and finally the entire swimming world. "Virginia just won the lottery," I'd told him last year, after he'd signed his letter of intent to swim for them. "I'm so proud of you, Smoosh."

Smoosh.

We'd had such silly nicknames for each other. Tag had been "Smoosh" because he gave the best hugs, wrapping me in a warm, cozy cocoon. They lasted for what felt like a wonderful forever.

Meanwhile, more girls than ever started showing up to swim meets and saying things like, "Tag Swell is a gold medal."

That had been a tamer one.

"Sorry," Tag said now, turning on his iPhone flashlight. "I was—"

"I mean, what a stupid place to sit," I blurted.

"But what a pretty place to fall," he quipped before coughing, remembering himself.

We were off to a roaring start. One of the reasons Tag and I couldn't be friends was because we were always in sync with each other. Here we were, already bantering. It should've been awkward because I'd buried our relationship, but instead I felt white-hot inside. I felt *alive.*

If we still did this every day, I'd never fall out of love with him.

One night, I felt myself flush. *One night, and one night only.*

I glanced away but caught a glimpse of him slipping something into his pocket. It looked sort of like the original iPod, but I knew it was his insulin pump. Tag had been diagnosed with type 1 diabetes when he was six.

I resisted the urge to ask if everything was okay. "Alright, so this is how it works," I would never forget him telling me when we were freshmen. "This monitor is connected to my body by a cannula..." He'd raised his T-shirt just enough to show me a thin cord. "And it acts as an insulin reservoir; it's programmed to administer a certain amount per hour." Then he patted the right side of his abdomen. "I also have a glucose sensor that is wirelessly linked to the pump. It tracks and measures my blood sugar and will notify me if it gets too high or too low..."

Now, Tag cleared his throat. "You're early."

I played it cool. "I could say the same about you."

"Well, I thought I should be," he said, lips curling into a half smile. The backs of my knees instantly betrayed me, tingling before going absolutely numb. "Since I'm running this show and all."

"Not without a set of keys you aren't," I pointed out.

His smile faltered. "You got them, right?"

I let him sweat for a few seconds, then removed my fist from my pullover's pocket and raised it as if about to perform a magic trick. When I opened it, my mom's ID and collection of keys tumbled out, all dangling from the Red Sox lanyard. "Ta-da," I deadpanned.

Tag exhaled. "Oh, thank god," he said and reached to touch them. His fingers lingered on the Cubs key chain before he made eye contact with me. "Listen, Lily, I—"

"Holy hell!" someone called. "Taggart Swell, *you're* the Jester?"

We turned to see Alex striding toward us in a black Adidas tracksuit. "Haha, very funny," I said. "You knew."

Alex widened his eyes with shock. "I did not," he said. "Why ever didn't you say anything, dear friend?"

"I would've, Alexander," Tag replied, putting a hand on his best friend's shoulder, "but it's against the rules. I made a vow to my predecessor."

I melodramatically groaned. "You two are *so...*"

"Okay, I knew," Alex caved. "I've known ever since he got the gig." He chuckled. "But in all fairness, I have no fucking clue what we're doing tonight."

"Really?" I asked, doubtful.

"Really." He elbowed Tag in the ribs. "So can you please tell us what the fuck we're doing tonight?"

"Yes," Tag said, but before we could get too excited, he added, "When everyone gets here."

"How many more are we waiting on?" I asked as Alex checked the time on his phone.

"Three, but two will probably arrive together."

"Huh?" Alex and I said, but it soon made sense.

"Lily, I *knew* something was off yesterday!" Zoe exclaimed after squealing at Tag and his jester's hat. She smiled, but it turned sympathetic as she squeezed her close-to-miserable-looking girlfriend's hand. "Maya's the one off now, though."

Holding up his flashlight, would-be Dr. Alex Nguyen conducted an assessment. "You do look peaked, if not a little green," he concluded. "Did you eat the meatloaf tonight?"

"No, I didn't." Maya Rivera waved him away. "But I'm pretty sure I have a bug," she told Tag. "I've thrown up twice and feel like more's on the way."

"It's coming out of both ends," Zoe whispered to me.

Tag was quiet, contemplating. "Do you want out?" he asked.

"Not necessarily," Maya answered. "Does the prank involve a bathroom break?"

"It must," Zoe said supportively while I tried to make the connection here. Tag was the Jester and had tapped Alex for obvious reasons. He'd tapped me to get my mom's keys, but why were Zoe and Maya here? They weren't friends with him. I mean, Tag and Zoe saw each other in the gym all the time— Zoe was queen of the basketball court—but Maya practically lived in the art building, a talented metalworker and glass-blower. I didn't understand. Did she and Tag talk when he went to develop photos in the darkroom? What was I missing?

Tag's phone alarm sounded at midnight. He'd set the sound effect to "Bell Tower."

Alex and I made eye contact. He smirked and I smirked back. Tag was such a nerd.

But we were still missing our final crew member—our final fool.

"He has until 12:01," Tag said, seemingly unconcerned. "I suspected he'd be last."

"Oh, so it's half-and-half, then?" Zoe said. "Three guys, three girls?"

Tag nodded. "You all bring something critical to the table."

I suddenly wanted to shake him. *What is on this freaking table?!*

Alex sighed. "Just tell us what's going on already, Jester."

"Yeah—Jester! I'm here... I'm—ready!" a new but familiar voice said. Manik Patel was panting like he'd just run a marathon. More confused than ever, I watched him edge in between Alex and Zoe. He pointed at Tag and his ridiculous hat. "You were my third guess." He turned to Alex. "You were my first."

"Who was your second?" Zoe asked.

"Blair Greenberg."

I couldn't have rolled my eyes harder.

"Well, congratulations," Alex said acerbically. "Two out of your top three are here." He flicked one of Tag's bells. "Jester, the floor is yours."

"Thank you." Tag took off his hat and stuffed it in his backpack. What happened to not wanting noise? "Alright, it's simple," he said. "Complex, but ultimately simple."

His five fools leaned in, eager as ever. What were we doing that involved keys?

I held my breath as our Jester took a deep one, then said, "We're going to steal the Almanacs."

SIX

"What?!" everyone exclaimed before shushing one another. "Steal the Almanacs?" we said in lower voices. "You want us to *steal* the Almanacs?"

Tag winked. "Yes."

No one knew how to respond except Manik, who let out a legitimate *squawk*...and for a fair reason. He was the yearbook's *editor in chief*. If Tag wanted us to commit this crime, why had he invited one of the people it affected most?

"We don't have time to fully unpack this," Tag said quickly, "but think about it. The Jester's previous pranks have always been *immediate*." He subtly glanced at me. "We woke up, heard about the prank, had a good laugh, and then it was over." He paused. "What if we were to draw things out more? Someone will notice that the Almanacs are gone when they unbox them tomorrow for distribution, but that doesn't mean they're going to get them back right away. It'll spread that they're missing, and campus will go wild." He gave us a look. "We know how much Ames loves the Almanacs."

Again, nobody spoke. It was true; we cherished the yearbooks, poring over their pages for days.

"I'm in," Alex declared. "I'm totally in."

Zoe and Maya giggled. "So we're going to hide the Almanacs and hold them hostage?"

"In a sense," Tag answered before explaining the second phase of his plan. Which, I had to admit, smirking a little, was mastermind-level genius. Even Alex had a dreamy grin on his face.

But again, Manik was here. Why was Manik here? "Tag, is that why you called FedEx and demanded to speak to their supervisor?" he asked. "Was it to ensure the Almanacs were delivered on time for this?"

"*You* asked *me* to handle it, Manik," Tag reminded him coolly as something twisted in my stomach. I remembered Daniel telling me about the recent delayed delivery and how assistant photo editor Tag had been the hero.

He got the yearbooks, I thought, *just to steal them.*

"I'm sorry," Manik said, adjusting his glasses, "but I don't know if I can condone this. The Almanac…"

"…is your pride and joy," Tag said. "The yearbook is your baby, Patel."

He nodded. "Pretty much."

"Then why should someone else have the honor of handing out the Almanacs?"

My heart rate sped up. This was a dig against Daniel. It was an age-old Ames tradition that the president gifted each and every yearbook to his schoolmates. Three hundred copies.

Manik gave Tag a questioning look. "Why did you choose me to help?"

"Because I don't want you to worry when they go missing," Tag replied. "You did so much work, so I want you to know they're safe." He paused. "And I trust you to keep a secret."

We're all linked to Daniel, I suddenly realized. Tag had said we each brought something special to the metaphorical "table," but everyone also had some link to Daniel.

I looked around our circle. Tag had truly assembled a motivated crew. Manik was our unsung Almanac editor. Alex Nguyen had shockingly lost last year's election to Daniel and was still peeved. Zoe Wright considered him about as interesting as a leaf of lettuce. And Maya—Maya Rivera was his fraternal twin!

"Come on, Manik," she said now. "It's been a while since my brother's been humbled."

But what am I doing here? I wondered. Daniel could be pretty pompous, but I didn't really have anything against him. Everyone else had a vendetta while I was his prom date.

The jingle of my mom's keys swiftly reminded me.

"Okay," Manik finally agreed. "Let's do it."

"Hell, yeah," Zoe said, and then Tag's eyes met mine. It wasn't until I nodded that his tensed shoulders relaxed.

"Right," he resumed. "Before we head out…" He unzipped his backpack and pulled out a silver flask. "A salute."

"Sweet." Alex took the flask first, unwound its cap, and took a pull. Everyone jumped backward when liquid came spewing out of his mouth. "What *is* this?" he asked Tag. "Diet..." He choked. "Coke?"

"Excellent deduction skills, Alexander," Tag said as Zoe grumbled. She liked soda about as much as I liked coffee. "I think it's best if we kept our wits about us, don't you?"

Alex rolled his eyes and passed the flask to Manik, who gulped before giving it to Zoe. Maya, still looking ill, smiled and raised the flask in solidarity instead of drinking. I took a sip of Tag's favorite drink and then handed it back to him. Our fingertips brushed. *Did he feel that?* I wondered, sparks flickering through my veins.

"Cheers, fools," he said and drained the flask before stowing it back in his backpack. "Now it's time to take the stage."

The six of us silently said farewell to King's Court, creeping across the cobblestones and making our way back to Ames's main paved road. "Stay out of the light beams," Tag cautioned, so we zigzagged around the streetlamps' dangerous pools of light. With the yearbook office in the student center, Hubbard Hall was our first stop.

"Crap, someone's at their window," Zoe whispered as we passed the sophomore girls' dorm, and I stopped to see my friend was right. A girl sat on her window seat; we had a clear view of her, which meant she had a clear view of *us*.

"Don't worry about it," Tag whispered back. "She's holding up her phone, see?" He pointed. "FaceTiming."

Zoe released a breath, but I sucked one in…because I could hear the jester hat's jingling bells in Tag's backpack. They weren't loud per se, but the sound was consistent and made the hair on the back of my neck stand up. Quickly, I sidled next to him. "Why do you still have the hat?" I asked in a low voice that only Alex could hear. "Your email said you didn't want noise."

Alex snorted. "I *knew* your emails would get personal."

Tag ignored him. "We need it for one more thing," he said through gritted teeth. The hat was bothering him too. "If I could stop the chiming, I would."

"Okay," I said, but instead of falling back in line, I stayed next to him and Alex, who patted my shoulder. That was one of the things I loved most about Alex Nguyen: He put you at ease. He calmed you. Tag always said that too. "If Alex isn't nervous, then I tell myself I have no reason to be either," he once said, then added, "And I feel safest with you, Hopscotch."

Hopscotch, I recalled like a distant dream. "What kind of celebration dance is that?" Tag had asked during a sophomore whiffle ball game in the Circle. I'd scored a home run for our team and been a little smug about it, bouncing up and down on my feet. "It looks like you're playing an invisible game of hop—"

"Don't!" I'd read his beautiful mind. "Don't even think about it!"

But he smirked, as if to say, *Too late*.

It hadn't taken me long to warm to the nickname. I was Lily to everyone but Hopscotch to him. Every day, all day, always. He'd only started calling me by my name again when Blair and the other girls had started swooping in like vultures. *Don't let him pull away*, I told myself, but it soon grew harder and harder to hang on to him.

My heart tumbled even now as our band successfully reached the front entrance of Hubbard Hall. Its columns looked especially intimidating, glowing pearly white from the moonlight and towering above us. I held my breath until someone gently nudged me. Tag.

It was go time.

Sorry, Mom, I thought before I pulled her lanyard from my pocket and flashed her ID card across the door's sensor. There was a soft *beep* as the red light turned green and then the *click* of the lock. We were in.

The student center was pitch-black. "We can't turn on the lights, can we?" Manik asked once we'd all slipped inside and carefully closed the door behind us.

"No way," Zoe said. "Lighting up the whole first floor? Campo would be on us in seconds. There are so many windows here."

"How are we supposed do this, then?" Manik countered.

"Fear not," Tag said, "for we have the magic of flashlights."

I heard him unzip his backpack again and someone else unzip theirs too.

"You said you didn't know what we were originally doing," I muttered to Alex.

"I didn't," he muttered back. "My email said to come equipped with flashlights."

He and Tag began switching them on while the rest of us watched. Why did Tag and Alex have so many mini flashlights?

It was a rhetorical question. Just, of course they did. They had everything, including a contraband cat. Rumor was that they'd found a stray kitten in town and smuggled it into their dorm room.

"Turn on your phone lights too," Tag instructed. "We're going to line these up from the yearbook office to the storage room—"

"We're hiding the Almanacs in the storage room?" I blurted as the others simultaneously asked, "*What* storage room?"

"The storage room at the other end of the lounge," he answered. "Right behind the Hub." I recognized something wry in his voice. He was pleased, pleased that most of the group had no idea what he was talking about; it boded well for the prank.

"But that's so close," Maya said, her voice strained. She was definitely going to puke again. "Why hide them here when we could hide them across campus?"

"Because transporting them would be too much work," I guessed. "Carrying all those heavy boxes for that long would slow us down and pose more of a risk of getting caught."

"Exactly," Tag said. "Hiding the Almanacs as close to the office as possible is the safest and most unexpected move."

"And the funniest," Alex said with a laugh, and again, I suspected he knew more about this prank than he was letting on.

"I like it." Manik nodded. "I've never seen this storage room before, but it sounds secure enough." He reached for a flashlight. "I'll head to the office."

"Zoe and Maya, if you could go too?" Tag asked as I handed Manik my mom's keys. The yearbook office was locked. "Start moving some of the boxes? Alex and I should have the runway finished soon."

"Oh my god," Zoe said. "Are we the muscle, Swell?"

Tag chuckled. "I wasn't going to put a label on it, Wright, but…"

"I love it," she said and exchanged a grin with Maya. "Instead of two lacrosse lugs, you chose us."

"I've seen you in the gym and Maya in the workshop," Tag said. "You're both much more capable."

Egos extremely boosted, Zoe and Maya turned to follow Manik to the yearbook office. Although Maya soon made a detour to the restroom.

Uh-oh.

I blinked when I heard Tag ask if I could go open the door to the storage room. "Sure," I said softly, remembering when we had first explored it together. It was down the hall and around the corner from the Hub, its door partly covered by a large blue-red-and-gold Ames flag. We'd never given it a thought until Josh had brought it up at dinner at my house one night. Apparently he and the Alumni Relations office were in a heated battle over who deserved use of the space. "They have *plenty* of room in their offices upstairs," he'd said, stabbing his pork loin in frustration, "while I don't have *nearly* enough in the kitchen!"

Tag and I'd checked it out to find the room filled to the brim with supplies for reunion weekend. Storage shelves lined the walls, housing boxes of table linens, graduation flags, and even old class T-shirts. Circular tables, folding chairs, speakers, and DO NOT PARK HERE signs covered the floorspace. "I'm sorry, but I have to side with Alumni Relations," Tag had said. "This is a lot of crap."

"*A lot*," I'd agreed, suddenly very aware that we were *very* alone.

Tag had thrown back his head and laughed as I backed him into a dusty corner. We'd had to brush some dirt and cobwebs from our clothes before leaving.

Yes, I concluded with a twinge in my ribs. *It's safe to say no one will find the Almanacs in here.*

After kicking the door stopper into place, I reunited with the others in the yearbook office. About thirty cardboard boxes were in the far corner, and Manik looked like he was about to tear his hair out, watching as Zoe and Tag each hefted a heavy box onto their shoulders. "Where's Maya?" I asked, even though I had a pretty good guess.

Zoe smiled faintly. "Bathroom, with Alex holding her hair back."

"I knew he wouldn't be any help in the transport depart-ment," Tag said with mirth. While you couldn't get Tag out of the gym, Alex was all but allergic to it. Instead of playing sports, he was Ames's favorite student commentator.

"Well, he *does* want to be a doctor someday," I said slyly. "He might as well work on his bedside manner." I looked at a fretful Manik and gestured to the boxes. "May I?"

He nodded slowly. "Just don't drop it," he said. "You might dent the books' covers or crack their spines."

My brows knitted together. Maybe I didn't hit the gym regularly, but I'd run the Chicago and Boston marathons and danced in every school musical. "I can handle it," I told him at the same time as Tag called back, "She can handle it!"

Then he pretended to fumble his box, catching it just before it fell to the floor.

Manik sucked in a sharp breath, and I felt my lips twitch. There was goofy Tag.

Zoe, as predicted, was a workhorse, moving her boxes in half the time I moved mine. They *were* extremely heavy and I didn't want Manik to have a meltdown if I did accidentally drop one, so I took it slow and steady. "I don't understand why Alumni Relations gets this room," Zoe said as we deposited boxes. The center had been cleared, supplies moved aside, and concrete floor swept. *When did Tag find the time do this?* I wondered. "It seems like it should belong to the Hub."

"We wouldn't be able to use it if this was the Hub's territory,"

Tag said, carrying the last box with Manik, Alex, and a seriously pale Maya. "Josh—I mean, Mr. Bauer—would be in and out of here all the time. Alumni Relations doesn't set foot in this place after the class reunions in May." He placed the final box on top of the fortress we built. Together, we watched in awe. It was a perfect pyramid.

"Damn." Alex whistled. "This is worthy of Giza."

"It needs one more thing," Tag said before jogging out of the room. A minute later, he returned with none other than his kooky hat. We laughed when he crowned the pyramid.

Ames's Jester had spoken.

"Alright, alright, everyone out," Tag said afterward, his cheeks a little red. "It's time to move on to the scavenger hunt."

The scavenger hunt was the second phase of the prank. "We can't *really* deprive Ames of the Almanacs," Tag had said back at King's Court. "I'm sure as hell not graduating without mine, so after we hide them, we're going to set up clues all over campus that'll send our esteemed president on a treasure hunt to *find* them."

"I love that journey for him," I'd said, which had made Tag bite his lip so he didn't laugh. But Alex did. He cackled. *Schitt's Creek* was their favorite, and my Alexis impression was apparently scary good. I used to greet Alex every day by booping him on the nose.

Now though, it struck me again that this was Daniel we were pranking. It was *Daniel* who would be going on this treasure hunt. My stomach stirred. Even though I didn't like him the way he liked me, he was still...

Well, he was still.

We shuttled out of the storage room and quickly disassembled the lighted pathway, collecting the flashlights and phones. Everyone turned their lights off except for Alex, who shined his on the Jester's backpack so Tag could dig through it. It seemed to be bottomless. "What's the first clue?" Manik asked excitedly. "Where does it lead?"

"Someone's sure changed their tune," I mumbled and felt Zoe pinch my arm in amusement.

Tag pulled out a nondescript manila folder. I squinted to see that it was full of unsealed black envelopes, the same ones used for the Jester's invitation. But instead of names, each envelope was numbered. It seemed like everyone was holding their breath as we watched Tag tug out the first clue. Again, there was no handwriting—only the magazine letters.

We all huddled together to read:

To Our Fearless Leader:
If there's something you seek,
visit Cassiopeia at the peak.
Meet her at midnight for your second clue.

"There's a catch with this first one, though," Tag said mildly as I deciphered the clue to mean the observatory. Most

Ames students took astronomy at one point or another. It had a reputation of being easy.

"What is it?" Maya asked.

"I'm going to slip it in his mailbox…" Tag gestured to the darkened mail room. "But not tonight. We want him to discover the Almanacs are missing and then sweat for a few days before following the bread crumbs. If we give him the clue now, he might find it before noticing the yearbooks are gone."

"And what's wrong with that?" I heard myself say as Maya gave him a thumbs-up before sprinting for the bathroom again. Zoe followed her. "The Almanacs will still be MIA."

"Yes, but the point is to draw out the prank," Tag said. "If he recovers the yearbooks only a night after students were supposed to get them, it isn't very—"

I cut him off, my heart thumping hard. "I don't get why you're doing this," I said. "Why are you picking on Daniel?"

"Manik, let's do some recon," Alex chirped. "Check and see if there's any activity outside." He grabbed the yearbook editor's shirtsleeve and dragged him over to a window.

Tag dropped his voice. "I'm not *picking* on Daniel," he said. "I'm pulling a prank that happens to heavily involve the school president. If Alex had won the election, we would still be standing here right now." He shook his head. "In fact, I wish it were Alex. It would be a lot funnier—he would have an open breakdown while I'm sure Rivera's gonna put up a front that everything's fine."

"But everyone helping has an issue with Daniel," I whispered.

Tag raised an exaggerated eyebrow. "You have an issue with Daniel?"

The back of my neck heated. *Yes*, I thought. *I don't want to go to prom with him.*

"No, of course not," I stammered. "I meant the others do. You only need me for the keys."

"Lily, you don't actually believe that, do you? That you're just the key holder?"

I didn't respond.

"Alex and I have watched many a YouTube video on how to pick locks. Leda's ID makes things infinitely easier, but we could've managed without it." He reached out as if to touch me but ended up running a hand through his hair. "I asked you because..."

"We should get going," I said when he trailed off. From the sound of his voice, I knew he had an answer, but I also knew it wouldn't be what I so dreamed of hearing.

I asked you because I trust you.

I asked you because I miss you.

I asked you because I love you.

Maybe Tag trusted me, but there was no way he missed or loved me anymore. He'd moved on after that day in his room last spring. "I think it's for the best," I'd told him as he sat on his bed, head in his hands. "Because I'm really tired, Tag. I'm really tired of playing all these games and tuning out the noise. I love you so much, but I can't do this anymore."

"I just don't get what you're talking about," he eventually said, green eyes glassy. "What games? What noise? Am I doing something wrong? Hops, please tell me…"

But I didn't tell him. If he didn't realize the gold rush of attention he got from girls and how hard it was for me to handle, it meant he was enjoying it. Breaking up, then, really was for the best.

"I don't know where the Jester's clues lead," I said now, throat thickening, "but I imagine we're about to embark on a campus tour?"

"Yeah," he murmured, giving me a half-hearted smile right when Alex and Manik returned. Zoe also reappeared, but without Maya. She was still in the bathroom.

"Coast is clear, Captain," Alex reported, then turned to Zoe. "Can the last troop be rallied?"

Zoe shook her head. "I don't think so," she said. "She's, um, made camp in there." She sighed. "And I'm sorry, but I'm going to stay with her. I don't want her sneaking back to her room alone later. Maybe I can meet up with you after?"

Everyone looked at Tag. I caught his jaw just barely twitch, but other than that, he appeared unfazed. "No worries," he said. "Tell her I hope she feels better."

Alex, Manik, and I echoed him.

Zoe nodded.

"And please ask her to text me," Tag added. "Or have you text me."

"Text you what?"

"Four digits," Tag said, then thanked her for the heavy lifting. They exchanged a fist bump, and Zoe affectionately tugged my ponytail before hauling ass back to the restrooms.

No one else moved.

"Is anyone else out?" Tag asked after a beat. "Feel free to speak now."

My hands shook a little, knowing he was talking to me. I thought for a moment. Was it unfair that Daniel was going to take the brunt of this bank job? No. It was *unfortunate*, but not unfair. The Almanacs were the president's responsibility, and Daniel just so happened to be the president.

This isn't personal, I reassured myself. *It's a prank.*

"Brilliant," Tag said. "Who's ready to count constellations?"

CLUE ONE

TO OUR FEARLESS LEADER:
IF THERE'S SOMETHING YOU SEEK,
VISIT CASSIOPEIA AT THE PEAK.
MEET HER AT MIDNIGHT FOR
YOUR SECOND CLUE.

SEVEN

My lungs quivered with nerves when we headed back to Hubbard Hall's entrance. Sneaking out of my house, sprinting through the faculty neighborhood, and breaking into a school building were one thing, but trekking across Ames's four-hundred-acre campus? That felt like another quest entirely.

"Now the *real* fun begins," Alex whispered as I walked straight into Tag's back when he stopped short near one of the windows. Both his arms swooped back to steady me in case I wobbled. It was like being wrapped in a backward hug; I had to fight the urge to lean into it. He smelled faintly of chlorine and his flannel shirt was so soft.

"Headlights," Tag murmured. Alex motioned for us to retreat to the nearby stairwell before we listened for the mechanic *hum* of an engine to pass. Once Tag had double-checked that the nocturnal streets were again quiet, we slid out a side exit.

"Harvey is on duty tonight," I told Tag. "With Guardhouse Gabe shadowing him. He told me the other day."

"I know," Tag said.

"You do?"

"Lily, you aren't the only one who talks to Gabe."

"We mostly discuss chess," Alex cheerfully chimed in. "Believe it or not, he's really into it. Sometimes we'll play during my free periods. Taggart comes and watches..."

I rolled my eyes. "And subtly takes pictures of the weekly guard schedule?"

"I'll neither confirm nor deny," Tag said.

"You knew but didn't plan this for Mr. Harvey's day off?" Manik asked. "Or during his retirement party?"

"Oh, shitballs," I said. "My mom and I are supposed to bring dessert to that."

Tag chuckled. "Leda wears an apron now?"

"Only for dramatic effect," I said. "I'll whip up brownies or something while she supervises and then taste tests. Same as always."

Tag was silent for a beat. "She's going to miss you next year."

A lump formed in my throat. I was going to miss her too once I left for Georgetown. "She'll be okay," I whispered. "She has Josh to keep her well fed."

Especially since he was finally moving in this fall. It was perfect timing because I'd be gone, and he'd have fulfilled his five-year housemaster requirement. Most Ames faculty members lived in a dorm before they graduated to the neighborhood. At twenty-four, my mom had arrived on campus with a toddler on her hip and became housemaster in the junior girls' house. "Everyone was very eager to babysit you," she once told me. "Although after you turned six, it became difficult wrangling you into bed with Taylor Swift blasting on the other side of the door. You always wanted to go dance with the girls in the common room."

Honestly, it explained why my go-to karaoke song was "The Story of Us." One of the girls must've been going through a tough breakup.

The Galloway Observatory sat atop the big hill behind two boys' houses, and while it sounded grand, alas, it was not. White brick with arched windows and a small rotunda, it desperately needed a new paint job, and sections of brick were eroding.

No one spoke as we crossed the Circle toward the dorms. Biting my tongue, I felt like we were in the Hunger Games, creeping through the arena with all eyes trained on us. There were no Campo cars in sight, but dorm housemasters…they were different from neighborhood faculty members. They kept unusual hours since they both parented and policed students. I caught Manik glancing over at the darkened Bates House and knew he had the same thought. My mom and I'd lived there once upon a time, and now it was home to the Epstein-Foxes. My physics teacher was probably asleep, but I couldn't help but imagine her and her fellow housemasters armed to the teeth with knives, ready to hunt us down and skin us alive.

Get a grip, I told myself, hugging my pullover closer. The breeze had picked up and I again wished I'd worn a sweatshirt.

A second later, Tag was behind me and draping something over my shoulders. The flannel he'd been wearing over his sweatshirt. "Right on schedule," he said after popping the collar for the finishing touch.

My eyes prickled a little. Tag—he'd remembered how easily I became an icicle. When we were together, I'd always be running my hands up his sleeves to get warm. "Thank you," I told him, slipping into the shirt. It felt like chestnuts roasting on an open fire.

We kept walking until we reached the base of the hill. A twisting and turning stone stairway had been carved into the side; it was wide with repurposed driftwood banisters, and tonight it felt like Mount Everest. Save for Tag's iPhone flashlight, we were surrounded by darkness so there was seemingly no end in sight. "God, I'm so happy my parents never let me take astronomy," Alex commented. "This climb is…"

He went silent. We'd reached the top of the hill, and while the observatory was dark, the cedar-shingled cottage just a few leaps and bounds away was *not*. It was entirely illuminated, as if expecting someone.

As if expecting *us*.

"Holy hell," Alex breathed. "Was he supposed to be home?"

Nobody responded; we were too busy staring speechless at the house…Bunker Hill's house. Several years ago, he'd informed Ames's administration that he was going to have a cottage built on campus. "It'll have a classroom too," he'd told my mom. "I'm tired of teaching in the language building after all these years."

"No, he was not," Tag eventually answered as a man's silhouette became visible through one of the front windows. "He's supposed to be in New York. He's been bragging for *months* about these opera tickets he scored—opening night of *La bohème* at the Met. Just the other day, I asked if his tux was ready, and he told me it was looking better than ever."

"But he changed his mind," I whispered. "I helped him sell the tickets on StubHub this afternoon because he's sick. His seasonal allergies have evolved into a sinus infection."

Alex groaned. "Hasn't he heard of Zyrtec?"

"I'm sorry," I said. "If I'd known…"

If I'd known the Jester's plan, I would've warned him.

"Well, we're screwed," Manik declared, pointing to the house as Tag rubbed his forehead. Bunker was now comfortably settled in an armchair with a glass of something and a book. "There's no way he won't see us."

We stood there at a loss. "No, screw being screwed," I said a few moments later, my stomach spinning. "We're not. We can still do this."

The boys gave me incredulous looks. "Come again?" Manik squeaked.

"We'll go on with the Jester's plan." I swallowed hard. "Bunker…" I felt guilty for what I was about to say, but it was true. "That glass he's holding isn't filled with water. Even if he does see us—which he *won't*, because it's not like we're going to ding-dong-ditch his door—he won't remember it."

Manik took an audible breath. "Should we all go?" he asked. "Even if he is drunk, four people on your front lawn is a lot to miss."

"Agreed, so you guys wait here," Tag said. "I'll hide the clue." Alex opened his mouth in protest, but Tag shook his head. "You *need* to stay. We can't risk it."

We can't risk it.

I didn't need to ask to know what that meant. Ames had a two-strike disciplinary policy, and Alex already had one tally in his file. He and some guys had been caught red-handed with a six-pack after a dance last year, so if he got caught tonight, he'd be making an early exit from campus.

"Plus, you take Russian, Alex," I quickly said. "Not Latin."

"*Da.*" He smirked. "I don't study your *dead* language."

Tag and I rolled our eyes. Latin students were teased on campus because we had all the basics of a dark academia novel down, including an enigmatic professor who taught a coterie of seven seniors in his own home. Bunker wrote on an old-fashioned blackboard while we sipped freshly brewed tea. "When's the murder happening?" everyone always asked.

"No body, no crime," we always answered.

I didn't think Bunker would catch us, but if he *did*, my hope was he'd cut two of his students a break and at least give us a head start before calling Campo.

"Fine," Alex said once I'd explained. He nodded. "I'll chill with Manik."

"Ready?" I asked Tag, already picturing us doing some sort of army crawl to stay in the shadows.

He hesitated. He didn't want me to come.

And to be honest, I didn't really want him to go. He had a strike too. A strike for something stupid. If anything, this clue should be my responsibility.

But that was out of the question.

I pretended to cough. "Keys."

"Are you kidding?" Alex said as Tag sighed. "Don't tell me Leda has a key to the gate too?"

"But of course." I shrugged.

And then tugged Tag out of the trees.

EIGHT

After indeed army crawling our way to the observatory, Tag and I stood up and brushed ourselves off before swiping into the spooky building and climbing the spiral staircase that led up to the telescopes. Its outer wrought iron gate barred us from the balcony, so I shuffled through my mom's collection of metal keys until I found the right one. But Tag hadn't spoken since we'd left the trees, so I did what first came to mind once the gate creaked open. "Tag!" I whisper-yelled, then slapped his arm and took off down the long flagstone overlook.

I heard him let out a surprised laugh before hightailing it after me. My heart was still racing when we'd both made it to the end of the line and the last telescope in the row. "*Lux*," Tag said. "Light" in Latin, so I moved close to shine my mom's key chain flashlight into his backpack. He pulled out another unsealed envelope, marked with a hodgepodge of letters spelling out **CLUE TWO**.

"Where did you get all the magazines?" I asked when he handed me the envelope.

"Here and there," he replied vaguely.

"Shall we do a dramatic reading?"

"Eh, I don't think so," he said as he retrieved a roll of duct tape from his backpack. "I've read these clues a hundred times."

"But I haven't," I said.

"You don't need to." He tried reaching for the envelope. "They're stupid."

I held on tight. "I highly doubt that."

Then I pulled out the envelope's contents: another sturdy piece of cardstock, but this time adorned with red-and-black letters. I shook my head at Tag's meticulous handiwork, cleared my throat, and began to read:

> *Let's talk about sex, baby.*
> *You know who's doing it and you know where.*
> *If you don't hurry, Tag and Blair*
> *might even beat you there...*

My voice was a whisper by the end, and afterward, I put the clue back in its envelope and licked the flap to seal it. "Lily, they're stupid," Tag repeated, but his voice was gravelly this time. "These riddles..." His throat bobbed. "They're all ridiculous."

I acted like everything was fine, like there wasn't a chord being painfully plucked in my rib cage. "No, they're not," I said. "I actually think this one's pretty funny."

A beat of silence, and then, "Really?"

"Yeah." I nodded and handed the envelope back to him. "I mean, I don't understand why you'd put yourself in a clue, but…" I shrugged. "Whatever."

Again, Tag didn't immediately respond. All I heard was the sound of duct tape being unrolled. "It's so people don't guess I'm the Jester," he said while securing the clue to the telescope's underbelly. "Like Manik said earlier, I'm a front-runner." He ripped the tape with his teeth. "I figured a joke about myself would throw everyone off."

I opened my mouth, then closed it. He was right. If I read this riddle as a bystander, I'd *never* guess Tag was the Jester. Blair either. It made too much fun of them.

When did he write this? I wondered. *Before or after they broke up?*

Then something else struck me. "Wait, throw *everyone* off?" I said. "You think Daniel is going to show Ames these clues? After he solves the mystery?"

Tag half shrugged. "Debatable."

I folded my arms over my chest. "*Debatable?*"

"Yes," he said, but he wasn't looking at me. His focus was still on the tape and telescope. "Part of me can see him keeping it professional and close to the vest, but another part…" He paused. "Well, I've never laughed at his jokes, but he does have a sense of humor—or at least a shred of one—so I can see him showing some people. His prom date, definitely."

"Lucky her," I replied offhandedly before remembering that *I* was Daniel's prom date. There was way too much going on right now to remember anything except *right now*. I bit my pinkie nail, then said, "I'll make sure my laugh is convincing."

"Convincing?" Tag stuffed the duct tape roll back into his backpack before rising up to his full height. He cocked his head. "Didn't you say this clue was funny?"

I pulled my baseball hat brim lower, which made him chuckle. "It *is* funny," I admitted, because it was—objectively. Objectively speaking, Tag and Blair's roller-coaster relationship was flipping hilarious. Ames would eat it up like Tag did his scrambled eggs with ketchup. "It's funny, but not to…"

Me, I wanted to say. *It's not funny to me.*

Even if they'd broken up for good, I hated seeing their names linked.

"Not to…?" Tag tried to tease out when I dropped off, but my stomach swished. I didn't have the guts to tell him the truth.

And we didn't have time. There wasn't time for the truth. We had a mission to accomplish.

"Blair," I mumbled. "It won't be funny to Blair."

Like I really cared.

Tag snorted. "Believe me," he said, "Blair will not only survive, but she will *thrive*." I raised my brim to see his brows comically furrow. "You truly haven't noticed how much she likes her name in the papers?"

Blair Greenberg did love people buzzing about her, whether it was thanks to one of her bylines in the school newspaper or a TikTok. Or even better, school gossip. She lived for the publicity.

I couldn't help but give Tag a tiny smirk.

He gave me a tiny smirk back. The exchange was so natural that I wasn't surprised when his hand suddenly swiped my arm. "You're it!" he said and went dashing down the balcony.

I followed as fast as I could, hoping to leave all thoughts of Blair Greenberg behind us.

Although I swore I saw her ghost ahead of me.

⁓

Tag beat me to the gate but chivalrously held it open before I took over, slamming it shut and then wincing at the wrought iron clanging against its frame. The echo made me fumble with my mom's key. How was Daniel going to get through later? I had no idea but knew he would figure something out. He was Daniel Rivera. "His ID has full access," Tag said, reading my mind. "The administration gives the president full campus access. As for the gate…" He eyed it. "I think he can climb it. I could climb it."

"Oh, really?" I said airily but also kind of annoyed. "Care to demonstrate?"

It took him less than fifteen seconds.

I refused to acknowledge it. "We should hurry," I said once his feet were firmly back on the ground. "The sculpture sanctuary isn't exactly close."

Ames's sculpture sanctuary, where Tag and Blair were

infamous for doing "yoga" early in the mornings and reconciling from fights on Saturday nights. Even the faculty was aware of their routine because they knew *everything*. "If it affects his performance in the pool," Josh once said, "I'm going to—"

"You can't knock his teeth out, Josh," Headmaster Bickford had interrupted. She sighed dreamily. "The boy has such beautiful teeth."

Yes, the many wonders of orthodontics! I'd thought. Tag had spent freshman year in braces but sophomore year searching for his retainer. Alex constantly hid it.

But somehow his smile had stayed straight.

Soon, Tag and I were spiraling back down to the observatory's first floor. I led the way with Tag's hand latching onto my flannel to better navigate the staircase. When his fingertips grazed the back of my neck, I wondered if he felt the goose bumps bursting on my skin. They were breathtaking like fireworks. That initial jolt of surprise, but then a dazzling crackle.

Together we raced across the worn black-and-white tile floor toward the door and exploded into the night. Still dazed from the twisting stairs and Tag's touch, I stumbled over the building's crumbling front steps. Tag stayed silent as I dramatically dropped every expletive in the book, but then he broke down laughing and said, "Man, I've missed your mouth."

I took one step forward and then froze, going as still as a statue...but my mind did not turn to stone with it. *Man, I've missed your mouth.*

I told myself not to overanalyze; I knew what he meant. "You've got a real seafarer there, bud," I remembered Josh joking when Tag and I'd started dating, because while I didn't curse in front of the neighbors, I swore like a sailor at home.

Tag had always found it hilarious.

A deep ache settled in my stomach. Because I missed Tag's voice too. I missed his confident cadence. I missed his soft whispers. I missed his easy laugh.

I also missed kissing him. Sad, maybe…but true. I missed his lips on mine and my skin. "Isn't it a bit warm for a scarf, Lily?" Zoe and Pravika giggled two Septembers ago, and all I could do was smile at the ground. The picnic Tag and I'd packed the day before had gone untouched; we'd spread out the blanket on a far-flung stretch of campus but then ended up devouring each other instead of the food. "Best picnic ever," Tag said while we'd walked back to main campus hand in hand. His hair was a mess and his Henley on backward, but he twirled me around in his arms before I could tell him. We both laughed when his stomach rumbled halfway home.

Man, I've missed your mouth.

I stood there, waiting for the tips of Tag's ears to burn red and for him to backtrack and clarify what he meant. "We need to hurry," I said when it didn't dawn on him. "Alex and Manik are probably wondering where we are."

Tag murmured something that sounded like, "I don't think Alex is worried."

"Well, he should be," I said, now stalking across the grass. "This isn't some…" I searched for the right phrase and, after a second, ironically found it. "This isn't some silly prank."

It took only three bounds for Tag to catch up to me. "Technically, it is," he said. "So let's embrace the silliness and lighten up a little."

I turned on him, my voice sharp. "Lighten up a little?"

The Jester nodded merrily. "Yes, it'll be easier if—"

The sound of a door swinging open brought our conversation to an abrupt halt. Tag and I both lurched as a deep and congested voice called, "Who's out there?"

His words were slightly slurred.

Run! my muscles screamed, but Tag and I didn't get the chance; the light from Bunker Hill's high-powered lantern captured us in its beam almost immediately. It was big and bright, practically blinding.

"Miss Hopper, is that you?" Bunker asked from his front stoop. He was dressed in a black-and-gray smoking jacket with his flashlight in one hand and a tumbler of brown liquid in the other. Probably the bourbon my mom had recommended the other night.

Even though I'd run through this scenario earlier, my heart hammered and I could hear the blood pumping through my ears. Tag had told Alex to stay in the trees to avoid a second strike, and I'd mentioned Latin to keep him there…although truthfully, being Bunker's students wouldn't carry much weight (despite what dark academia dictated). I knew that. If we were caught, Latin wouldn't save us. My surrogate grandfather would definitely call my mom.

"Do you trust me?" I whispered to Tag.

A heartbeat later, he'd threaded his fingers through mine. The movement was so smooth and effortless that I needed to pull away and stretch my tingling hand before finding his fingers again. My eyelids fluttered. The moment took me back to a different time—a better time.

We took several steps toward the cottage. "Yes, it's me, Mr. Hill," I said as if I weren't shaking in my sneakers. I lifted an arm in greeting, and once Tag and I reached the base of the porch, I noticed our teacher's disheveled white hair and the red rings around his weathered eyes.

"Now, Lily…" he began before he raised an intrigued brow at who was at my side. I moved closer to Tag, and Bunker let a small smile slip. "I know that young love has a mind of its own," he said, bemused, "but don't you think it's a bit late for you and Mr. Swell to be taking in the moonlight together?" He squinted at his watch, as if to confirm Tag's curfew had indeed come and gone. Part of me wondered if he knew when the boarders' curfew actually was and if he even cared. He looked up and gave Tag a drunkenly solemn stare. "I assume the rumors are true? You and Miss Greenberg have said farewell?"

"Yes sir," Tag said. "For the last time."

Bunker raised his glass. "Then cheers."

I felt Tag shift from one foot to the other, so I let go of his hand to casually rub the back of his neck. My heart twinged when he leaned into it; afterward, it was like he couldn't find my hand fast enough. *He's nervous*, I thought as our fingers intertwined again. *He's nervous about Bunker reporting us, about getting the damning second strike.*

I squeezed tight to tell him it was okay. I had this handled.

"Well, then," Bunker said, "it's probably best that you two weren't here earlier." He sipped his drink. "It would've made for a rather awkward gathering."

"Gathering?" Tag and I both asked.

"Oh, yes." Another swig of bourbon. "President Rivera was here—"

I gasped. "Daniel? *Daniel* was here?"

"Indeed. He stopped by for a chat."

"When?" I asked gravely as our teacher's words sunk in, as every ounce of blood drained from my face. Daniel was another one of the seven "murderous" Latin students. He too was close with Bunker, though I knew Bunker found Daniel's essays "contrived" (even if his grammar was perfect). "When was he here?"

Bunker studied his watch again. "This evening" was what he settled on, waving us off and swaying in place. His glass was almost empty.

Tag, back in control, moved to steady the old man. "Why don't we get you inside, Mr. Hill? I heard you have a sinus infection?"

Bunker pinched his nose and nodded. However, I stayed where I was, watching through the window as Tag helped him into a worn leather armchair before disappearing into another part of the house. He returned with a glass of water. "Now, Taggart," I heard Bunker say, his voice much too loud, "you and Lily be careful. Roger Harvey's trainee is itching to make his first arrest. You're ten days away from graduation, and I don't want to see either of you mess it up! Lily's not just our salutatorian, she's our *crown jewel*." He sighed. "And you...we both know what a time you've had. I want you to finish strong, son."

Tag gave Bunker a wan smile and a pat on the shoulder. I also saw him mouth something, but his voice was too low to hear. When he reemerged from the cottage, all traces of the smile were gone, lips now in a flat line. "Do you want to punch the editor?" he said as we made eye contact and started walking resolutely toward the trees, where Alex and Manik waited. "Or should I?"

My voice trembled. "Do you think it's true?"

Tag nodded. "He left his hat. His fucking Harvard hat was sitting on the coffee table."

"Gentlemen do not wear hats indoors," I remembered Bunker saying to the boys in Latin.

I gritted my teeth and picked up my pace. Tag upped his too. Our hand-holding was finished, our show over.

"Okay, *what* happened?" Alex said once we reached the copse of trees. "Where have you guys been?"

We ignored him. "Patel!" Tag all but barked. "Patel, where are you?"

Manik appeared from behind a tree, basically vibrating like Madame Hoffman's toy poodles in December. "There you guys are. We were getting worried—"

I didn't let him finish; instead, I stepped forward and surprised myself by poking him in the chest. "Where was Daniel, Manik?" Tag asked from behind me, his voice sounding somewhere between irked and infuriated. "Where was Daniel when you snuck out tonight?"

NINE

Manik's eyes widened—or at least, I imagined they did. The trees were a whirl of darkness. "What?" he asked. "What are you talking about?"

"Daniel," Tag repeated. "Daniel Rivera? Your friend, fellow prefect, *and* our school president? Maybe you've heard of him?"

"Okay, seriously," Alex tried again. "*What* happened?"

"Bunker happened!" I couldn't help but snap, suddenly realizing why *else* the Jester had tapped Manik for tonight. It wasn't only because he was the Almanac's hardworking helmsman; he was also Daniel's roommate, which made him perfect for recon. He could ensure nothing was amiss before the prank had officially begun.

Although something told me Tag hadn't spelled that out for him.

"We hid the clue," Tag started to explain. His tone was now precise, all business. "But Mr. Hill caught us afterward—" He dropped off, as if unsure whether to share the details about our encounter with Bunker. I waited with wavering lungs, only exhaling when he skipped over our showmance. I didn't want to hear the word "pretend" leave his lips.

Even if that was what we'd been doing.

"That's really what he said?" Alex asked once Tag had finished. "'President Rivera stopped by for a chat this evening.'"

"Direct quote," I confirmed.

Alex sucked in a breath. "Did you tell him, Manik?" he said. "Did you let *anything* slip?"

"No!" Manik exclaimed. "How could I? I had no idea about any of this! Once I accepted the prank bid, all I got was the email about wearing black and the midnight rendezvous. That's *it*."

"And that's not *at all* telling," Alex deadpanned, though no one laughed. I wanted to believe Manik, I did, but...

"Daniel likes to take walks," I said, readjusting my baseball hat. "He goes on walks when he wants to clear his head."

"What does he need to clear his head about?" Alex muttered to Tag. "He's achieved nearly everything this school has to offer."

Except valedictorian, I thought.

Blair had beaten him there.

I couldn't hear what Tag muttered back, but even in the dark, I felt his eyes on me, and my heart rate hitched. Sometimes after we studied, Daniel asked me to join him on his meanders. He did most of the talking and I did most of the nodding along while keeping my hands in my pockets so he wouldn't try holding one.

Sneaking out to take a moonlit stroll didn't sound like Daniel, but it was late May. The end of senior year gave people incentive to take chances.

I mean, here I was.

"Manik, did you *see* Daniel?" Tag asked inquisitively.

"Of course," he said. "We live together. Of course I saw him; I see him all the time."

"*No,*" I said, taking more of a bad cop stance. We needed to get to the bottom of this. "He means did you see him *tonight*? Your rooms have an adjoining door, right? Did you see him brush his teeth? Climb into bed and close his eyes? Did you *see* Daniel before you left?"

Manik sighed. "No," he admitted. "I didn't. Our connecting door was closed because I lied that I was going to bed early, but Daniel needed to stay up to finish his English essay." He coughed. "His light was off when I snuck out onto the fire escape, but I didn't check if he was in his room or not." He was quiet for a few seconds, *guilty* for a few seconds. "I'm sorry."

Alex groaned while my stomach squirmed. There was a possibility Daniel was wandering campus—and that possibility, the possibility of running into him didn't add to the thrill of tonight. It only made it more dangerous. "Maybe we should hide the rest of the clues tomorrow morning?" I gently suggested. "Our building access will have been restored, so we won't need my mom's keys—"

"But he's asleep!" Manik insisted. "He *has* to be. I said his light was out when I left and now that I think about it, I remember hearing some snoring…"

After a second of deliberation, Alex snapped his fingers. "Alright, devil's advocate," he said. "Let's say Manik is right that Daniel's all tucked in for the night, snoring and hugging his teddy bear." He took a breath. "Was Mr. Hill plastered, Lily? Like you predicted?"

"Um…" I thought of Bunker's rumpled hair, red-ringed eyes, and bourbon-filled tumbler. "Pretty much."

"Then what does 'this evening' *really* mean?" Alex posed. "He's probably lost his sense of time. Daniel might've visited him at 8:30 or 9:00, and then it could've felt like you guys arrived right after he left. Minutes later…when it's actually been *hours*." He illuminated his phone to show that it was a little past 1:15. "What do you think?"

"I guess it's plausible…" I began. Seniors had a 10:30 curfew, so Daniel could've stopped by on the later side. And Bunker *had* consulted his watch after catching Tag and me, undoubtedly unsure about the time.

Tag didn't say anything. His silences were so loud that sometimes it was impossible to ignore him. You wanted to know what he was thinking.

Alex sighed. "Really, Taggart?"

"We have to check, Alexander. I don't want to chance it."

"Fine," Alex gritted out, "but I have to tell you, I don't

have much confidence in that old fire escape's weight-bearing capabilities…"

Over at Macalester House, the freshmen boys' dorm, there was a rusty fire escape that led directly up to Daniel and Manik's suite. "I can't believe you haven't had Buildings and Grounds dismantle it yet," my mom had told Josh at dinner right before school started in August. "It's practically an invitation for your prefects to sneak out or sneak others in."

"I'm aware," Josh said after finishing off his rack of ribs. "That's why I chose two guys who wouldn't even consider it. They're too responsible." He took a sip of beer. "And from what I can tell, they don't exactly have the biggest social lives."

"That's not true," I remembered saying. "Daniel Rivera was elected school president."

"A vote that definitely prioritized competency over likability…" My mom shook her head, still disappointed for Alex.

Josh shrugged. "Even better. He'll be too busy to get any action."

"Josh!" my mom and I both exclaimed, and I thought something similar now. One—possibly two—prefects had snuck out of the dorm from right under his nose. The fire escape was right above his first-floor apartment!

"Alright, let's go," Alex said flatly. "Preferably with our fingers crossed."

"No," Tag said before anyone could move. "We're not all doing this."

Alex groaned. "Taggart, you just said you wanted—"

"Yes, he wants confirmation," I blurted, surfing Tag's wavelength. "But not *all* of us need to confirm that Daniel's melatonin is doing its job."

"Exactly." Tag stepped closer to me. "Mack House is in the opposite direction, so everyone going will waste time. We'll be completely off course." He paused, then delivered the hard truth. "Manik, I think you should go check on Daniel and keep an eye on him."

Manik squeaked. "Really? Me?"

"Yes, it makes the most sense."

"How so?"

"Well, for starters, you live there."

"But what if he catches me coming back?"

"Have an alibi ready," Tag said, and I impulsively knocked his knuckles with mine. It was an old code between us. Two knocks meant, *You're funny.*

Tag flicked my arm. *Thanks.*

Manik was silent but contemplative. *Come on,* I thought, holding in a breath. *Come on, Manik. You'd be doing this for the greater good of the team...*

"Wait," Alex said. "Don't send him yet—we might be overthinking this." He laughed. "All we have to do is check Daniel's location on the Snap Map."

"Daniel doesn't have Snapchat," I said, hoping everyone else had set their profiles to Ghost Mode. We couldn't have a fellow student randomly checking the map in the middle of the night and not seeing us in our houses.

"Do you even know me?" Alex said when Tag confirmed that everyone was invisible. "I'm always in Ghost Mode."

"I'll check Find My Friends," I said, pulling my phone from my pocket. "He's on Find My Friends."

But Daniel's profile gave us virtually no information other than the fact that he had been in the dining hall at 6:34 p.m. for dinner. "No dice," Tag said, looking over my shoulder. "He has it set up so that his location isn't updated unless he's actively using the app."

I glanced up from my bright screen. "Please, Manik?"

"Okay, okay," he said, relenting. "I'll do it. I'll go." He huffed. "But is that it? After I spy on him for a while, am I supposed to stay there for the rest of the night?"

Tag avoided the question. He just gave Manik a fist bump and said, "Don't forget to text the chat as soon as you know."

Tag had created a group chat right before we'd left King's Court, and I hadn't thought much of it. But now...with Zoe and Maya staying behind in Hubbard and Manik striking out on his own operation, it was like Tag had considered us getting separated during the night.

Alex let out a slow whistle once Manik had disappeared. "That sucks," he said, then turned upbeat. "But hey, now it's officially the A team!"

My shoulders slumped. *Zoe,* I woefully thought. Where

was she? She *had* to have gotten Maya back to their dorm by now, right? Because selfishly, I needed her. Tag, Alex, and I might've been the A team once, but we weren't anymore. And there was suddenly no way I could handle spending the rest of the night with Tag without a buffer. He and I had fallen back into reading each other's rhythms as predicted, but *now*? After what had happened with Bunker? Pretending to be together? Holding his hand, if only for a moment?

It hurt, like I always knew it would.

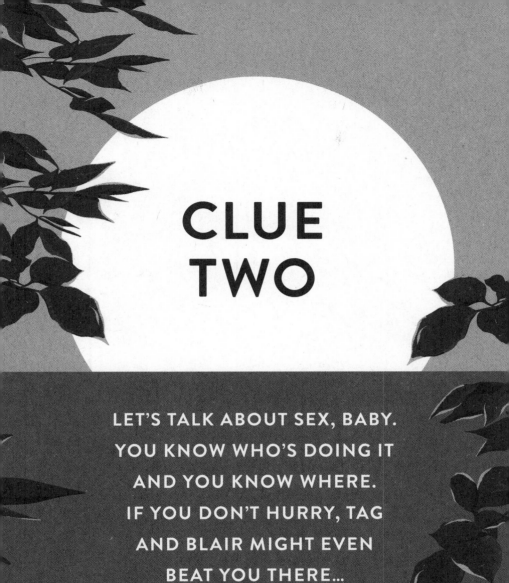

CLUE TWO

LET'S TALK ABOUT SEX, BABY.
YOU KNOW WHO'S DOING IT
AND YOU KNOW WHERE.
IF YOU DON'T HURRY, TAG
AND BLAIR MIGHT EVEN
BEAT YOU THERE...

TEN

Tag and Alex took the steps two at a time down the hill's stone stairway, but I lagged behind to send a private text to Zoe. She'd messaged me while Tag and I'd been playing Romeo and Juliet. Did you hide Clue #2?

Yes, but not without some complications, I typed back. Apparently Daniel felt the need for a late-night stroll...

Wait, he's on a walk right now? Zoe asked, along with (Maya says WHAT?!?!).

I filled Zoe in as I blindly bounded down the stairs, then she did the same. "Zoe and Maya made it back okay," I told the guys once I'd joined them. "Maya's still down for the count, though."

"God, what did she *eat*?" Alex said.

"Zoe said she'll try to meet up with us soon," I told Tag. "She wants Maya to fall asleep first." Maya had a single, but little did their aloof housemaster know that Zoe was in there all the time.

Tag nodded and said, "She's a really good girlfriend."

We looked at each other for a moment. *And you were a champion boyfriend,* I wanted to say, my heart aching. *During the best and worst times.*

One of the worst was junior fall. My mom and Josh had gone away for a long weekend. We'd agreed I was old enough to stay home, because I would be *far* from alone (the neighbors would find excuses to check in on me). "But I think I'm sick," I'd whispered to Tag during our nightly FaceTime. "My throat…"

I'd woken up the next morning with what I knew was strep. When I looked in the mirror and opened my mouth wide, you could see the bulbous red bumps. Go to the infirmary! my friends said, but I didn't. Why would I trade my own house for blank walls and starchy sheets? Instead, I hauled all my blankets downstairs and made a nest on the couch.

And after putting on a face for Headmaster Bickford, the DeLucas, and even Ames's married biology teachers, the doorbell rang yet again. "I brought fudgesicles!" Tag said, as if he knew I planned on ignoring any other visitors. "Ice cream's a legit remedy…or so says the internet!"

Then he just walked through the door, shucked off his jacket, and joined me on the couch. "Smoosh." I swallowed, my eyes welling up with tears. It hurt to talk. "I feel like a flaming pile of fucking shit."

"But my oh my, do you *look* radiant!" Tag grinned impishly and pulled me into his arms, cuddling me close before I settled my head on his lap and started sobbing. He kissed the top of my head and then slid his hand up my grandfather's old fisherman cable cardigan to rub slow circles on my back. "Close your eyes, Hopscotch," he said like a hypnotist. "Close your eyes and—"

A beeping noise cut him off. His glucose sensor. "Perfect timing," he mumbled, and I felt him shift so he could pull his insulin pump from his pocket to check his blood sugar. "Too low," he said after he'd silenced the device. "I need something to boost it."

"Gatorade's in the back of the fridge," I said. Neither my mom nor I drank the stuff, but we kept the house stocked for Tag.

"Cool Blue?" he asked.

"Of course," I answered as he carefully slid out from under me. "Because you're the coolest."

Tag laughed and took my hand.

"You'll come back?" I murmured hazily.

"When have I ever not?" he murmured back, raising our laced fingers to kiss the inside of my wrist. It sent sweet shivers through me. "And why would I ever stop?"

Because I told you to, I thought now. Only several months later, I'd told him to stop coming back, or coming in general. I could feel him pulling away and wanted to protect myself.

"So..." Alex ventured once the three of us had started walking. "What's next?"

"Sculpture sanctuary," Tag said right as I deadpanned, "Dropping the act."

Alex kept his voice light, innocent. "Pardon, Lily?"

I sighed. "Alex, come on. You know everything that's planned for tonight." The final tip-off had been seeing Bunker at home. Alex had been surprised—*shocked*, even. Like Tag, he clearly believed the old man would be gone for the night.

"Listen, I *may* have consulted a little," Alex allowed, which made Tag chuckle. "Everyone knows that sounding boards are helpful." He clapped Tag on the back. "But really, this is all the Jester." He pretended to weep. "And I couldn't be prouder."

I shook my head. "You guys never cease to amaze," I said, then randomly felt the need to ask, "Do you *actually* have a cat? Or was that a rumor?"

Tag answered. "No, it's true," he said. "We found Stevie hiding behind Provisions' dumpster and convinced her to come home with us."

"Stevie after *the* Stevie?" I guessed, jettisoning Stevie Nicks. There was only one Stevie in Tag and Alex's life: Stevie Budd from *Schitt's Creek*.

He nodded. "It fits her. You wouldn't think a cat could be so sardonic, but…" He pointed to the left, which meant we were taking the scenic route to the sculpture sanctuary. It would take longer but would be worth it.

There was the "beach side" of Ames and the "wood side." The sculpture sanctuary was wood side, but the most direct path there involved parading back through the academic village and cutting across the Circle again. Tag was smart; it was better to keep to the outskirts. Ames's paved roads only extended so far, so the outer buildings and fields weren't monitored as habit-ually by Campo.

But watch rookie Gabe get overeager and want to sweep the fields, I thought. *Watch him borrow Madame Hoffman's toy poodles for the first-ever Ames School K9 unit.*

They knew the Jester's prank was happening sooner or later. What a way for Gabe to be welcomed to the squad and what a way for Mr. Harvey to go out if they caught its culprits…

I barely let myself breathe as the three of us fell into a game of follow the leader. Tag was on point with me in the middle and Alex bringing up the rear. I was on high alert for any suspicious sounds, still feeling whiplash from our tête-à-tête with Bunker and the chance that Daniel was on tonight's chessboard. If we ran into any other roadblocks, I worried there would be no escaping them. Hence, I almost cried out when I felt Alex's hand on my shoulder. "Shh, it's only me," he whispered.

Instead of screaming, I sighed.

"Thank you for asking about Stevie," he said in a hushed voice.

He doesn't want Tag to hear, I realized and, with one quick glance, confirmed that the Jester was still scouting ahead of us.

"No worries," I whispered back. "I'd been wondering for a while, so…yeah."

"It chilled him out," Alex said. "You noticed that, right? How fired up he was on the hill, especially after giving Manik new marching orders?"

"Yeah," I grumbled. "Considering I was equally fired up, I'd say I noticed."

And I'd noticed Tag thaw too. We were both rattled, and if Alex's mere presence didn't do the trick, the best way to calm Tag was to get him talking about something he loved. All I needed to do was ask questions and listen...which was, well, how my heartbeat steadied. I'd been so nervous for *The Sound of Music* sophomore year, but by the time I walked into the auditorium on opening night, I was fine. I was nothing but excited, because Tag had come over after classes and analyzed *Dune*—his favorite book—for an hour straight. "*Dune* is to sci-fi what *The Lord of the Rings* is to fantasy," I'd never forget him saying.

His voice vaporized my nerves.

"He's head over heels for your cat," I told Alex. "It's so cute that he wants—"

Alex snorted. "He wants a girlfriend."

My stomach somersaulted. "What?"

"A girlfriend," Alex repeated. "What he wants is a girlfriend."

"Alex, if he wanted a girlfriend, he wouldn't have broken up with Blair for the..." I did a quick calculation. "Gajillionth time."

"She doesn't count," he replied. "Blair isn't a girlfriend, Lily. Blair is a Band-Aid." He paused. "Well, more like a *box* of Band-Aids."

I stopped in my tracks. "A box of Band-Aids? What does that even mean?"

"Hey, does Lily need a Band-Aid?" Tag whisper-shouted back to us. "I've got some in my backpack."

"Nah, she's fine," Alex answered as I tried to decipher his weird metaphor. Blair was a box of Band-Aids? Because even after all the arguing between them, he still reached for her to patch up the hurt? Over and over again?

I rolled my eyes and resumed walking.

———

Slowly but surely, we passed various checkpoints. The darkened art building, music hall, and then the deserted baseball fields and other practice fields. During a recent game of truth or dare, Zoe had admitted that she and Maya had hooked up in one of the lacrosse goals. "Well, I'm glad the season's over," Pravika had joked. "Because now that I know you've scored there, I don't ever want to again!"

I wished I could tease her about it now because I needed a distraction. Tag and Alex were muttering about how we hadn't heard from Manik yet, so Blair floated through my mind. For our first couple years at Ames, I'd only known her as the pretty popular girl who got great grades, wrote for the school paper, and was worshipped by guys. We didn't talk until junior year, after one of Tag's swim meets. "Lily, hi!" I remembered her saying. "Tag had an awesome relay today!"

She'd been really nice, but now I knew it had all been

so calculated. Most girls had been so obvious with Tag; they smiled and said hello in the halls, interrupted our conversations, and some were bold enough to touch his arm while giggling at his jokes. *Stop it*, I always thought. *Stop it, stop it, stop it!*

Blair hadn't thrown herself in his face. She'd casually talk to me alone, then Tag and me together. It wasn't until she wrote a profile on him for the newspaper's sports section that I wondered if something was up. Blair was features, not sports. "The two of us are also partners for a stats project," Tag had mentioned after his interview with her. "We both hate that class, so we've decided to suffer together."

My heart had sunk. *She likes him*, I realized. The incessant attention from the others was testing my nerves, but *this*? Blair making all the right moves to get Tag to fall for her?

Leave Lily, I could hear her saying. *Break Lily's heart and be with me.*

"Mom, I have to end things with Tag," I'd whispered to her late one night. "Nothing has happened, but I feel so sick. There's this knot inside me…"

She'd nodded like she knew it'd been coming. "Then let him go, Lil." She gave me a bittersweet smile and a big hug. "Let him go for now."

The three of us soon reached the mouth of the woods. They were far from welcoming, pitch-black with tree branches audibly swaying in the breeze. Tag and Alex switched on their iPhones, but my hand was shaking so hard that I couldn't tap the flashlight icon. Instead, I slipped my phone back into my pocket and made a fist around it.

Tag's eyebrows furrowed. "Your battery isn't dead, is it?"

"No, it's alive and well," I said, then shrugged. "I just can't do this."

"Because of the skunks?" Alex asked. "Because no lie, I'm kinda freaking out too. We should've brought tomato juice—"

"Lily, what do you mean?" Tag spoke over his friend. "You can't do what?"

My stomach started churning, and I couldn't ignore it. "I mean I can't pop by the place where you and Blair used to have wild sex," I said. "I know I'm your ex-girlfriend, and she's also your ex-girlfriend, but it's not okay, Tag. I don't care how stupid you say that clue is." I swallowed. "I'm not okay."

Tag glanced at the ground. Alex awkwardly patted his shoulder before vanishing into the woods, but Tag stayed quiet. "Wild sex, huh?" he eventually said. "I thought it was 'sunrise yoga.'"

I folded my arms across my chest. "You know it's a euphemism."

"Well, yeah, but a completely off-base one," he said, sighing heavily. "We actually *were* doing yoga, Lily. Blair is not the most relaxed person, so that's how she starts her day, and since I'm not all that relaxed either, I joined her."

"Oh," I said.

Tag forced a smile. "To be honest, it's not that effective."

"Why aren't you relaxed?" I whispered. "What's wrong?"

He yawned. "It doesn't matter."

Yes, it does, I thought, but instead I asked what they did there at night. "After you argue in front of everyone?"

God, I was so jealous. Desperately jealous. He didn't owe me any explanations, but I wanted them anyway.

"It depends," Tag said. "Usually, we'll apologize to each other or call it quits." He ran a hand through his hair. "Lily, there is a place where Blair and I would…" He trailed off, letting me fill in that blank space. "But it's not the sculpture sanctuary, I swear."

I waited a second, then nodded. "Alright," I whispered, and in an even smaller voice, I said, "Thanks for telling me."

"You're welcome," he replied. "And I'm sorry. I didn't realize how loyal Ames is to *People* magazine."

"Oh my god, I hate you," I said. Tag knew how much my mom and I loved *People*. His favorite joke was that our weekly subscription was "keeping the lights on" at their headquarters.

"I don't believe you," he said back.

"Why not?" I asked, heart now hammering.

But before he could respond, our phones simultaneously buzzed. Finally, a message from Manik. Back at Mack, his text read. Daniel is on-site.

My pulse slowed. *Phew*. Daniel was asleep, not wandering around Ames.

Roger that, Tag replied. Update us if anything changes.

My brows knitted together. "What could possibly change?"

"Hmm…" he mused as Manik sent back a thumbs-up emoji. "He could wake up?"

"Manik's not coming back," I guessed, switching on my flashlight. "You're going to have him monitor Daniel for the rest of the night, aren't you?"

"Preferably without blinking," he deadpanned when the two of us entered the woods to find Alex. Twigs and other forest floor remnants crunched under our feet, and little animals luckily scattered and scuttled away before I caught them in my beam. Tag cleared his throat. "We wasted so much time on the hill trying to figure out where he was, Lily. That type of clusterfuck can't happen again. Not if I—or in this case, Manik—can help it."

"But he knows where the Almanacs are," I warned. "If we cut him out…"

"He won't tell," Tag said. "Once you join the Jester, you're loyal to the Jester."

True, I thought while we walked in silence, feeling surer of myself now that we knew Daniel was snoring into his pillow.

"Alright, here we go." Tag slowed to a stop several minutes later and shined his light to reveal a raised plank walkway. The entrance to the sculpture sanctuary, which had been a collaborative project between one of Ames's old art classes and faculty volunteers. And Headmaster Bickford, naturally. Forget a landscape architect; she had impeccable taste and a vision. "But it's turned into *such* a headache," she'd complained once, and my mom and I had cracked up because the whole point of the sanctuary was to promote *tranquility*.

The walkway led to a hexagonal deck surrounded by students' work. Some sculptures were abstract and impressive, others abstract and awful (but because they were so abstract, you couldn't put your finger on why they were so awful). True talent and tradition were there too. Certain Italian- and Indian-inspired pieces were so lifelike it was beautifully haunting.

All the sculptures were artfully arranged in the area with viewing benches rounding the deck and a bubbling fountain in the center, one filled with wishes. You weren't supposed to toss coins in, but students did it anyway. I remembered Tag flipping in a shiny penny during the final days of sophomore year. Pretty much everyone on campus had gathered in the Circle to watch the senior prom processional, but we'd slipped into the woods. "What did you wish for?" I'd asked and rolled my eyes when he refused to tell me.

Or else it won't come true!

"Yes, it will," I said, sliding my arms around his waist. "Don't be so superstitious, Smoosh."

Tag laughed and threaded his fingers through my three-second braid before kissing me. We'd been dating a year; we were mad for each other. "I wished to take you to prom," he said afterward. "You know, when it's our turn—senior year."

I playfully swatted him. "What a wasted wish! Of course we're going to prom together. I mean, who else would I go with?"

Tag shrugged. "Somebody."

"Nobody," I corrected. "The answer is *nobody*."

The corners of Tag's mouth twitched.

"*You're* my prom date," I told his glinting green eyes, a smirk on my face. "Because, Tag, you know you're the—"

"Hey," someone said, and I snapped back to attention to see Alex leaning against a nearby tree. "We have a situation."

"A situation?" I asked. "What do you mean? The situation's under control. Manik texted that Daniel's asleep."

"Yes, I saw, but now we have *another* situation," Alex clarified. "A *problem*." He dropped his voice. "Listen."

Only ten seconds passed before Tag tightly inhaled and my spine straightened, both of us hearing laughter. "It's coming from the end of the walkway," I whispered. "Someone's here."

"More like *a lot* of someones," Tag whispered back. The three of us listened to at least five or six voices going back and forth. We were far enough away that their conversation sounded like gibberish, but it was clear each participant was male…and *young*. For every deep voice, there was a high-pitched one.

"Might as well alert Manik," Alex grumbled. "Daniel might be asleep, but there was still a jailbreak from Mack tonight."

No way, Manik said after I texted that a bunch of freshmen boys had snuck out of Macalester. Daniel has our kids on lockdown. It must be the sophomores. You know their prefects do nothing.

I sighed. Being an Ames prefect was a J-O-B *job*. You were

a mentor, an older sibling, and police officer all at once. You dealt with the fears, the tears, and the cheers. It was a huge responsibility, so I hadn't understood why Daniel had applied for the position last spring. "You're already running for president," I'd commented while he sped through his application and I color-coded Latin flash cards. "Why this too?"

"Because what if I don't win the election?" he'd posed. "You know I need to pad my résumé for Harvard. If I'm not president, prefect is the next best thing."

I hadn't said anything. Maybe because I had always pictured Tag and Alex as the freshmen prefects. They'd talked about it a lot over the years. But now Alex was running against Daniel for president, and everyone knew he and Tag were a package deal. If Alex didn't apply to be a prefect, Tag wouldn't either.

"What if you get both?" I asked. "Then what?"

Daniel shrugged. "Then I'll get both."

I tried to hide how irked I was. Not only because he didn't need both positions, but also because it didn't even sound like he *wanted* the second one! Someone who genuinely wanted to be a prefect deserved the role. It was about more than just bolstering your college application.

Please just apply, Tag, I'd thought, because he would be so good at it. But we weren't together anymore, and since we couldn't be friends, I'd said nothing.

ELEVEN

"Okay, time to regroup," Alex said after Tag and I had carefully backed away from the sanctuary's entrance and huddled under Alex's tree, hiding his flashlight beam. "It sounds like those guys are all over the deck, which we needed for the *Hour Glass*." He gave Tag a look. "Unless you want to change the location?"

Tag shook his head. The aforementioned *Hour Glass* was the best place to hide the next clue, because it was a Maya Rivera original. Ten feet tall, the sculpture was a mixture of light sea-green glass and melded metals. There was even sand inside, on the top, bottom, and somehow suspended in between. Daniel's twin had outdone herself.

And Tag, once again, understood the assignment. If we didn't choose Maya's installation, Daniel would be checking every single sculpture here. Which could take hours.

There was only one catch.

"He'll suspect it's Maya," I pointed out. "Daniel will think Maya's the Jester."

"Well, at the end of the day, he's going to peg *somebody* as the Jester," Alex said.

"And it *won't* be Maya," Tag said, showing us his phone screen. Zoe had buzzed in: Maya's going to the infirmary. Take cover. Housemaster is driving her over now.

"Excellent," Alex whispered excitedly. "Awful but excellent."

Can we ensure word is spread? Tag wrote back.

"Uh, who are you?" I joked. "*People* magazine?"

"It's her alibi," he responded after Zoe liked his message. "It'll eliminate her as a Jester possibility." He locked his phone and nodded at the sanctuary. "Okay, now let's solve this."

We *needed* the deck. Unfortunately, none of us were tall enough to reach the top of Maya's sculpture without standing on one of the deck's benches.

"I say we split up," Alex said. "You two can hide the clue from the sculpture's other side while I create a diversion. I'm a senior, they're freshmen—or, if Manik's right, sophomores. Either way, I outrank them."

"But you're not an *authority figure*," I said. "It's not like you can send them racing for their rooms. They might leave, but they *also* might sit and stay a while."

Alex was unfazed. "Then I'll shoot the shit with them."

I sighed. "Alex, even if you play it cool now, those guys will immediately remember you when Ames finds out the Almanacs are missing. What are you supposed to be doing out here alone? Unless you have recreational drugs in your backpack..."

Alex tilted his head. "Lily."

"No!" I whisper-yelled. "You have recreational drugs in your backpack?!" Alex had gotten his strike for drinking, but I'd also caught a whiff of a Dave Matthews concert once or twice. He occasionally partook in a joint.

I looked at Tag. He never smoked and rarely drank, but a bathtub and champagne flashed through my mind. After crossing the Chicago Marathon's finish line, we'd celebrated with the bottle of nonalcoholic champagne that my mom had hidden in my suitcase—she knew how hard I'd been training for that race. 26.2! its tag had read. In Tag's empty house, I'd been lounging in a decadent bubble bath while he'd sat freshly showered on the edge of the clawfoot tub. Back and forth, back and forth, the bottle had passed between us until our stomachs fizzed and we couldn't stop laughing. He became so naturally tipsy that he'd leaned far over the edge of the tub. Any second, he would slip. "What a stupid place to sit," I'd giggled, to which he grinned and said, "But what a pretty place to fall!"

Then he'd slid into the water, T-shirt and boxers and all. And my heart—well, my heart had swelled so much I thought it would burst from my chest. I could still see us splashing each other in between soapy kisses.

"Blame me, Lily," Tag now said. "I told him to bring some in case we ran into students. We need as many explanations as possible. If they see Alex light up, they won't think he's the Jester." He gave his friend a shove. "They'll just think he's an *idiot.*"

I considered for a beat. *It* would *knock off another Jester prospect,* I realized. *Tag put himself in a clue, Maya's now safe in the infirmary, and Alex would be sneaking out for a smoke...*

We needed a distraction. The freshmen were talking, but unless someone purposely kept the conversation flowing, they would break off if they heard too many sticks snap or the faintest of whispers.

"Okay," I mumbled. "Fine, but promise you won't share with anyone?" Watching Alex smoke would already be giving them the wrong idea.

Alex held out his pinkie. "Promise."

Our makeshift scheme came together quickly. Alex would casually run into the underclassmen while Tag and I handled the clue. We didn't have the time or privacy for a clue reading, so after Tag showed it to me, he tucked it inside its envelope before licking the seal. "What's that for?" I asked when he dropped the envelope into a plastic sandwich bag.

"Protection from the outdoor elements," he answered as I vaguely remembered him performing the same ritual on the telescope balcony. I'd just been too wrapped up in his Blair clue to really notice.

"Alright," Alex said. "Wait until you hear my voice."

I shifted from one foot to the other. My mom always said

that Alex could make conversation with a chair, but that didn't make me feel better tonight.

Tag nodded, and my pulse sped up once Alex left. The walkway's first step squeaked, and by the time Alex and his flashlight had rounded the bend, the boyish babble had quieted.

"Whoa there!" Alex exclaimed seconds later. He was nearly shouting to ensure we'd hear him. "You guys scared me..."

"Ready, set, go," Tag said, and after a deep breath, the two of us headed for the walkway. But instead of climbing the low-slung steps, we skirted around them and dropped to our knees. Even with the deep and dark woods for cover, we had no choice but to crawl around the deck. Alex also knew to aim his flashlight above the *Hour Glass* since we couldn't risk lighting our way.

There were both sharp-edged twigs and soft pine needles under my palms and soon I came across something wet. "Watch out," Tag warned too late, my hands already soaked. "There's a mud puddle."

I got my revenge when we stood up, wiping them on his sweatshirt.

Meanwhile, Alex had officially taken over the party on the deck. I could smell his pot. "This is purely for medicinal purposes," he told the boys as Tag and I navigated around a sculpture of Poseidon together. "My insomnia tends to hit me pretty hard, so I came out here to hopefully chill out."

"Can I take a hit?" one boy asked boldly.

"Nope," Alex answered, then said to someone else, "Here,

scoot over, bud. It's important to treat your elders with respect. Offering them a seat would be a strong start."

Only Alex, I thought as Tag and I dodged some tangled tree roots.

Whoever Alex had politely pushed aside on the bench didn't complain, because after a moment, Maya's sculpture appeared in all its glory. Our beautiful beacon of light.

But Alex's beam did not go unnoticed. "Why the flashlight?" someone asked, giving me goose bumps. I could feel all six gazes turn toward us. "Is someone out there?"

"On the ground!" I told Tag at the same time he said, "Plank position!"

Both of us fell to the earth. Dirt went straight up my nose, and I worried my heart would give us away. It thumped wildly against the ground.

"Nah, I don't think so," Alex said easily. "At least not *yet*." He turned off his flashlight, not really having a choice. "Tag Swell and Blair Greenberg could arrive in a few hours, though. It depends if they've gotten back together." He paused. "Are you interested in joining their *yoga* class?"

I felt Tag tense next to me.

The boys laughed, a buoyant enough chorus that Tag and I could stand and snap sticks in the process. Now on our feet, we broke into a jog. I could still envision where the *Hour Glass* was, but if I blinked a few times, it would disappear.

Keep talking, I thought. *Alex, keep talking.*

But I knew he had to be careful. If he talked too much, asked too many questions, the guys would grow suspicious. It was a risk we'd been willing to take.

"No, no, we aren't here for yoga class," one boy said. His voice hadn't dropped yet. "We came to pull a prank."

"A prank?" Alex sounded as surprised as I was. "Color me intrigued. Shocked, but intrigued."

"Yeah, there's like a week left in school and this so-called Jester hasn't done anything," another kid said. "We thought it was time we took matters into our own hands."

I imagined Alex exhaling some smoke. "What did you have in mind?"

All six boys spoke at once, so Tag and I made one last loud push for Maya's sculpture. I couldn't follow what anyone was saying, but by the time we arrived, one boy had been elected to speak. His voice sounded so close that I could step around the sculpture and tap his shoulder. He was talking about the Circle's iconic scattering of Adirondack chairs.

"And do *what* with them?" Alex asked.

Tag handed me the duct tape and third clue before crouching down and whispering for me to climb onto his shoulders, pool party chicken fight-style. *You're joking*, I almost said, but then remembered this job required a dynamic duo. The *Hour Glass* was ten feet tall. Daniel would hop up on a bench, but Tag and I didn't have that luxury.

So I gingerly threw a leg over his shoulder.

"Build a tower out of them," the freshman told Alex. "Picture a Jenga game—"

"Which will upset all the upperclassmen!" another couldn't help but jump in. "Because we all know you *live* for those chairs."

"We also want to steal some chairs from inside the buildings," the first kid added. "Enough that classes get canceled, because it's like, where will we sit?"

Tag and I swayed together for a second when he rose to his full height. I was trying really hard not to think about his hands on my thighs, so I didn't realize I had grabbed two tufts of his thick hair and was holding on for dear life.

"Lily, you're squeezing my skull," he whispered.

"Shit, sorry," I whispered back, but after letting go, it only got worse. I crossed my ankles for better support while Tag's hands moved farther up my thighs, and his lips pressed against the inside of my knee as if to anchor himself.

A lightning bolt crackled through my body before it settled into an electric hum, a longing ache. "Okay," I breathed. "Just a little closer..." I swallowed hard, my pulse pounding. "Just a little closer and I'll be able to reach the top."

"We'll be in their crosshairs," Tag warned, mouth moving on my skin. A few more steps forward and we would be in plain sight. Alex had turned off his flashlight, but someone else's glowed so they weren't in total darkness.

A distraction, I thought. *We need a diversion within a diversion.*

Tag shuddered as I clung closer to him to pull my phone

from my pocket. Thankfully, I'd turned my brightness level down ahead of time. We are right behind the HG, I texted Alex. Can you somehow turn their heads?

My heart thudded three times before a deep-voiced boy asked Alex who'd texted him. He definitely thought something was amiss. "My dearest friend," Alex lied smoothly. "Instead of keeping a dream journal, Taggart likes to text me his."

Tag snorted. "Try the other way around."

"Oh…" all the guys said, and that was when I knew for sure they were freshmen. Freshmen idolized Tag because he was so nice to them. Even watching from afar, I knew he always had a fist bump ready and knew almost everyone's name.

He would've made a damn good prefect.

A sudden beeping noise snapped me back to the sculpture situation. "Fuck," Tag was mumbling. "Fuck me." He let go of my left leg to dig something out of his pocket. Not his phone but his insulin pump. Did he have a notification?

I squeezed my eyes shut. *Don't hear us*, I prayed as he silenced it. *Please don't hear us—*

Alex immediately did, attuned to the sound, but swooped in to save us. He sprung up from his bench, sneakers slamming against the deck's wooden planks. "So you want to move all the chairs…" I could tell from his tone that he was pacing. "That's a pretty big job, guys. Especially at this time of night." He let out a low whistle.

A signal.

Tag's hand went to my leg again to regain our balance,

and he edged us around the *Hour Glass*. *Slow and steady*, I told myself, even though I wanted to go fast and furious.

"The buildings are all locked," Alex reminded the boys. "How do you plan on getting inside to take those chairs?"

No one offered up an answer except the trusting tinny-voiced kid. If I were to suddenly go toppling over, I would land on him. "Brendan stole our prefect's ID," he said. "He snuck into his room while he was in the bathroom brushing his teeth. He stays up late, so that's why we got out here so late."

Oh, how marvelous, I internally groaned. Something told me it wasn't Manik they'd robbed.

"You good, Lily?" Tag asked, and I stilled my shaking fingers long enough to secure the Ziploc bag on top of the sculpture. Alex continued to pace and ask questions, so his audience didn't hear me ripping strips of duct tape. He somehow managed to sound interested instead of interrogative.

"How about the plan of attack?" Alex asked. "Dividing and conquering won't work, because you only have one key."

I shifted on Tag's shoulders. "Done," I said, and he moved so abruptly that I went swinging, and when he tried to stop me from tumbling to the ground entirely, he stumbled over a stray branch.

With Alex still in the sanctuary, Tag and I could forgo our army crawling and just make a quick and quiet run back to the main trail. I was afraid to check the time once we finally made it back to the tree where we'd stowed his and Alex's backpacks. The gnawing in my gut told me it was after 2:00 a.m.

We both sighed in relief. "Well, that was fun," I joked weakly.

"I'm going to update Alex," Tag said, unlocking his phone. "Since I'm apparently sending him my dreams…"

His text appeared in our group chat several seconds later: Mission accomplished.

Alex quickly responded: You guys should go ahead without me.

My heart rate skyrocketed. NO! I wrote before Tag could.

I can't just get up and leave, Alex said. It'll look suspicious.

"But he only brought one joint," I said to Tag. "Hasn't he finished it yet?"

Plus, Alex added, I really should dismantle this bomb. We can't have these guys wandering around. I need to convince them to go back to Mack.

Then Manik decided to join the conversation.

Wait, those are seriously my guys?!

Don't worry, we're taking care of it, I wrote when Tag didn't. He seemed to have switched to a separate conversation with Alex. Stay on the fire escape.

Zoe then privately texted me: WTF is going on?

What's your twenty? I replied. Any chance you can meet us?

Because the next clue's hiding place…well, I imagined it was another reason Tag had tapped Zoe. There was a reason my mom had nicknamed her "Wonder Woman." She was heroic.

Sneaking out my window now! she wrote. Where am I heading?

The ropes course, I wrote, my legs wobbling at the thought. Heights—oh, how I hated them. Meet us at the ropes course.

CLUE
THREE

HEY, HEY, I KNOW IT'S
BEEN A LONG DAY,
SO HOW 'BOUT YOU BELAY,
BELAY ALL YOUR CARES AWAY?
OR CLIMB HIGH AND
GRAB YOUR GEAR,
FOR SOMETHING MAGIC
MIGHT APPEAR.

TWELVE

Tag and I didn't talk much while we navigated the woods, both of us mourning the loss of Alex. What was his plan? "He'll catch up to us," I told Tag as some way of comfort. "He knows where we're going…" I paused. "And where we're headed after that?"

"Yeah," Tag said quietly. "He knows the entire route."

"Zoe's on her way," I added. "We'll have her."

That made him chuckle. "Phew, because we *need* her."

I smiled. "That's an understatement."

Our trail would soon spill out of the woods into a large clearing, which was one of my least favorite places on campus: the ropes course. My mom and I rarely disagreed on things, but our "likes" did not align when it came to Ames's ropes course. She loved climbing the various apparatuses and was the faculty ropes course instructor, while my knees buckled at the thought of a heavy-duty harness. I'd only climbed the rock wall once, during freshmen orientation. "Come on, Lily, keep going!" I remembered one of the student RCIs cheering, but after I'd rung the bell at its peak and clambered downward, I said I needed to go to the bathroom.

But instead, I made a detour to the back side of the storage shelter and collapsed in the shade. My legs were still wobbling. *Deep breaths*, I'd told myself. *In through the nose, out through the mouth—*

"Oh, nice," someone said. "Is this the designated hiding place?"

My heart lurched. The boy had scared me.

"If we're afraid of heights?" he tried again.

All I could do was nod, and he took that as the go-ahead to join me. I noticed he wasn't much taller, skinny with thick brown hair and gray-green eyes. "I'm Tag," he said.

"Like the game?" I replied.

He smiled, revealing a set of silver braces. "It's short for Taggart," he explained. The tips of his ears pinkened. "But yeah, Tag like the worldwide recess phenomenon."

I laughed. "Well, I'm Lily, but ironically I'm allergic to the flower…"

This is where we met, I thought once the footpath ended and we were dumped out into the dark meadow. *This is where Tag and I first met.*

My heart twisted, wishing and wondering if he was thinking the same thing.

The moon was bright enough to highlight the ropes course's five climbing apparatuses. They looked like they soared all the way to the stars. I morbidly imagined myself falling to my death from one of them.

But that was why we had Zoe! She and her family went rock climbing out west every year. Even in the dark, Ames's ropes course would be a piece of cake.

Tag was really making Daniel work for the Almanacs.

"What's the plan?" I asked. "Should we unlock the storage shelter and grab equipment for Zoe? Which one of us is going to belay?"

Back at the freshmen climb, Tag and I learned to belay so we wouldn't have to climb anymore. Few people volunteered for the job because belaying had none of the *glamour* that climbing did. It meant you stood at the bottom of a structure to control a climber's rope. You gave them slack to climb higher but also enough friction to ensure they didn't fall.

"Not necessary," Tag replied, then pointed to the far corner of the field where another copse of strong and sturdy trees stood tall. His arm shook a little. At least four trees were connected by a building fifteen feet off the ground. "We're breaking into the Hideout."

The Hideout was a tricked-out tree house where the senior RCIs conducted meetings and stored all their personal climbing equipment. I'd never been up there, but I'd heard enough to know it was a great hangout space. Three walls were decorated with past RCIs' signatures while the fourth was lined with five sacred equipment stalls.

My guess was the next clue was going straight into Daniel's stall. "Oh my god," I couldn't help but blurt. "This is absurd!"

"What's absurd?" Tag asked. "Planting it in the Hideout?"

"No!" I exclaimed. "This!" I flung an arm at nothing in particular. "The fact that he's president, a prefect, *and* a senior RCI? I mean…" I trailed off, flummoxed. "How is that even remotely fair?"

Tag shrugged, but there was a tightness in his voice when he spoke. "The faculty considered him best suited for the positions. The student body too. They elected him president."

I shook my head. "You should've applied to be a Mack prefect," I said. "I'm sorry, but you should've. Tag, you would've been brilliant."

"How do you know I didn't apply?" he asked.

"Because Josh…" I started before realizing Josh had never gone into detail about his applicants. He just said why he'd chosen Manik and Daniel.

Had Tag actually applied?

And if he did, why wouldn't Josh have appointed him? They were so close. He was Tag's swim coach, and we'd shared so many dinners together at my house. It made no sense.

We reached the base of the tree house, and I assessed the narrow metal ladder leading up to the Hideout's trapdoor entrance. My stomach turned at the height. "I hope Zoe gets here soon," I said.

"Yeah," Tag replied, "since this stunner wasn't cheap."

I glanced away from the ladder to see him pull a

goofy-looking headlamp out of his backpack. "Holy shitballs," I breathed. "That crown is befitting of a *queen*."

"Right?" Tag giggled, really giggled like a little boy. "I know we could've used it earlier, but I thought it should be saved for a special occasion."

"Zoe's going to flip," I said, smiling. "Before making you take about a thousand photos."

"I'll agree to the requisite three," Tag said. "We don't have time for a thousand." He sighed. "I wish she'd get here too."

"May I read the next clue?" I asked when Zoe didn't magically appear.

"Yeah, yeah, of course." Tag handed me the envelope. "My bad, I thought you already had…" He yawned. Someone was getting tired. "Remember, I'm no poet."

I smirked. It was true, but I couldn't begin to imagine coming up with these clues myself. This piece of cardstock had a jumble of blue-and-white letters and read:

> *Trim the sails and take the helm*
> *You are comfortable in this realm*
> *O' Captain, starboard ho!*
> *Remember to lock up before you go.*

"Nice," I said. "Boathouse?"

"Yep." Tag clenched his jaw. "I thought we'd throw him an easy one."

I slid the cardstock back into its envelope. "Beach side isn't so simple, you know." We needed to cross Campo's favorite patrol road to get to the ocean.

"Well, he'll figure it out," Tag said. "Just like we'll figure it out." He paused. "At least I'm not making him *climb* anything else."

I laughed. From Bunker's hill to the telescope balcony's locked gate to the Hideout's ladder, Daniel would need to channel his inner monkey.

We kept waiting for Zoe, this time in silence. Two minutes, five minutes, maybe even ten. "I'll text her," I said when we were nearing fifteen. We couldn't spend much more time here. Our deadline was sunrise, and it would arrive soon.

Tag & I are here, I wrote. Where are you?

Her iPhone's typing dots instantly appeared, and after a blink, so did her reply. You'll never believe this, she said. I'm literally in the hydrangea bush outside Leda's classroom!

More dots.

I hid after seeing a Campo headlight, but instead of cruising by, the car ran into the fire hydrant. Not bad, only a graze, but I think it's because the driver got distracted? Maybe he saw me? They stopped the car and are now inspecting the damage. It's Mr. Harvey and the guy from the guardhouse.

I grimaced and showed the text to Tag, who sighed. "Why would Harvey let Gabe drive on his first shift?"

"Because Gabe probably said, 'pretty please with cherries

on top,'" I deadpanned as Zoe's third message appeared: I'm so sorry, Lily, but I can't leave until they do.

No, of course, I typed. Stay safe!

Zoe promised she would be back in touch, and I shot her a heart emoji before shoving my phone back in my pocket. "So," I said to Tag.

"So," he said back.

We both knew what was coming.

"Have you heard from Alex?" I asked as a last-ditch effort.

He shook his head. "I told him not to text until he was free. The more he has his phone out, the sketchier it'll seem."

I sighed. "Where's Manik when you need him?"

Tag ran an unsteady hand through his hair, and my stomach felt like it was about to drop like an EDM song. Neither of us wanted to make this climb. Getting on Tag's shoulders was one thing, but this...this was fifteen fucking feet.

"Should we flip a coin?" I asked.

"Do you have one to flip?" he answered.

I shook my head.

"Lily, I don't think I can do it," he said, looking at the ground but then looking back up with a pale face. "The thought is actually making me dizzy." He rubbed his eyes. "I, um, never made it up to the high swing that day. Right before I found..."

Me, I thought with bittersweetness. *Right before you found me.*

"Give me the crown," I said, holding out my hand for the

headlamp. "Give me the clue and the crown so I can ascend and achieve everlasting glory."

———

I told Tag no commentary while I climbed. That had been one of the worst parts of climbing as a freshman. While the *Keep going, Lily!* and *Yay, Lily!* cheers were meant to be encouraging, I also couldn't help but feel like I was being peer pressured. "I'm ready," I'd said at one point on the rock wall, feeling bile rise in my throat. "I'm ready to come down!"

"No, you aren't!" my RCI had called back. "You haven't reached the top and rung the bell yet!"

I'm going to vomit all over her, I'd thought.

Tag stayed silent as I stepped up to the ladder, closed my eyes, and inhaled a deep breath of the crisp night air before grabbing the first cold, metal rung. Then I began to climb. One rung, two rungs, three rungs. I forced myself to stare straight ahead, refusing to look up or down, and only when my lungs started screaming did I exhale. But soon, fear paralyzed me—I froze. How long had I been climbing? How much farther?

Do not look down, I told myself. *Do* not *look down…*

But unfortunately, I looked *up* and saw that I had a long way to go.

"Commentary!" I called to Tag. "I need some commentary—or a distraction. Yeah, I need a distraction!"

"What's my favorite color?" he called back, but before I could answer, he added, "Yours is pink." He chuckled. "Remember that furry pink coat freshman year?"

"Yes, the teddy bear coat," I replied, a little dazed he remembered. Tag and I'd gotten together at the end of spring term; we'd spent most of the year smiling at—then shying away from—each other. "It was originally my mom's," I told him, grabbing the next ladder rung and pulling myself upward. "Your favorite color is gold, because of the autumn leaves..." I fleetingly thought of my freshman formal dress. "And the late afternoon light, when campus is painted gold—it's your favorite time to take pictures."

It didn't matter if it was his Nikon or his Polaroid or some antique camera that only he knew how to use, but Tag always walked around with a camera slung over his shoulder. So many of his photos were still on my bedroom wall. He'd tack up a new one without saying anything, instead waiting for me to notice. I swallowed hard.

"What's my favorite drink, Mr. Diet Coke?" I asked.

"Ginger ale with a slice of lemon and sprig of mint. You love flipping through Josh's cocktail book and trying to make mocktails out of them." He paused; I climbed. "Most prized possession?"

"I don't have one," I said honestly, even though I'd kept our Chicago Marathon champagne bottle. It had returned to Rhode Island with me and now sat on my bookshelf. "And you...I can't decide if it's still your cameras, or now Stevie the cat, or just ketchup."

"Oh, *obviously* ketchup," he said, and I swore I heard his stomach grumble from a million feet below me. "Ketchup elevates every culinary experience." A beat, and then, "Something that scares you?"

I felt a pang in my chest. Something that scared me? The question was too loaded; there was too much to unpack. From getting caught tonight to giving my currently nonexistent salutatorian speech to going away to college, my list was long.

So I tried to make a joke. "This!" I knocked my fist against the tree house's aluminum ladder. "Right here, right now!"

Tag didn't laugh. "You're almost there," he said instead.

"What about you?" I asked. "What scares you?"

"Never talking to you again," he answered.

Just.

Like.

That.

"The Jester didn't tap you to get Leda's keys," he continued as my heart twinged. His cadence was hurried—nervously so. I forced myself to keep climbing. "We never talk anymore, Lily. I know I should be used to it by now, but I'm not, so I wanted to see if we could be..."

Blood pumped through my ears. *Don't say friends*, I thought. *We* can't *be friends.*

Because there were only two options when it came to

Taggart Swell: loving him with every bone in my body and beat of my heart or cutting ties with him completely. For me, we were everything or we were nothing. I couldn't fathom how he thought we could meet somewhere in the middle.

"Fuck!" I exclaimed when my head banged against something, otherwise known as the Hideout's trapdoor. "Fucking hell!"

Tag didn't laugh or cheer or anything; instead, he shifted back into Jester mode. "There should be a four-digit combination lock on the door."

"Affirmative," I replied, reaching for the lock. "Did Maya get those magic numbers?"

I remembered much earlier in the evening before we'd left Hubbard Hall. Tag had reminded Maya to text him the lock combination because rumor was the senior RCI chose it.

Tag sighed. "She sent me some ideas," he said. "I would've preferred the facts, but she's confident one of these is right. Unlike her, Daniel's not that creative a person."

I snorted. Maya could be brutal. "Okay, well, what's first on list?"

"The year Ames was founded." He didn't specify, knowing I was good with dates.

1-8-0-3.

After inputting the numbers, I gave the lock an unrelenting tug. "Incorrect!"

"Okay, the twins' birthday," he said, and after that didn't

work, he gave me the Rivera family's street address and our graduation year. We even tried what was allegedly Daniel's debit card PIN, but to no avail.

Both of us were silent once we'd tried all Maya's guesses. Then Tag groaned and dropped a couple choice words. I was right there with him. Ames believed they were rewarding Daniel for all his hard work but *come on*. He'd amassed more power than a student should ever possess. Full-on ID access as president, prefect status, and senior RCI perks? Choosing the lock combination for the tree house?

My heart suddenly jumped into my throat. "Wait, he didn't choose it!" I nearly squealed, excited. "Daniel might be the *senior* RCI, but he's outranked by the *faculty* RCI." I smiled. "And I doubt she'd let him forget it."

Tag cheered. "Leda!"

I nodded. My mother with all her special keys and combinations. I should've known better. She'd once made an offhanded comment that Daniel was her most capable RCI, but that didn't mean he needed to know *everything* about the ropes course.

Quickly, I tried various dates. Her birthday, my birthday, the year we came to Ames. No, no, and no!

What is it? I wondered, rubbing my temples as if to summon the answer. My mom's comment about Daniel not knowing everything about the ropes course—it was true in the sense that he didn't know the lock's code but also that he didn't know all that had happened here. Nobody ever would, but my mom knew one special thing that *did*.

"Any luck?" Tag called up to me.

My fingers trembled as I reset the dials and then immediately input: 1-0-2-5.

October 25th, the day the course closed to students for the fall.

October 25th, the day she and Josh went on their annual climbing date.

Please, I thought before shutting my eyes and tugging the lock.

This time, there was no resistance. It willingly popped open for me.

"I'm in!" I shouted as I unhooked the lock and shoved it in my pocket before pushing the trapdoor upward. Its squeaky hinges drowned out Tag's reaction.

After hoisting myself into the darkened Hideout, I aimed my headlamp straight at the far locker-lined wall. Because of the lock trouble, there wasn't time to see the sights or check out how comfy the couch was. I needed to hide the clue and then scramble back down the ladder. Hopefully Alex would be waiting with Tag at the bottom. Had the freshmen boys gone home to Mack?

Sure enough, each equipment stall had a weathered brass nameplate. D. RIVERA, the one in the middle read. I rolled my eyes before pulling the clue from the back of my shorts and tucking it on the stall's top shelf, under Daniel's red climbing helmet.

Goodbye, little one.

Then I retreated to the trapdoor and tediously lowered myself down through the hole, taking care *not* to lock up behind me. It was probably best to throw Daniel a bone.

Because he would never guess that code.

THIRTEEN

Tag was ecstatic once my feet were safely back on the ground. "You did it!" he whooped and then lost it when I celebrated a victory the only way I knew how: playing an invisible game of hopscotch. The headlamp beam danced up and down as I bounced, heart rate riding my rhythm. Tag laughed. "Hopscotch," he said, voice almost hoarse. "Hopscotch for the win!"

I grinned, but before we could share it, he hugged me. A congratulatory hug, not a romantic one. Tag clapped me on the back like we'd won a swim meet, although I imagined most of his teammates shook off the slap after a second or two.

Not me. Even through a couple layers of fabric, his handprint branded itself on my back. I felt it there, burning red. "Take off your sweatshirt," I said.

Tag abruptly pulled back. "What?"

Shit, I thought. *It's "Man, I've missed your mouth" all over again.*

"You're hot," I told him, then cringed. "I mean, you're *sweaty*." I backed up to see him in my headlamp. His face, ears, and neck were flushed. "Do you feel okay?"

"Yeah, fine." Tag nodded. "I was just really nervous that the code couldn't be cracked, so that's why—"

"But your pump went off," I suddenly remembered. "It beeped back in the sculpture sanctuary. What did the notification say?"

Tag gave me a lopsided smile. "It was kindly asking for a BG calibration," he said, putting a hand to his heart. "Impeccable manners, as ever."

I smiled back in relief. Tag's pump just needed a blood glucose reading to ensure he was receiving the right amount of insulin. Nothing was up with his blood sugar, and even if he got an alert later, I'd wager his backpack contained at least one Gatorade and some snacks.

He was always so prepared.

My phone pinged in my pocket—hopefully a status update from Zoe or Alex—but I ignored it, watching Tag shrug off his sweatshirt. The headlamp must've looked like a stage spotlight, but he didn't say anything—actually, he was having trouble. His T-shirt clung to the sweatshirt; my legs went weak when a slice of bare skin was exposed, that swimmer's six-pack. "Where is Tag Swell?" I'd once said, when it was clear all those gym sessions were doing the trick. His second growth spurt too. "Where is my Bambi boyfriend?"

He'd blushed. "Yeah, I don't really look like myself anymore, do I?" He ran an awkward hand through his hair. "Do you still like me like this?"

"Smoosh, that's the most absurd question I've ever heard," I replied. "You're the next Sexiest Man Alive."

Tag pretended to groan. "Please don't put me in *People* magazine."

I'd laughed and stretched to kiss him. "Too late."

Eventually he managed to shuck off the sweatshirt and pull his T-shirt back down, and that was when I caught it on his bicep: the tattoo. A lump formed in my throat. Alex had said Tag had gotten it on his eighteenth birthday this past summer. Blair wasn't shy about expressing her distaste for it while old Bunker thought it was the best thing ever. *AUT VIAM INVENIAM AUT FACIUM*, it said in Tag's concise block-letter handwriting.

Latin for "I shall either find a way or make one."

The words were bracketed by an ivy wreath, which had been sketched by…well, me. Sophomore year in history class, I'd been doodling and gave him the sheet of loose-leaf paper afterward. Maybe the saying was Roman general Hannibal Barca's maxim, but it sounded like Tag. Strong, smart, determined.

Although I never imagined he would someday ink it on his skin.

Tag tied his sweatshirt around his waist and then glanced up to find me looking at him. My heart quickened when he tilted his head, but the moment didn't last long. "Hey!" someone called, but before Tag and I could bolt, Zoe jogged out of the darkness and into my ray of light. "You didn't answer my text."

"Sorry!" I blurted. "I'm sorry. We, um, well…" I trailed

off when she hugged me, a tighter one than normal. She was shaken up, so I squeezed her back.

"Everything's okay?" I asked. "How did you slip by Campo?"

Zoe sighed. "While Gabe dented the hood, Mr. Harvey deemed the Prius was still drivable for tonight, so they got back in and zoomed off toward the freshmen dorms."

Tag and I shared a telepathic look. The freshmen dorms. Would Manik be spotted on the fire escape?

"I see there's been a couple more casualties," Zoe commented. "I tried to follow what was happening in the group chat, but it was confusing. Where are Manik and Alex?"

Tag relayed everything that had happened since we'd stolen the Almanacs: Bunker Hill, the rumor about Daniel being on the loose, sending Manik home to spy, and Alex staying in the sculpture sanctuary with the freshmen boys.

"How delightful," she said sarcastically, then tapped my headlamp. "You look adorable, though. Am I too late to save you from whatever climbing expedition is on the agenda? Your legs are probably mush."

"Hopscotch killed it," Tag said. He was pulling on his backpack, ready to leave for the next checkpoint. "She was a superstar up there."

Zoe didn't verbally respond. Instead, she nudged me, as if to say, *Hopscotch, huh?*

I fumbled to take off the headlamp, not wanting either one to see the redness creeping up my neck. Soon it would sting my cheeks. Maybe under different circumstances, Tag calling me Hopscotch would mean something, but here and now, it didn't. He was just on a high from me managing to crack the trapdoor's code and hiding the clue. My friends read too much into things.

Didn't they?

"What was the code, anyway?" Zoe asked. "One of Maya's guesses?"

"No, Leda actually set it," Tag answered. "It was…"

He trailed off, realizing I hadn't told him.

"My birthday," I quickly lied. "0-1-1-4."

That code was between my mom and Josh.

"Hmm," Zoe mused. "I would've thought she'd do something a little more secretive. Everyone knows your birthday, Lil."

She was right. "Lily Hopper's Birthday" might as well have been a national holiday. Ames's dining hall always served my favorite foods for lunch.

"We should head out," Tag said. "I wanted to wait for Alex, but he hasn't made contact yet, so—"

"So it's good I'm back, then!" another voice called, and with my headlamp still in my hands, I shined my light on the new face—or the *returning* face.

"Manik," Tag said. "What are you doing here?"

"Circling back with the regiment," Manik replied, chuckling. "And let me tell you, it was *not* easy to get here. Campo is all over the place tonight."

Tag closed his eyes. "What happened to watching Daniel?"

"It was a waste of time," Manik said. "He's following his normal nighttime routine like clockwork."

Normal nighttime routine? I thought, stomach stirring. *What does that mean?*

Zoe asked as much.

"He sleeps," Manik began, "then wakes up, walks to the bathroom like a zombie, and then pulls up Netflix and watches something before falling back asleep."

"I don't like the sound of that," Zoe said.

"Neither do I." Manik nodded, clueless. "*Stranger Things* kept me up for hours once."

"What was he doing when you left?" Tag asked, somehow keeping his cool.

Meanwhile, I just lost it. "How did you find us?"

Manik shrugged. "He was halfway through some documentary, but I'm pretty sure he was asleep." He gestured to Zoe. "And I followed Zoe. All I had to do was check Snapchat."

Tag and I didn't bother hiding our groans. Zoe hadn't been with us when we'd confirmed everyone's invisibility on the app's map, and we hadn't thought to search for her way-too-accurate avatar.

"God, I'm sorry," she whispered. "I didn't even think about it. I was too worried about Maya…"

I tugged her dark braids to let her know it was okay. I mean, we would make it okay. It had been a mistake, but Tag would fix it.

"Go back to Mack," he told Manik.

"No," Manik said. "I want to help."

"You *were* helping," Tag countered. "Having eyes on Rivera was crucial."

"All we needed to know was that he was in his room," Manik said as an imaginary snake slithered up my spine. My mom called it my "sixth sense." It told me when something was off or about to go wrong. I switched off the headlamp before moving closer to Tag.

"Serpents," I muttered.

"You sure?" he muttered back.

"And I confirmed it," Manik continued. "He's in our house, in our room, and it's what? Like 2:45? Why would he leave?"

"Oh, I don't know," I said caustically. "Maybe because all your kids are on the loose?"

"Yeah, um, how did you miss that?" Zoe asked. "Them sneaking out?"

Manik sighed. "They probably went through the kitchen window," he said. "It's ground-level and as far away from Mr. Bauer's apartment as you can get, on the opposite side of the house." He shook his head. "I'd never be able to see them from the fire escape."

"Whoever designed Mack's layout is an idiot," Zoe mumbled as Tag said, "Word on campus is they nicked Daniel's keys too."

"Brendan Foley!" Manik exclaimed indignantly as Tag put

both hands on my shoulders. Through his flannel, I felt his thumb trace a swift circle on my shoulder blade—our code for *relax*—before he began backing us into the trees.

"Serpents indeed," he murmured. "Do you see that light over there?"

I squinted, then shivered when I saw the dim iPhone light across the course. "Alex?" I whispered.

"He would've texted," Tag said. "Not to mention, also come from the woods."

I swallowed hard. Whoever was out there was walking up from the ropes course's main entrance, right off a campus road. My heart pounded. Who was it?

"Oh my god," Zoe breathed when the newcomer called out, and then in one quick kick-ass motion, she shoved Manik into the meadow before diving in the shadows and rolling into a crouch next to Tag and me. I grabbed her hand. The chances of everything going to shit had suddenly soared.

"For fuck's sake, there you are!" an extremely irritable Daniel Rivera said. "Where have you been and why haven't you answered your phone?"

"Uh…" was Manik's strong start.

"Stop putting your ringer on silent," Daniel went on. "I called you like ten times." He released an exasperated sigh. "Greg banged on my door and told me that he'd woken up to find his three roommates gone. He'd already checked the bathroom, so we went down to the common room, only to find Ross, who said his were gone as well. He was on his way to tell Mr. Bauer, but luckily I intercepted him." He exploded. "Six guys! Six unaccounted-for guys, Manik! Do you know how much trouble we'll be in if Mr. Bauer finds out they've escaped?"

They're not prisoners, Daniel, I wanted to say. *They're kids. We're all kids.*

And stop being such a jerk to Manik! It's both your faults!

"Yeah, yeah, I know," Manik said. "That's why I've been out looking for them. I fell asleep basically right after closing our door, but I woke up later craving ice cream, so I went down to the kitchen and saw that the window was wide open." He forced a laugh. "They should really put bars on it, right?"

Daniel ignored that last part. "Why the hell didn't you wake me up?"

Manik was silent for a few seconds. "I tried," he lied. "I tried, but you said to go away. You mumbled some mumbo-jumbo about needing to finish your English essay...about how Leda wasn't going to let you take Lily to prom if you, uh, didn't finish it on time?"

"Oh," Daniel said as my cheeks began to simmer. "That sounds sort of familiar. I think she said I had to get an A-plus too."

"Only in your dreams," Zoe muttered, and I found myself nodding. Next to me, Tag was as still as a statue. Was he even breathing?

"Together?" Manik said a few seconds later. Daniel had

suggested they leave and check the natatorium next. "We're sticking together?"

"We gotta, Manik," Daniel said. "Not only because you don't answer your phone but also because my keys are gone. I think that asshole Brendan robbed me."

Suddenly I felt Tag's broad shoulders knock against mine. They were bobbing up and down from silent laughter, so I covered his mouth with my hand just to be safe. And I couldn't help but grin when some of his chuckles escaped and swirled in my palm.

CLUE
FOUR

TRIM THE SAILS AND
TAKE THE HELM
YOU ARE COMFORTABLE
IN THIS REALM
O' CAPTAIN, STARBOARD HO!
REMEMBER TO LOCK UP
BEFORE YOU GO.

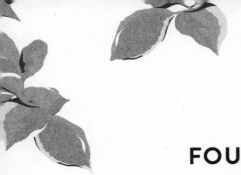

FOURTEEN

"Alrighty," Zoe said once we were sure Manik and Daniel were gone. "What's next on this wild goose chase, Swell?"

"Certainly not chasing *that* goose," I replied, gesturing in Daniel's wake. He and Manik had taken off at a run and so had the blood in my veins. "No way."

Zoe laughed while Tag spoke softly. "The boathouse," he said, "but Alex…" He trailed off, almost mournful. "Alex hasn't checked in; he said he would when he was on his way to catch up with us. He's probably still in the sculpture sanctuary."

I nodded, wishing Alex wasn't a ghost on Snapchat's map so we could locate him. "Guys, of course he is," Zoe said. "Imagine you're a freshman, and the coolest, most enchanting—"

"Enchanting?" Tag interrupted, bemused.

Zoe responded with her middle finger. "And the most enchanting senior showed up and started to talking to you. Would you let him get away so easily?"

Tag and I were silent for a few seconds, both knowing the answer was no. Because Alex Nguyen *was* enchanting. He was fascinating and funny and could captivate an audience with only one sentence.

He should be salutatorian, I thought. Alex would write—or, let's be honest, *wing*—a better speech than I ever would.

And I knew for a fact that he'd been next in line. While grilling hot dogs and burgers at last weekend's neighborhood pool party, Dean DeLuca had let the top academic rankings slip. If I didn't exist, Ames would've awarded Alex the title.

Tag sighed. "You're right. He's trapped."

Zoe shook her head. "Not if the biggest buzzkill crashes the party."

"Um, did you just call yourself a buzzkill?" I asked. Zoe was anything but.

"In this instance, yes," Zoe said. "It's no secret they're afraid of me."

"*Intimidated* by you," I corrected, although it was true. All the freshmen boys feared Ames's basketball captain. She was incredibly poised, marched through the halls with a purpose, and had what vaguely resembled a resting bitch face. (Her words, not mine.)

"You two go ahead to the boathouse," Zoe said. "I'll extract Alex from the sculpture sanctuary, and then we'll rendezvous."

After Zoe beelined for the woods, Tag nodded his head toward the ropes course's main entrance. I didn't like the idea of directly following Daniel and Manik, and I also didn't like the idea of navigating one of Campo's favorite patrol routes, but it was the fastest way to the boathouse.

Gilmore Lane was the border between campus's wood side and beach side, and it was also the reason for Tag's disciplinary strike. The day after I'd gotten my driver's license, I'd asked Tag if he wanted to come to Whole Foods with me. All he had to do was get permission to leave campus from his housemaster. It wasn't until Campo spotted him riding shotgun on our way back that I found out he'd never gotten the green light; he couldn't get ahold of his housemaster, so he'd chanced it and ended up in both Headmaster Bickford's office and in one of our biggest fights. Tag lying to me was unacceptable, even if he did want to carry my groceries.

"Wait, where are you going?" I asked when he turned left on Gilmore. We were supposed to go right, walk a quarter mile up the road, and then peel off onto the boathouse's long drive. "Tag, stop." I caught up to him. "Tell me where—"

"Shh," he cut me off and took one of my hands. I barely felt him tug me along, instead noticing how clammy his palm was. Why was he so nervous?

Then I heard it—the unmistakable, motorized *hum* of a Campo car. "Christ, why does *everything* happen on this street?" I muttered as Tag and I dove behind a tree together. Was it a good enough hiding spot?

We were about to find out. The Prius was getting closer, its engine growing louder, and its headlights now shining bright. The moment it caught a nearby patch of grass in its beams, I spun. This tree trunk wasn't big enough to conceal us side by side, so I twirled to press myself up against Tag. He inhaled a sharp breath, but I tried to soften it. "Hey there, cowboy," I whispered casually. "You on the run from the law or something?"

"Depends on who's asking," Tag whispered back, and when the Prius rolled up, I hid my face in his chest as he slid his arms around my waist to pull me closer. His touch was achingly familiar, so intoxicating that it made my heart throb.

Smoosh, I wanted to whisper before I forced myself to focus on *something else*. But the only something else was the approaching Campo car. We were going to get caught.

"How close is it?" I asked.

"By my best estimate," Tag said, "pretty damn close."

I peeked over his shoulder to see a white Prius and then lost all sense of space and time when the car not only reached us but also *stopped* in the middle of the road.

Tag's arms tightened around me, his lips brushing my ear. "Don't move," he breathed as the driver door popped open and a patrolman climbed out with his flashlight. I couldn't make out who it was, but the car wasn't dented, so it wasn't Harvey and Gabe.

Brian, I realized when I heard him speak. He wore a pair of AirPods. "Yeah, Gabe, I'm not sure what Sal saw," he said, "but tell Harvey it seems to be clear on Gilmore." There was a soft click, and then a ray of light slowly scanned our area. I burrowed into Tag's T-shirt again, trying to find comfort in his frantic heartbeat. "No sign of any—" He dropped off, then snorted. "No, no, you definitely said *Gilmore*." He switched off his flashlight. "Gabe, put Harvey on the line…"

"He's getting back into his car," Tag murmured. Sure enough, the car door soon slammed shut. We both exhaled deep sighs of relief but clung to each other until the Prius had roved out of sight.

"I've never seen a more chill-inducing horror movie," I said, cold sweat sliding down my spine. "Who do you think we have to thank for that tip-off?"

Tag pretended to shiver. "Toss-up between Zoe, Manik, or Rivera. They did say Campo was on the prowl."

I bit my pinkie nail. "Try up their asses."

"Yeah…" Tag said a little distantly, then looked at me. "Should we, uh, keep going?"

I nodded before quickly dashing off a warning text to Zoe and Alex, wherever they were. "Let's not get our directions mixed up this time, though," I joked. "Alright?"

Tag's eyebrows furrowed.

"Before," I said. "The boathouse is to the right, but you went left. Buildings and Grounds is to the left."

"So I've been told," Tag said lightly. "I've also been told that Leda has a key to their garage."

A key to their garage.

I immediately caught his drift. "We couldn't."

Tag shrugged. "You called me a cowboy."

"Bandit would've been better."

Because you've broken almost all Ames's laws.

Yet so had I.

Tag tipped an invisible Stetson. "I like cowboy. Cowboys are loyal, bandits are not."

My throat thickened. *Loyal.* "Tag…"

"There's only three clues left, but a lot of ground to cover," he said. "What's the harm, Hops?"

We stood in a standoff for several seconds before I dug my mom's keys from my pocket. "Okay, partner," I said, swinging around the heavy lanyard like a lasso. "Let's ride."

~

Predictably, Ames's squadron of golf carts awaited us once Tag and I weaved our way through the Buildings and Grounds offices and reached the small hangar. Each golf cart was white with Ames's insignia on its hood. Tag tut-tutted like a disapproving grandmother because the fleet was used only three times a year and never for golf. During Alumni Weekend's festivities three weeks ago, student council had circulated in the golf carts to answer any questions and get older alums off their feet.

"There's only one problem," I said while Tag inspected the carts. He stopped and looked at me with a questioning brow. "We don't have any keys."

"Oh…" Tag said, dragging out the word before swiping

something from the golf cart's cupholder. "You mean keys like these?"

I rolled my eyes, then stalked away to hit the button that raised the garage door. Now with a golf cart, we couldn't exactly exit the way we'd entered. My phone pinged in my pocket as the door rose, and I unlocked it to see an update from Zoe: I've collected the package. He was in the middle of a Q&A session about acing English exams when I got there.

So? Alex replied. We were in a new group chat that didn't include Manik. At least I stopped their prank! (Long-winded summaries of each book/play/poem they read, btw.)

I couldn't help it; I shook my head and smiled, knowing my mom was worried some freshmen wouldn't be ready for their exam. Just maybe, Alex's improvised lecture would give them a boost.

Even if he was a bit high.

We're now camouflaged in some bushes, Zoe wrote. The boys are gone, but Daniel and Manik are stomping around nearby.

I'm so getting poison ivy, Alex said.

You have my greatest sympathies, Alexander, Tag typed. Circle back to the ropes course when you can.

Both Zoe and Alex: ???

They won't check there twice, I responded. The boathouse was too far for them to meet us. Hang tight.

Tag had made himself comfortable in the passenger seat by the time I made it over to his cart of choice, the engine already rumbling. "You don't want to drive?" I asked, surprised. One of the things Tag actually missed about home was cruising around town in his beloved Grand Cherokee. When you lived at boarding school, you never drove. Some kids joked that when they went home for breaks, they had to relearn how to drive.

"Nah." He shook his head. "Better your fingerprints on the wheel than mine."

"True, forensics doesn't have a file on me yet," I deadpanned, knowing someone would eventually discover the golf cart wherever we chose to ditch it tonight. And since Ames *refused* to institute a forensics lab in the science department, it would be impossible to trace the robbery back to Bonnie and Clyde.

Unless we got caught.

I slid into the driver's seat and flipped on the headlights, then second-guessed myself and flicked them off. We didn't want to attract any attention. Instead, I propped my phone up in the cupholder; its glow would have to be enough to guide us.

But before I even shifted into drive and hit the golf cart's gas pedal, sirens sounded. My heart lurched. Had raising the garage door set off some kind of alarm?

Then I realized it wasn't sirens. Tag's insulin pump was beeping.

"What's it saying?" I asked, even though I already had an idea and felt stupid for not realizing it sooner. Tag's profuse sweating and clamminess weren't entirely due to nerves; it was because he was...

"Low," he finished for me, silencing the notification. "Blood sugar's low."

My grip on the steering wheel tightened while Tag unzipped the front pocket of his backpack, and I watched him pull out a packet of Welch's fruit snacks. "How much have you eaten today?" I whispered as he chewed and swallowed the gummies.

I remembered him and Alex talking before we set off on our journey to the sculpture sanctuary, murmuring about Tag drowning his meatloaf in ketchup earlier. What time had he had dinner? 6:00?

"Not as much as I should've," Tag admitted, then crumpled up the empty plastic packet. He nodded at the whorl of darkness in front of us. "Onward."

"But, Tag—"

"Onward!" he repeated, this time hopping up in his seat. The golf cart shook under his weight, and he pointed outside as if he were a sea captain shouting, *Land ho!*

"Use your magic words," I singsonged.

"Onward, *please!*"

"Oh, right away." I fumbled with the gearshift like the fool in a fifties movie. "Right away!"

And then we laughed as I pressed down on the gas.

FIFTEEN

My pulse set the pace on our way to the boathouse. Instead of creeping along at a snail-like speed, I quickly turned onto the gravel driveway, soon flew over a speed bump. Our golf cart caught some serious air. "I *swear* you just took us to outer space," Tag said through his laughter. The fruit snacks seemed to have done the trick. "We went to the moon; we went to Saturn…"

I smirked and took one hand off the wheel. *You're funny*, I said by knocking my knuckles twice against his knee. Our old code again.

Tag shifted in his seat.

We couldn't see it in the dark, but Ames's boathouse was beautiful. "Traditional," our school brochures liked to say, "with a modern twist." Its faded cedar exterior was classic, but the glass statement wall that let you see the sailboats and surfboards systematically stored inside was brand new. A glass-sided overlook had also been recently added; there was no better view for a regatta.

Ocean waves swishing and swirling, I sucked in a deep

breath of salt air after parking the golf cart. Tonight's wind really ripped this close to the water; I had to keep a hand clamped down on my baseball hat so it wasn't suddenly stolen away and flung out to sea.

My mom didn't have a key to the boathouse, but that was okay because Tag knew the garage door's code. "Once a sailor, always a sailor," he said, because Ames's sailing coach never changed the keypad's passcode. It was the same as when Tag had been on the team. Nothing creative, just the last year Ames had won Nationals…way too long ago. "It all comes down to coaching," Josh once insisted, a comment my mom deciphered to mean *he* wanted to take over the team. "Josh, you don't know the first thing about coaching sailing," she said, to which he casually responded, "I can learn."

Once the door had groaned to a stop and Tag and I crossed the threshold, overhead lights flickered on, courtesy of a motion sensor. Surfboard racks lined the walls and various victory flags hung from the ceiling. NATIONAL CHAMPIONS 2010 was the most prominent, but its colors were beginning to fade.

"Hello, old friend," Tag said, and I turned to see him by one of the sailboats. He held his duct tape and the next clue but was lovingly looking at the boat. I immediately knew it was the one he used to sail with Daniel, the one Daniel now sailed with my fellow fac brat Anthony DeLuca. Even though swimming was more important, I'd never quite understood why Tag had given up sailing. "This won't hurt, I promise."

"Wait," I said as he dropped into a crouch. It looked like he was going to tape the clue inside the hull. "I want to read the riddle."

"Ah," he replied. "I already licked the envelope."

"Then unlick it," I said, moving toward him. There was no way I was missing a clue. Because while their scansion would probably make a poet laureate cry, they were perfect for the prank's scavenger hunt. Jesters made fun of their kingdoms.

Ames was a kingdom of sorts.

Tag stilled when I held out my hand for the envelope. After a few beats, he stiffly handed it over, but the serious expression on his face...

My stomach sank. "You sealed this on purpose," I guessed. "Whatever's in here..." I sighed. "You don't want me reading it. Just like you didn't want me reading the clue about you and Blair."

Let's talk about sex, baby, echoed in my mind.

Tag didn't correct me. "Of course you can read it" was all he said. So without thinking twice, I did. The envelope's seal was still damp from Tag's saliva, and I had to finesse the flap back open, taking care so it wouldn't tear. The cardstock was covered in its familiar jumble of letters, and I couldn't read the clue fast enough:

> *Roses are red,*
> *The ocean is blue,*

Go to the Hoppers' mailbox...
Where clue six waits for you!

"Oh my god..." I said, shock shooting up my spine. "What *is* this?"

Tag didn't say anything. I waited for him to again reassure me that the riddle was ridiculous—that *all* the riddles were ridiculous—but he didn't.

Blood thumped through my ears. "What is this, Tag?" I repeated sharply. "What the hell kind of clue is this? Some shitty Valentine?"

He rose from his crouch. "Lily—"

"You said this prank wasn't a dig against Daniel," I cut him off before he could begin. "But it is—it *totally* is!" I gestured to the sailboat. "This, for example. Every team member and clue location is connected to him."

"Yes," Tag said simply.

"What?" I blinked, having expected the Jester to put up more of an argument.

"This prank revolves around Rivera's ties to Ames," he continued. "You called me on it while we were moving the Almanacs." His voice was level. "None of this is new information, and I maintain that if Alex were president, we would be hiding a clue in the commentator's box in the ice rink right now."

"But Alex *isn't* president," I countered. "*Daniel* is."

"So?" Tag said through gritted teeth. "He's just your prom date, Lily. It's not like you're the First Lady."

Just your prom date.

I didn't know why the words made me so angry, but they did. Maybe because once upon a time, prom meant so much to Tag and now it meant nothing. My pulse pounded so hard that I lost control over what I said next. "For some reason, you have it out for Daniel, and fine, we're helping you on this mission. But putting a clue in my mailbox makes this much more personal to me, Tag! I will be your Jester's fool but *not* your pawn."

He didn't react at first; there were at least five beats before Tag said, "Why are you always defending him? He's such an asshole."

I rolled my eyes. "He's not that bad."

"Oh, really?" Tag said airily, but I noticed the tips of his ears redden. "Frying my pump isn't that bad?" He nodded to himself. "Okay, yeah, thanks for the perspective."

My heart slid into my stomach. "What are you talking about?"

"Sailing last spring."

"Yeah, Alex told me you were retiring after the season to focus on swimming..." I trailed off when Tag's gray-green eyes fixed on mine. "What happened?" I asked, suddenly anxious. "Something happened, didn't it?"

"It was the last practice before the Bexley regatta," he said. "We were doing a run-through, and I hadn't removed my pump beforehand—my levels had been up and down that day, which I told him. He *knew* I was still wearing it. But later we got into an argument that ended with him knocking me overboard. I hit the water *hard*."

I opened my mouth, but Tag shook his head.

"I lost it. I fucking shouted that he needed to help me, but he didn't listen, even though he knew my pump wasn't water-proof." Tag's face twisted like a grotesque gargoyle. "He watched me panic and then laughed while I pulled myself back onto the boat. I was so out of it that it took me three tries."

My lungs beat like a bird's wings, almost unable to breathe. *How dare Daniel? How dare he let Tag struggle like that?*

Tag rubbed his eyes as mine began to sting. "I was fine, but my pump…the battery was completely soaked." He sighed. "And to make matters worse, my replacement pump got lost in the mail, so I was stuck with finger pricks and backup shots for a while."

I winced. Tag hated needles, but it was the only other way to monitor his levels and inject insulin when needed.

"After we finally got back to shore, he clapped me on the shoulder and said I had no reason to be so dramatic." He paused. "I advised he find a new sailing partner before shoving him off the dock."

"How dramatic of you," I attempted over the lump in my throat. I let a beat pass. "Did you get in trouble?"

He shook his head. "Not really. Coach Burns pulled my prefect recommendation, but that's it."

My stomach stirred. Tag *had* applied for prefect.

"Oh, and my parents reached out to ensure I knew how irresponsible I'd been."

"That's sickening," I said softly. "I want to vomit."

"Be my guest," he croaked as he dropped back down to his knees and grabbed the duct tape off the concrete floor. "Like I said, Daniel's an asshole."

I blinked away my tears. It all made sense now, the motivation behind tonight's prank. But still, somehow, I heard myself say, "Please don't use that clue."

Tag closed his eyes and gritted his teeth. "You're kidding me. You still don't think—"

"No, I just don't want to be associated," I cut in quickly. "You're right; he's a dickhead and deserves this, but I don't want to be associated beyond being an anonymous fool."

"But you *need* to be," he countered. "Everyone has been taken off the suspect list, Lily. I called myself—and Blair— out in a clue, Maya is in the infirmary, Alex lit up and gave some twisted TED talk to six witnesses, Manik's literally *with* Daniel trying to find said witnesses…and, let's face it, Zoe's just a badass. As of now, everyone's name will be crossed off in red ink." He gave me a look. "Except yours."

"Except *mine*?" I gave him a look right back. "Come on. I was never on the list to begin with, Tag." I shook my head, thinking of my angel-on-top-of-the-Christmas-tree image. "Jeez."

"You will be when Daniel *really* thinks about it, and so will the rest of campus, because there's a chance he *is* going to share the clues." Tag held up the envelope. "Lily, if we don't hide this one, which I do admit is middle school-level mean—"

"Translation: pure evil."

"Yes, the purest of strains," Tag agreed with a nod. "Which means if we use it, Ames will never nail you as the Jester. Daniel's your prom date. Why would you ever write something like this?" He let out a breath. "But if we skip it and reconfigure things…" He grimaced. "Hops, I worry you're fucked."

I crouched down next to him, feeling like a complete idiot. Why? Why would I be fucked? What would give my involvement away?

"Building access," Tag murmured. "No Jester has ever pulled an indoor prank before because student IDs are powerless after sundown. The only student who still has approval is our commander in chief, but he's the one solving the puzzle. And while that freshman stole his keys, I think pegging him as the prank mastermind would be a stretch." He sighed. "We both know those obnoxious alarms go off if doors are open for too long and how Campo never misses them. And there won't be any signs of forced entry. If we're lucky, a few classroom windows were accidentally left open, but we didn't exactly break any for shits and giggles. The only other logical explanation is a faculty ID."

"And that means me," I muttered bitterly, then swore. "Shitballs."

Tag was right; we needed to use the casually cruel Valentine's Day card. Daniel would recognize that it didn't sound like me at all, and if the clues went public, I doubted anyone else would point fingers. They'd wonder how the culprits successfully got into Hubbard and the observatory, but because of my reputation, they'd probably conclude that a daring daytime heist was more likely than recruiting me to provide a faculty ID.

Lily Hopper would never! I could imagine Blair saying.

I held the envelope in place while Tag taped it to the boat's hull, and then he quickly zipped up his backpack before we silently said goodbye to the sailboats and surfboards. Neither of us spoke until the boathouse's door had been fully lowered. "There are other reasons why Ames would think you're the Jester," Tag said. "It's not just because of Leda's golden ticket."

"Okay, yeah." I snorted, starting toward our golf cart. "Sure."

But Tag's sudden hand on my arm stopped me in my tracks. He was already speaking, already rattling off adjectives at a speed that suggested he was extremely nervous. I barely caught any of them thanks to the roaring ocean. "I told Alex after I was chosen!" I finally heard him shout. "It was at the very end of last year, and we pretty much laughed the entire summer about the ensuing madness when it was my turn. I refused to do any concrete brainstorming, of course."

I gave him a single nod. "Of course."

"Because I wanted to talk to *you*, Hopscotch. It was you I wanted to scheme with…" He dropped off, the wind whipping his hair. "I procrastinated playing Jester for months, because I didn't trust myself not to walk over to your house, knock on your door, and ask you to write in a stupid spiral notebook with me. I know prank collaboration goes against code, but I didn't care about painting by the numbers. All I wanted was to make bullet-pointed lists and annotate campus maps and write ridiculous riddles with you." He sighed. "If Alex hadn't locked me in our room one weekend to work out the logistics, I don't know if we'd be here right now. Nothing about being the Jester seemed worth it if you couldn't be my partner in crime."

He was shaking by the time he'd finished speaking, and while part of me wanted to throw myself into his arms, the other part told me to stay put and say, "Yet somehow I wasn't good enough for you."

Maybe it had been a mistake, to dig up our relationship's grave, but...

So it goes, I thought.

Tag's eyes widened. "What? What are you talking about?"

"You would've come over if I was good enough for you," I said, gathering as much courage as I could. "Tag, you would've walked into my house and grinned as you presented me with a brand new notebook after giving the *greatest* hello hug. You would've chased me up the stairs, and we would've put on our invisible jester hats and made some magic."

God, I could see it. I could see it so easily, right down to the way he would've flopped down on my unmade bed and how I would've tackled him once he revealed his secret.

"But I already knew I wasn't good enough for you," I said, nodding resolutely. "So it's cool. Totally and completely—"

"Why would you think that?" Tag blurted. "Why would you *ever* think you weren't enough?"

"Because of Blair!" I screamed over the ocean's rushing waves. "Because you decided to go out with the *gorgeous* and *glamorous* and intellectually *superior* Blair Greenberg!"

"But you dumped me," Tag stated matter-of-factly. "After two months of pushing me away—"

"I did not!" I said.

"You did too!" he said back. "You started hanging at home on Saturday nights instead of coming to dances, and whenever I also wanted to skip, you told me not to worry about it—to just go have fun with Alex." His throat bobbed. "It's like you didn't want to spend any time with me. You'd always be doing homework when I came over for Josh's neighborhood brunch the next morning, and then you invited friends to go to the movies with us later. Sunday matinée showings were ours, Lily. They were *our* tradition."

"Yeah." I glanced at the ground. "Until you stood me up for one."

Tag released a long breath. "I did that on purpose," he eventually said. "I'm not proud of it, but I wanted to see if you'd care." He shrugged. "You didn't."

Tears pooled in my eyes. "That's not true." I swallowed hard, remembering. "I sat in my room and stared at my phone for almost the whole afternoon, wondering if I should call you."

"Why didn't you?" he asked.

"Because I thought you'd found something better to do," I admitted. "Something better to do with someone better than me."

Tag put down his backpack, and my breath caught when he moved closer to pop my flannel's collar. "What could be better," he said, "than spending my entire afternoon seeing some strange foreign film…" His fingertips fiddled with the shirt's cuff, so close to my bare wrist. Something began building up in my chest, as if water were filling my lungs. "With approximately four senior citizens and my one and only—"

I didn't let him finish; instead, I grabbed his face and all but smashed my mouth against his. "Christ," I mumbled when it didn't go as planned. Our heads had bounced off each other.

Tag let go of the flannel and laughed into the night. "What was that?"

My voice was weak. "A kiss."

I glanced away from embarrassment but then felt him coaxing me back. His knuckles brushed mine before our fingers mingled and soon entwined. Tag raised them, and I blushed as he swept me into his arms. One calm hand went to my lower back, the other splayed wide between my shoulder blades. "I wish you had come over," I whispered. "I would've loved to make bullet points and annotate maps and consult a rhyming dictionary with you."

"I wish I'd come over too," he whispered back, the two of us slowly swaying from the sea breeze. His muscles tensed. "But tonight has been okay, right? Besides some shit hitting the fan?"

"It's been more than okay, Jester," I said. "It's even been— dare I say it—*fun*." I felt him relax when I smiled. "Let's just pray there's no more shit."

Tag smiled back. "All's well that ends well," he murmured, lightly kissing both my dimples before stepping back to look at me.

You've got my favorite smile on your face.

There was a moment of silence between us.

And then...

And *then*.

Tag and I were kissing, and oh—oh, his lips were soft and gentle but also sizzled like summer sparklers against mine. My stomach somersaulted as the kiss deepened, and it cartwheeled when Tag slid his hands around my waist to pull me closer. I rose up on my tiptoes and tangled my hands in his dark hair. "Hopscotch," he breathed after several hammering heartbeats. "I don't want this to fall apart. We need to—"

"I know," I said, kissing his neck. "We need to get back to the clues." I sighed. "Just not yet, Tag. Please. A little longer."

For over a year, he'd been untouchable, but now—now I couldn't help but throw caution to the ocean winds. The twinkling stars behind my eyes told me this was worth it.

"No, that's not what I—" Tag began, but when I kissed him again, he released a groan and slipped his hands under my Dri-FIT. Everything in me *ached*. We still weren't close enough, even though our hips were now digging into each other. It felt excruciatingly wondrous.

"There's the upstairs trophy room," Tag whispered in my ear.

"Excuse me?" I smirked and slung my arms around his neck, sweat beading on my forehead. "Since when does the sailing team have enough trophies to fill a room?"

We stumbled back against the boathouse's outer wall, laughing like the sun would never rise. "There might not be many recent ones," Tag said after a fierce kiss. "But you'll see plenty of first-place finishes from the sixties and seventies."

I latched my fingers onto his belt loops. Another kiss, another kiss, another kaleidoscopic kiss. "Do you have one?" I asked breathlessly. "In your backpack?"

Tag's shoulders sagged. "No," he said, then coughed. "They didn't, uh, make tonight's packing list."

And that was when it hit us like a gunshot—what exactly we were doing. Trying to make up for lost time when there wasn't any to spare. We sprang apart and stared at each other, scared shitless. "Get your backpack!" I shrieked at the same time as he shouted, "Grab the keys!"

The only thing we had time for was a great escape.

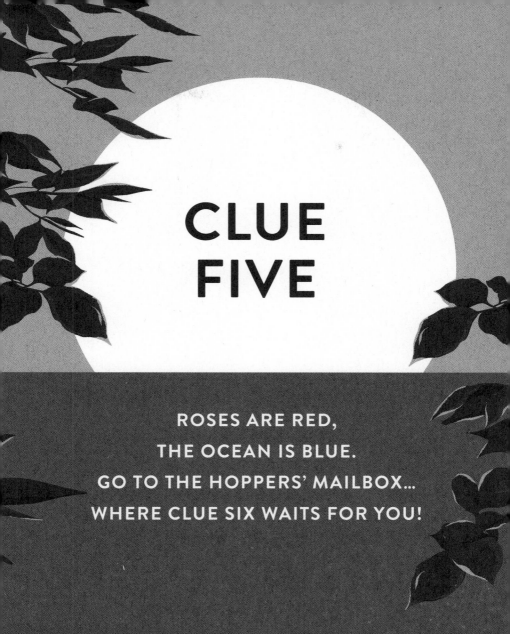

CLUE FIVE

ROSES ARE RED,
THE OCEAN IS BLUE.
GO TO THE HOPPERS' MAILBOX...
WHERE CLUE SIX WAITS FOR YOU!

SIXTEEN

The golf cart served as our getaway car, but it turned out a getaway car wasn't truly a getaway car if you were taking what you wanted to get away from with you. Tag and I sat stone-cold silent, staring straight ahead as I drove. *What is he thinking?* I wondered, my pulse jetting away with the golf cart. *Tell me, Tag. What are you thinking?*

Although I didn't even know what *I* was thinking. At least not clearly. Those fast and furious minutes between us had been amazing, but they now felt confusing. I still loved Tag, but did he feel the same way? Or his favorite partner in crime because we worked well together?

And what about Blair? Was I just the best person to distract him from her? Even if it was for the trillionth time, Tag *had* broken up with Blair, but he had *also* protected her in a clue.

Had we only been caught up in the excitement?

My heart twisted. We'd created quite the mess.

And thus, I realized sadly, *we won't be discussing it.*

There was no time for discussion if we were to finish hiding the clues by sunrise.

We did not return to Gilmore Lane; instead, I kept close to the water, driving on the widespread boardwalk that rambled along Ames's beach. It would eventually pass my house. The perfect shortcut, especially at 4:00 a.m.

When Tag finally spoke, my body quaked. "I think we should hide the cart here," he said, pointing to the upcoming gap between two rocky, sandy dunes. "Get back on foot."

"Okay." I nodded. Better in the dunes than in my backyard, and the boardwalk was a favorite campus running route, so it would be reported and returned to Buildings and Grounds within a day. "You really think of everything," I said after Tag wiped the steering wheel and seats down with Clorox disinfecting wipes from his backpack.

"It would be better if they were bleach," he said as my phone vibrated, and an invisible snake slithered up my spine when I saw a new message from Zoe. For some reason, I had a bad feeling about this one.

The rest of your clues better be brutal, Swell, she'd texted. Because thanks to Daniel FREAKING Rivera, I just broke my ankle.

"Oh, no," I said, shaking my head. "No, no, absolutely not..."

Zoe already taped her ankles before basketball games; she didn't need anything serious jeopardizing her career. With four years at Duke ahead of her, she was only getting started.

You didn't break your ankle, Zoe, Alex wrote, even though they were undoubtedly right next to each other. You twisted it.

Since when do you have a medical degree, Alex? she fired back. Ligaments have been torn!

Tag sighed and typed: What happened?

Then he looked at me as if to say, *We need to keep moving.*

Our speed walking jumped into a jog, and by the time we neared my house, Zoe had explained that she and Alex never made it to our planned rally point at the ropes course because Daniel and Manik had gotten too close to them in the woods. They'd decided to run, which had set Daniel off like a German shepherd. He chased us until Manik called him off, she'd written. He told Daniel it was probably Tag and Blair messing around since we were near the sculpture sanctuary. He heard they got back together tonight...

I glanced up from my phone and over at Tag, heart heaving. He and Blair had gotten back together? Earlier he'd told Bunker that he and Blair had said "farewell" for the final time.

Was he lying? I wondered. *To keep up our lovers-in-the-moonlight charade?*

"No," he said before I could ask for the truth. "No, we're not back together. No way. Don't listen to *People* magazine."

"But...?" I whispered, hearing the word in his voice.

Tag slowed to a walk. "But we did sit together at dinner," he said, "and she propositioned me for prom."

"Oh," I said, feeling clueless. I'd eaten dinner at home instead of in the dining hall, so I hadn't heard. Zoe and Pravika probably had, but maybe they'd wanted to spare me. The corners of my eyes needled. Our stolen moment at the boathouse meant nothing.

I wanted to crawl under my covers and cry. Yes, Tag had said I'd always been good enough for him, but it was too late now. I had dumped him and he'd moved on; the best we could be was friends.

But we couldn't be friends. *I* couldn't be friends.

"Lily?" Tag said, but I ignored him, scanning the rest of the text to read that Zoe had tripped over a fallen tree branch and now could barely walk. Alex was slowly sneaking her back to her dorm as well as concocting a convincing story of how she'd managed to injure her ankle while in her room.

I didn't speak until we'd reached my backyard. The cottage was dark, my mom hopefully asleep. "Alright, let's make this snappy," I told Tag, hurrying across the lawn. He was several steps behind me. "Clue in the envelope, tape at the ready."

"You...um, don't want to read it?" Tag asked.

"Nope," I answered as we passed under the back stoop's dusk-to-dawn light. "Alex said he's going to Admissions after helping Zoe, so I assume it leads there." I paused. "That's the last one, right?"

"Yeah, lucky number seven," Tag said softly.

We moved like two spies across the driveway, and Tag had the envelope sealed and strips of tape ripped once we made it to my mailbox. I couldn't help but glance back at the house as Tag pulled open the mailbox's small door; my mom's bedroom overlooked the front lawn. "Try taping it up top," I suggested, not taking my eyes off the windows. "Mom and I never have stuff to send, but the mailman's a busybody, and Josh collects the daily take because he has his mail delivered to our house now."

"When's the wedding?" Tag inquired.

"This fall," I said excitedly. "October."

Then I gasped, horrified. My mom and Josh hadn't announced their engagement yet. Only Bunker and Penny Bickford knew because they were like family.

Tag chuckled. "Relax, I've known for months. Josh is terrible at keeping secrets. I had dinner at his place one night—" He dropped off and let out a frustrated sigh, and I turned to see him shuddering. "My hands won't stay steady," he said. "Can you please do it?"

"Only if you eat more fruit snacks," I replied with a sour stomach. "Right now, Tag."

His pump was going to go off again any second for another low reading.

"I don't have any," he told me. "That was the last pack."

"Then something else," I said, elbows deep in the mailbox. "Eat something else."

Tag didn't unzip his backpack.

"No!" I whisper-yelled, pressing the last piece of tape into place and then quietly slamming the mailbox door shut. "That's it? Those fruit snacks were really the *only* food you brought?"

He shrugged half-heartedly. "I've had to force myself to eat today because of nerves."

"Well, what about a drink?" I asked. "You must have a Gatorade or something."

"Alex's backpack. There wasn't enough room in mine."

I groaned. "God, Tag, I take my earlier statement back. You did a *terrible* job packing."

"I know." He said. "First no condom, now this…"

Blood burned in my veins. *First no condom.*

Was he trying to be funny? I held myself back from shoving him. There couldn't be a worse way to lighten the mood.

When his pump inevitably went off, he silenced it…but that far from solved the problem. "Follow me." I beckoned Tag back to my house. "We *need* to get you some food."

———

You can do it, I told myself. *You can break into your own house.*

And technically, the voice in the back of my head said, *you aren't even breaking in since you left the back door unlocked…*

Yes! I straightened my shoulders. *Capital point!*

Christ, it was late. An imaginary conversation admonished me that I should be in bed.

"What would you like?" I asked a pale-faced Tag after

settling him at the base of the tire swing tree. We were right under my window, and I could hear the white noise machine I'd put on a loop. "We might have Gatorade, but—"

I dropped off once I twisted the doorknob, but it refused to turn. It was locked? *How* could it be locked? I'd made sure to leave it *un*locked before I left!

This could not be happening.

Mom, I thought. Had my mom woken up earlier and gone downstairs for a glass of water or more tea? Maybe I hadn't shut the door tightly enough, and the wind had blown it open? I pictured her half-comatose, closing the door and flipping the lock with a yawn.

"There's always the doggie door," Tag pointed out when I visibly started squirming, my neck flushing. "You could fit through there, no problem."

I glanced at the doggie door. The teachers who'd lived in the cottage before us installed it, and while my mom and I didn't have any pets, Josh's coonhound loved it. She was always going in and out, in and out...

"Promise you won't tell anyone," I said. "Alex included."

He nodded seriously. "Yes, Alex excluded."

I glared at him before dropping down on the back stoop to crawl through the door. It was easy enough to get myself in position, but I felt so stupid when my head popped through the rubber flap and into the kitchen. *I could've gone through the actual door*, I realized. *I could've* unlocked *the actual door, because there's a goddamn house key on the goddamn key ring in my goddamn pocket.*

Outside, Tag was laughing as if I'd voiced my revelation.

But I couldn't go back. Nope, I'd committed to the doggie door.

My heart rate quickened when I noticed the kitchen's overhead lights were not like I'd left them. They were now dimmed instead of fully turned off. My mom had definitely visited the kitchen since I'd skipped town. "Super," I whispered, then scrambled through the doggie door and shot up into a standing position.

The fridge was against the far wall, so I slipped off my sneakers and took it one step at a time in my socks. There was a burst of light when I finally pulled the refrigerator door open, but the deep breath I took was premature. Everywhere I looked, there were takeout containers and Tupperware full of leftovers. They were all systematically sorted and stacked but there nonetheless. We hadn't done inventory in a while.

I shuffled various things as I dug my way to the very back to confirm that we indeed had no Gatorade, which probably would've been expired by now. We'd only ever bought it for Tag.

Two minutes later, I crawled back out the doggie door to find Tag sweating bullets. "Here," I whispered, offering him both an unopened jug of Ocean Spray's ruby red grapefruit blend and a sandwich-ready pretzel bun. "Take your pick."

As an incentive, I also produced a bottle of ketchup and

squirted it all over the pretzel roll. A glop even dripped onto my thigh. "You know me," Tag said with a bemused tilt of his head.

"Yes, I do," I deadpanned. "Quite well, it seems." I handed him the ketchup-drenched bread. "Now eat, please."

Tag didn't argue. He devoured the roll in only a few bites, then licked the excess ketchup from his fingertips. My gut twisted, half sick to my stomach but also half lovesick. Even after four years, I was still completely and utterly unable to fathom his ketchup obsession, yet without it, he wouldn't be his ridiculous self.

"You ready to go?" I asked a couple minutes later, after he'd taken a sip of juice to wash down the bread and I'd stuffed a Capri Sun in his heavy backpack. Just in case.

Tag opened his mouth, but instead of his voice, I heard a distinct *meow*. "Was that a cat?" he asked, eyebrows furrowing as he glanced around the dark yard. "That sounded like a cat."

"Mm-hmm," I mumbled as a familiar ginger cat leapt up on the stoop. His hazel eyes were deceivingly innocent in the dusk-to-dawn light's glow. "Good evening, Mr. Goodfellow," I said, then turned to Tag. "Robin here is the neighborhood stray, but he favors our house because my mom pampers him."

"Josh must *love* that," Tag said before coaxing the cat over to the tree. It took a moment, but after I blinked a few times, the cat let him pet his head. "Pleased to meet you, Puck."

Robin Goodfellow, or "Puck," was the mischievous sprite from William Shakespeare's *A Midsummer Night's Dream*. It had taken my mom all of three visits to christen him. "Leda, I love you," Josh had said. "You know I love you and everything about you, but I can't condone this arrangement. First you feed him, then you continue to feed him as well as *name* him…" He groaned. "Soon he's going to think he lives here!"

Josh wasn't fond of cats.

"Okay, I'm good," I heard Tag say while I tracked Puck. Out of the corner of my eye, I saw him stand up and stretch. "One of us should text Alex we're on our way."

I nodded but then saw Tag unscrew the grapefruit juice's plastic cap and take two full-on *glugs*. "Shouldn't you stop?" I asked him. "Won't it be too much?"

From what Tag had told me about his diabetes, I'd brought out the bread and juice as an either/or option. Both were high in carbohydrates to raise his blood sugar, but together they might send it *too* high.

"Lily, it's cool," he said as I felt a twinge in my chest. "Believe me, I'm fine. I feel better—way better than earlier." He smiled at me. "You ready?"

SEVENTEEN

Ames's Admissions building was in the school's academic village, so Tag and I took deep breaths before setting off through my neighborhood. It was the fastest route to main campus, but while I'd felt safe and secure when making my dash to meet the Jester at midnight, I now felt less confident. Even though every house was asleep, the moon still gleamed, and I'd pulled my baseball hat low.

It might've had to do with Puck the cat following us.

"*Please* go," I begged him. "Go to the DeLucas' house. I know you hate their pool, but remember that nice swing set they have? Mrs. DeLuca has sent photos of you on the slide!"

"He might smell Stevie on me," Tag said when he stayed on our tail. "She kept winding herself through my legs before I left tonight."

"Or he might just like you," I grumbled.

Tag chuckled. "Maybe Alex and I can take him off the faculty's hands."

"Yeah, maybe," I said, pressing closer to him. We were

walking with our arms tightly hooked together, as if expecting to be pried apart any second. It went unsaid that we were both on edge about returning to campus, with its roaming Campo cars and shining dorm lights. I thought of Pravika and her habit of rising before the sun to finish assignments. Had her alarm gone off yet?

And what about Daniel and Manik and their freshmen? Where were they? For all we knew, Josh could now be involved.

"Are you sure we shouldn't text Manik?" I asked Tag. "To see what's happening there?"

"Positive," he answered as we rounded a bend in the road. "It would be unwise to distract him from his imperative search-and-rescue mission." He paused. "Not to mention very unfair to steal his attention back to our little prank."

I bumped his shoulder with mine. Goofy Tag was coming out to play, which made me smile. It was reassuring that he hadn't gone overboard with the juice, that he really was fine. "Do you regret tapping him?" I said suddenly. "Manik?"

"No way," Tag replied. "I meant what I said back at King's Court. He put his heart, soul, and every last bit of his *sanity* into being editor…he deserves to know the Almanacs are safe. I don't want him to waste one second worrying."

Our phones buzzed with a new text. I'm home, Zoe had messaged. Alex helped me into bed before going back downstairs and grabbing ice packs from the kitchen's freezer. He's now wrapping my mashed ankle in an ACE bandage.

RICE, baby, Alex chimed in. Rest, ice, compression, and elevation!

Thanks, doc, Tag texted before putting his phone back in his pocket. Neither of us spoke. We now walked in silence.

"I'm sorry I didn't read the clue," I eventually said. "I wish I did. I'm now curious why the Jester picked Admissions."

Tag didn't respond.

Please don't ask why I didn't read it, I thought, knowing he might. It was a valid question, after all. But I didn't want to answer it; I didn't want to explain that I was upset about Blair being his prom date.

"I believe the Jester has the clues memorized," Tag said after a few beats. "He's not only read them a hundred times but also thought it would be advantageous to memorize them." He gave me a smug look. "It appears he was correct."

"Only if he proves it," I prompted when he didn't say anything more.

Tag smirked, then began jumping up and down and waving his arms in the air as he jokingly announced:

Mr. President! Mr. President!
To an emergency cabinet meeting you are sent!
Its agenda contains quite the hook:
WHAT HAPPENED TO AMES'S
BELOVED YEARBOOK?

I quietly applauded his performance. "Not bad," I told him, giggling. "Not bad at all."

Admissions was not only the headquarters for prospective Ames students but also for all the school VIPs (as my mother called them). Dean DeLuca's office was on the second floor while Headmaster Bickford had the third all to herself. Daniel and the rest of student council also held their weekly meetings there, part of which were dedicated to pushing Ames to prospective parents in the waiting room before getting down to business in a first-floor conference room. According to Secretary Pravika, they lasted forever. The number of minutes she'd recorded on her laptop was mind-boggling.

"It's Alex's favorite clue," Tag said as he looped his arm through mine again.

Behind us, Puck hissed.

"But apparently not Puck's," I commented before glancing back to see if the stray had finally run off. Sure enough, I caught him scampering across Madame Hoffman's front lawn, the movement clear as day.

Because there was a light in the darkness. Not two car headlights but a single, slightly bouncing beam. It could've been a flashlight, but my money was on a headlamp like the one I'd worn back at the ropes course.

"Tag," I murmured. "Someone's coming."

"I know," he murmured back. "I hear feet pounding the pavement."

And heavy breathing, I thought as the runner called out, "Hey!"

Tag and I stopped in our tracks to see Anthony DeLuca slow in front of us. "Hey, Ant," Tag said casually as I half squeaked and skipped straight to, "I didn't know you ran at night."

Anthony fist bumped Tag. "Yeah, I run at night," he told me. "Or in the early mornings." He shrugged. "I accidentally fell asleep at 7:00 last night, so 4:30 is now morning to me."

4:30? I thought, resisting the urge to double-check my phone. *It's already 4:30?*

We had only two hours before sunrise.

"Anyway..." Anthony said, slyness seeping into his voice. "How'd it go?"

Three heavy heartbeats passed between us.

"Excuse me?" Tag feigned confusion since my tongue had gone completely slack in my mouth. "How'd *what* go?"

"Oh, please." Anthony stretched his arms over his head. "You know."

Did we? Because unless someone had swallowed truth serum, how could Anthony know about the prank? He was only a junior. The fact that Tag and I were together in the faculty neighborhood so late didn't exactly help the cause, but...

But nothing, I realized, relief washing over me. Anthony didn't know anything about the Jester and his plans; he was joking about something else.

Bunker Hill's deadly Latin students and the homicide they were destined to commit.

"No body, no crime," I said coolly, folding my arms across my chest.

"Are you sure?" Anthony asked, almost incredulously. "Because it certainly *looks* like there was."

He gestured at us, and for the first time in hours, Tag and I looked at each other—*studied* each other. And dear god, our appearances really did scream "brutally murdered our classmate and buried him in the woods." Tag's hair was wild from the wind while my ponytail had half fallen out, and our clothes were covered in sweat stains, dried mud, and leaves. The left knee of Tag's jeans had been busted and his T-shirt stretched out from our tryst at the boathouse. A mysterious bruise had blossomed blue on my shin, and—to top it off—I even had ketchup smeared down my thigh.

How convenient, I thought. *Blood.*

"I mean, where's the shovel?" Anthony said. "Am I right?"

"No body," I repeated.

"Yeah, because you buried it," he said, cracking up as I saw Tag pull his pump out of his pocket. My pulse quickened. Had it beeped? I hadn't heard anything. "Seriously, though," Anthony said once he'd pulled himself together. "What have you guys been…" He noticed Tag now pressing buttons on the pump. "Everything cool, Swell?"

"Yeah, all good," Tag said, trying to concentrate. "I just have to bolus."

Anthony nodded. "Gotcha."

I closed my eyes. Tag was pretty open with his friends about his diabetes, but never *this* open. He and Anthony swam together in the winter, and Josh liked joking that Tag was Anthony's hero, but as far as I knew, they weren't especially close. I doubted Anthony knew what having to "bolus" meant.

Which meant it needed to happen *now*.

He overdid it, I thought, tiny little needles pricking the back of my neck. Tag's pump knew how much insulin to administer regularly, but when his blood sugar spiked, he instructed it to deliver a bolus, which was a heavier dose of insulin to even out the rise in his blood glucose level. It was a one-time dosage, mostly deployed after meals...or, in this scenario, hastily thrown together snacks. Why had I brought out the grapefruit juice?

"Lily's just walking me home," Tag told Anthony after he'd slipped the pump back in his jeans. "We went camping in the woods last night."

"Camping?" Anthony asked. "Where're your pillows and sleeping bags?"

"With the shovel," I deadpanned.

"Which may or may not be buried with the body," Tag said smoothly, and I had to bite the inside of my cheek to stop myself from laughing. He shrugged. "Freshman year, I made a list of things I wanted to do before graduating, and camping was one of them."

I smiled. He wasn't lying, but he'd crossed that item off

the list a long time ago. It had been the summer between sophomore and junior year when we'd visited Josh's cabin in Montana—we'd slept under the sky three nights in a row. I'd never seen brighter stars.

Anthony soon asked the obvious question because no one was immune to Ames's gossip mill. "What about Blair?"

In response, Tag gave him a quizzical look. "Ant, come on," he said. "We both know Blair Greenberg doesn't camp."

And then he took my hand, laced his fingers through mine, and raised them so he could kiss the inside of my wrist. My heart swelled, absolutely spellbound.

It felt like magic had been injected into my veins.

Even if this was nothing but pretend.

I had to admit that now. Tag and I were playing pretend.

"Have a good rest of your run, Anthony," I said a few minutes later, and once he'd taken off toward the beach, I squeezed Tag's hand—*hard*. "You had to bolus."

Tag groaned. "Yeah, it wasn't my first choice to do it in front of him, but I suddenly felt like crap and needed to let you know. I'm never chugging grapefruit juice again."

"You have my full support on that front," I said, then swallowed. "You're sure you got it, though? The right dose? I mean, an accurate one based on—"

Tag covered my mouth with his hand. "Yes, I have it handled," he said. "Please stop worrying so much."

Please stop giving me reasons to, I thought, but I didn't say it; instead, I swatted his shoulder before beginning an invisible game of hopscotch up the street.

He laughed, then followed me.

Just before Tag and I reached the covered bridge, I texted Anthony: No body.

No crime, he wrote back.

CLUE
SIX

MR. PRESIDENT! MR. PRESIDENT!
TO AN EMERGENCY CABINET
MEETING YOU ARE SENT!
ITS AGENDA CONTAINS
QUITE THE HOOK:
WHAT HAPPENED TO AMES'S
BELOVED YEARBOOK?

EIGHTEEN

Not that Tag and I wanted to run into anyone, but we tried cleaning ourselves up before crossing the bridge to campus. I redid my ponytail while he smoothed down his hair and then pulled his sweatshirt back on before dipping his hand in the bubbling creek below to rub the ketchup off my leg. "I could've done that myself," I managed to say, my lungs refusing to release any air. It was too precious.

"I don't mind," Tag replied. "I know you don't like snakes."

A shiver went up my spine. There were somehow snakes all over Ames, but the creek bank was their haven. "Remember when I found one in my boot last year?" I asked. "And you didn't believe me?"

He chuckled, hand now resting on my thigh. I didn't have the strength to shake it off. "Yeah, because it was Halloween and you were *Jessie*."

Okay, fair. My friends and I had all gone to Ames's dance dressed as female Pixar characters, and of course I'd been Jessie from *Toy Story* because of my red hair. Tag and I had left the dance early, and after finding a quiet spot for some alone time, I'd walked home barefoot. "How was the dance?" my mom asked when I'd deposited my cowgirl boots in the family room, but before I could answer, a snake slithered out of one. It dove straight under our couch and Josh had gotten a broom to sweep it out. "Taggart Swell," I now said, "why would Jessie steal Woody's line?"

"'There's a snake in my boot!'" he answered in his best Tom Hanks impression, but then his voice dropped to a whisper. "Did you hear that?"

"Yes," I whispered back, taking Tag's sweatshirt sleeve and tugging him into one of the covered bridge's dark corners. Something was rustling nearby, and I couldn't tell if it was someone on foot or the breeze swirling through the trees or—

Meow.

I rolled my eyes. "You've *got* to be kidding me."

Tag took out his phone and tapped its sleeping screen so we could see Puck pattering toward us. "Hi, pal," he said when the cat sat at his feet.

"Don't encourage him," I said.

"He's only a cat."

"Yeah, and cats are independent thinkers," I said, quoting Josh. "Dogs are eager to please, but cats have hard opinions on things."

Tag considered. "I agree. Stevie can be narrow-minded at times."

I punched his arm. "And Puck seems hell-bent on joining us." I glanced across the bridge and sighed. "We should go, Tag."

Admissions was all the way across main campus; it was the first building you saw when you passed through Ames's front gates. Once we conquered the bridge, Tag and I would need to play tic-tac-toe past all the underclassmen dormitories and most of the academic village.

Together we shuffled sideways, feeling our way along the bridge's wall until we reached its far corner. Puck meowed again and even brushed himself up against our legs, but I refused to engage with him. Instead I spotted a Campo car cruising by the bridge before Tag and I stepped out into the shadows. The only problem was there weren't enough of them. "*How* did we do this earlier?" I breathed as we took in the shining streetlamps, cheery and bright dormitory windows, and imagined the other Campo guards circling. The day squad didn't start their shift until 6:30 a.m., when students were allowed out of their dorms.

"I have no fucking clue," Tag replied. "But somehow we're gonna do it again." He offered me his hand and squeezed my fingers tightly when I took it.

We began by edging around the streetlamps' stationary beams but had to dash behind some bushes when a seemingly nondescript Toyota RAV4 came into our crosshairs. Puck, naturally, stood right in the middle of a streetlamp as it drove by us. "I recognize that car," Tag said quietly. "It's Ms. Kathy's, isn't it?"

"Uh-huh." I gulped. Ms. Kathy managed the dining hall, whose food did not just magically appear when the doors unlocked at 6:30. More dining hall staff members would be driving onto campus soon. Not to mention...

"I think we need to get off the streets," Tag whispered.

I nodded. "Yeah, traffic's about to pick up." My stomach twisted. "What do you suggest we do, though? Taking the sports fields won't lead us to Admissions."

Tag was quiet for a moment, then said, "We use the dorms as cover."

"Are you blind?" I asked as Puck squeezed between us. "Have you *seen* the dorms?" I gestured to the freshmen girls' fortress with its gleaming windows. "Everyone's suddenly an early bird."

Because finals.

"Not everyone," Tag countered, nudging me so that I looked at the dorm across the street: Macalester House, our beloved freshmen *boys'* house. Almost every window was blackened.

I gritted my teeth. "That's because they're catching up on sleep."

We knew they'd made it back to Mack House without any incidents. Daniel and Manik are supervising everyone climbing through the kitchen window, Alex had texted a while ago, after he'd left Zoe and started on his own way to Admissions. The boys had snuck up on him, uncharacteristically quiet, but he'd managed to scramble up a tree to avoid detection.

"Right, they're all tuckered out," Tag said quickly. He wanted to make a move; I *knew* he wanted to make a move. "No one is going to notice us outside. We'll do it just like we did the bridge—shuffle sideways against the building, backs to the wall. Headlights only cover the front lawns." He shifted next to me. "What do you think?"

"I think Manik and Daniel are discussing what went bump in the night," I said and pointed to the prefects' suite on the right side of the house. Light streamed through the slats in their barely lowered shades.

Tag sighed and dug out his phone. "Once you join the Jester," he muttered as he tapped out a text, "you're loyal to the Jester."

Manik responded within a minute: Distraction already in place, boss. We're busy planning a mandatory house meeting to talk about tonight's events. It concerns me that you guys are still out there, but good luck. If you need to hide, the kitchen window is unlocked.

Tag hearted his message. "What?" he said. "I love him right now."

"Good." I sighed. "That's good."

"Yeah…" He stared at me over his iPhone screen. "Hops, what's wrong?"

"I have an idea for a shortcut," I said, "but I don't think you're going to like it."

"Why not?" Tag asked.

"Because it involves the Hub."

Tag glanced over at Mack again, this time at the housemaster's apartment. It was dark, but not because Josh was asleep... or even *there*.

After all, he had a job to do.

Just like the dining hall staff.

———

Tag's plan to skim Mack House was ingenious. Campo drove by us, and while the Prius's headlights swept across the yard, they did not stretch far enough to find even the toes of my sneakers. "We're invisible," Tag murmured, hugging his backpack to his chest so he could press himself as close to the cedar-shingled house as possible. "Nothing and no one can see us..."

It was smooth sneaking until we reached the end of the line at the side of the house. Puck was waiting patiently on a bench under yet another streetlamp. "Is the coast clear?" Tag pretended to ask him.

In response, the cat raised a paw and began daintily licking it.

That was good enough for me. I grabbed Tag's hand and we took a leap of faith, hauling ass over to the math building. Puck bounded off his bench and followed us. "I still don't know if I like this shortcut idea," Tag whispered when we'd hidden ourselves in one of the building's corner alcoves. "He'll be in there prepping breakfast."

"I know," I whispered back, because like the dining hall, the Hub opened at 6:30 sharp. Sometimes 6:45 if Josh felt like joking around with the seniors lined up outside the diner door. Whoever got there first was awarded a free breakfast. "But he'll be in the *kitchen*," I reminded Tag. "We'll sneak through the diner and out the student center's far door." I paused. "It would shave off some risk if we cut through Hubbard. We wouldn't need to spend as much time in no-man's-land."

No-man's-land, meaning the Circle. Forget about finding any safety there; it might as well be a wide-open prairie in Kansas. The sprinkling of trees was all too tall to climb in a pinch, and what good was an Adirondack chair or a hammock for a hiding spot?

"Alright, alright," Tag relented. "But let's touch base with Alex first."

I nodded, unlocked my phone, and wrote: Status update?

Admissions, he answered. Eagerly anticipating your arrival!

Good, Tag typed. I miss you, Alexander.

I miss you too, Taggart, Alex replied. But always remember that you're simply the best, okay?

"Tag, focus." I locked my phone and forced him to do the same. We had no time for needless *Schitt's Creek* references, even if Patrick's open-mic night performance never failed to warm my heart. Just like Tag and Alex's bromance did. I hoped things wouldn't be too rough for them next fall, with Tag in Virginia and Alex at Columbia. "There's no ID sensor on the

Hub's outside door," I said, "and I don't have a key." I thought about my mom's key ring. "Or I probably do, who knows." I took a breath. "But since Josh is there, it'll be unlocked…"

"Or just casually open to all," Tag noted once we'd crept over to Hubbard Hall. The building where the prank had begun was silent and secure, save for a propped-open black door and a dining hall delivery van idling on the street. "Did he mention if he was low on supplies?"

"Oh, he actually did," I said. "Flour, eggs, butter, bacon, just some basics. Although this kid has also completely cleaned him out of ketchup. Breakfast, lunch, dinner—I've heard he pretty much drinks it with a straw."

Tag threw me a glare but then knocked his knuckles against mine. *You're funny.*

I flicked his arm. *Thanks.*

We waited a couple more minutes for Josh or the delivery guy to appear, but when neither did, Tag and I tiptoed toward the doorway. From past backstage visits, I knew the kitchen would be to the left, the so-called too-small storage room to the right, and the diner floor straight ahead. We just had to strike at the perfect moment.

Which turned out not to be *this* moment.

Someone emerged from the building. Not Josh but Raymond from the dining hall. Tag and I both froze, backs against Hubbard's shadowed wall. "Hello, little fellow," Raymond said, spotting Puck over by his van. "You want to help unload?"

The damn cat, I thought. *Why must he insist on joining the team?*

"Hey, Ray, please tell me you brought..." I heard Josh call from inside, but he trailed off once he'd stepped out into the early morning air and spotted his archnemesis. "Nice try." He folded his arms over his chest and shook his head at Puck. "Nice try, but I'm not my fiancée."

Raymond gasped. "You and Leda are finally engaged?"

"You are not setting one paw in my diner," Josh told the cat, then looked at Raymond. "Yes, we are—have been, actually—but it's not public yet. We agreed to wait until after graduation." He smiled. "This is Lily's year."

Oh, Josh, I thought, my heart flaring with love for him. Ever since Josh had proposed in October, my mom had been saying they were waiting for the right time to tell people, and I kept wondering why it hadn't come around yet.

Now I knew.

"Still," Raymond said. "Congratulations!"

"Thank you, Ray," Josh said, running a hand through his bedhead. "That means a lot. We're really—sick of this con artist cat!"

Puck had pounced for the prize. I blinked to see the cat zig past Raymond, then zag around Josh and into the building.

"I knew it!" Josh shouted, stalking back inside with Raymond on his heels. "I told Leda!"

"Hurry, this is our chance," Tag told me. "Stevie's always

sniffing around Alex's and my snacks, so I bet Puck will go for the food and they'll follow him into the kitchen."

Together we ran for the door, and after throwing ourselves inside, I caught whiffs of sugar and spice and savories from the kitchen mixed with the sound of pots and pans clanging. Raymond was trying to mediate between a roaring Josh and a mischievous Puck. "No, Josh, violence is never the answer…"

Puck mewed mockingly.

"What an imp." Tag grinned while we weaved through the dark diner, booths empty and chairs still up on tables, and then flipped the lock to flee and fly across the student center. "We'll have to thank him later."

"If he's *alive* later," I said.

"Cats have nine lives," Tag shot back.

"But none of them have been hit by Josh's favorite frying pan," I quipped.

"Touché," Tag said, tickling my waist before we skidded through the side exit and back onto the street. All was still quiet except for a distinct *meow*.

"No," I whispered, spotting Puck sitting a few yards away with his tail swishing expectantly. "There's no way."

"Pet him," Tag said when the cat sauntered over to us. "He was willing to take a frying pan for you."

I shook my head and smiled when Puck let me scratch behind his ears. "Very nicely done," I told him. "Now let's go finish this."

NINETEEN

Somehow, some way, we made it to Admissions. Cutting through Hubbard had helped us avoid crossing the entire Circle, but we still had to army crawl through part of it, flattening ourselves like starfish whenever a headlight neared. Then we crouched by the Crescent's low wall before porch hopping between junior dorms and hiding behind the auditorium's pillars. "Better late than never," was how Alex greeted us when we finally arrived. He and his backpack popped out from the impeccably manicured boxwood hedges that framed the building. "What took you so long?"

"The Ames School equivalent of *American Ninja Warrior*," Tag said as the knot of anxiety in my chest began to unwind. We'd made it, although I swallowed hard when I checked my phone to see 5:22 displayed on-screen. I glanced at the guardhouse up the street. Gabe's old post faced the front gates, so his successor had their back to us.

"Oh man, who's this?" Alex asked, noticing Puck at my heels. He'd kept his distance on the way over but now had moved in close.

"Puck," I said. "Alex, this is Puck."

"As in hockey?" He raised an eyebrow. "Or *Midsummer*?"

"You'll find out soon enough," Tag said, then nodded his chin at the tulip-bordered flagstone pathway. "Shall we?"

"Don't!" Alex yelped before Tag could cross the lawn. "There's now a camera." He pointed to the elegant archway entrance. "We're out of range, but see? Over there?"

"Since when?" I asked after squinting at a security camera angled toward the front walk. My shoulders sagged. Not only was Ames considered old-fashioned because it had been founded in the nineteenth century but also because its buildings did not have cameras. The gated entrances and back delivery roads had electronic eyes twenty-four seven, but a fence ran around the entire campus. One too tall to climb unless you had a grappling hook on hand. Plus, the school's stalwart Campus Safety squad. How much more thorough did the coverage need to be?

After a couple beats, Tag sighed. "Eh, I get it," he said. "At least for this building. It's like a museum. Random people funnel in and out all day, every day. There should be more security."

"Wait a sec," I said. "Don't tell me you're giving up."

"I'm not." He glanced at Alex. "Someone leave a window open?"

"But of course," he said. "Associate Director of Admissions, I believe." He gestured to the side of the building. "This way."

"One more clue, Jester!" I tried to psych up Tag. "We're almost there—so, so close."

He was slow to respond. "How are you going to get back?" he asked. "I don't want you going through that maze again, and, Lily..." He yawned. "Lily, we barely have an hour."

Indeed, the sky had gone from inky black to a deep plum and was now lightening to violet. Sunrise was upon us. "Don't worry," I whispered. "I'll hide somewhere until 6:30, then simply walk home. If anyone asks, I'll say I'm taking a morning walk."

"But you never take morning walks."

"Well, there's a first time for everything."

"Here we go," Alex said, hoisting up an office window. Puck nimbly jumped up and dropped inside before the three of us followed suit.

Just not quite as nimbly.

The Associate Director of Admissions's office was dark with spooky shadows, which revealed themselves to be endless clutter when I switched on my phone's light. Piles of color-coded folders and paperwork, framed family photos, and multiple New England Patriots bobbleheads along with a freestanding globe and an Eiffel Tower-shaped floor lamp. "Mr. Hoffman has quite the eclectic vision," Alex commented. "I want the name of his decorator."

The lock *clicked* when we snuck out the door and into the first-floor atrium of offices. A twisting staircase was in the center, and if you tilted your head back and looked skyward, you could see the stained-glass ceiling of the building's rotunda. It was a depiction of Ames's coat of arms, a checkerboard of light blue-and-red panels with a gold seagull overtop.

I pointed diagonally across the atrium. "I think the conference room's the door on the left." I paused. "Or is it the right?"

"The left," Alex sighed, but before the presidential runner-up could trudge over to student council's base of operations, Puck started adamantly pawing at his leg. "What? What is it?"

A shiver went up my spine. "Someone's here," I whispered. "Someone's here and—"

The sudden but unmistakable sound of snoring finished my sentence. "Dear mother of god," Alex softly proclaimed. "*We* are supposed to surprise the people; the people are *not* supposed to surprise *us*."

"Aptly put, Alexander," Tag mumbled. "Now where's the Sandman camped out?"

Puck took that as his cue to tiptoe off, and I cupped my hand around my flashlight so we could track him. He stopped near a couch against the far wall, where a heavyset, bearded man was sleeping. "Is that...?" Alex asked.

"Yes," I said, mystified. Why was Mr. Hoffman here? "That's our Associate Director of Admissions."

"His colleagues should have plenty of fun with him later…" Alex said, but he trailed off as if unsure what to do next.

Truth be told, I wasn't sure either.

We gave it a full five minutes before linking arms like children and crossing the atrium floor, footsteps echoing off the walls no matter how lightly we tried to walk. My pulse pounded, even though Puck had not left Mr. Hoffman. *He'll sound the alarms*, I tried to reassure myself. *Puck will raise hell if he wakes.*

Tag began humming "The Final Countdown" once we'd ever so carefully closed the conference room's door behind us. I watched him flip on the lights but then immediately dim them until the room was almost dark again. An oval mahogany table sat in the center with a dozen matching chairs while the taupe walls were clean, save for several windows and a standard SMART Board. Alex wasted no time in helping himself to the conference room's sideboard, which was laden with fresh glasses and mugs. The water carafe was empty, but Alex popped a Starbucks Breakfast Blend pod into the Keurig.

Yuck. Coffee.

"*Alex*," I hissed. "Really?"

"Relax, Mom," he said. "It'll be ready by the time we're finished."

"And you will be abandoning it if not," Tag said dryly as he battled with his backpack's zipper. It looked like it kept getting stuck.

"Here, let me try," I said right before he won the war, but I joined him at the table anyway. He'd started rubbing his forehead, and when I put my hand on his back, his skin radiated heat. I could feel it even though his sweatshirt. My stomach stirred. "What can I do?" I asked.

"Clue," he said. "We need the clue envelope, and the tape—the duct tape." He sighed heavily. "I should've brought scissors. I'm so sick of ripping duct tape, Lily."

I nodded and pulled both the manila folder and roll of duct tape from his overstuffed backpack. "Heads up, Nguyen," I said, tossing the tape to Alex. "Use your teeth if you must."

"Are you going to read it?" Tag asked when I'd flipped the clue envelope to seal it. "Don't you want to read the riddle?"

"Yes," I answered honestly, "but there isn't time." I licked the flap and handed the clue off to Alex. "Why don't you perform it spoken word-style while Alex hides it?"

Tag opened his mouth, but only two words came out: "I couldn't."

"Don't be modest, Taggart," Alex said as he crawled under the table. "Spoken word poetry definitely puts you in a vulnerable position, but this is a safe space."

"And you memorized all the clues," I added. "Advantageous, remember?"

Tag ran a hand through his hair, then nodded. "Yeah, yeah,

no, I got it," he said, his laugh sounding more Jester than Tag. "Let me just…I need a stage…"

And before I could even grab his sweatshirt hood to stop him, he'd climbed onto the conference table. His legs wobbled a little like Bambi's once he stood tall above me. Alex crawled back out from underneath just in time to see Tag grin and sing:

> *Burgers, fries, milkshakes, oh my!*
> *Ready to know where the Almanacs lie?*
> *Well, say hello to the Hub,*
> *Behind where everyone gets their grub…*

Alex and I were both on the table before Tag could take a bow. Something was wrong. His opening stanza had been charmingly charismatic, but by the end of the poem, it was like a haze had engulfed him.

Alex took both of Tag's hands. "He's trembling," He said. "Lily, tell me why he's trembling!"

"Don't yell at her," Tag said sharply.

"I'm *not* yelling at her," Alex said while I tried to work Tag's soaked sweatshirt over his head. He was no longer warm but sopping wet with cold sweat. "I'd just like to review any recent medical history." He looked at me. "Please."

I told him everything, and his eyes widened when I mentioned the bolus. "But what's wrong with that?" I asked, heart lurching. "He does it regularly. He said he automated an accurate amount…"

"Well, being accurate is tricky," Alex said, unzipping his backpack. His hands were shaking too. "When you aren't carb-counting what you eat or drink, being accurate can be really fucking *tricky*." He rifled through his bag. "I'm sure he tried to be accurate, Lily, but I'm even *more* sure he overdid it. He gave himself too much insulin and now he's crashing."

Tag swayed on his feet, so I quickly wrapped my arms around his waist to steady him. "Is this true?" I asked, because as much as Alex sounded like a doctor, he wasn't one. And nobody knew Tag's diabetes better than Tag. "Did you overshoot?"

"I shouldn't have done it in front of Anthony," he said by way of an answer. "I wasn't fully focusing…I was nervous he was going to put the pieces together and confront us about the prank." He groaned. "Can we leave? This room is so hot. I feel like I'm in a…a place with lava." His throat bobbed. "A volcano."

I held Tag tighter, realizing that he'd gone from a cold sweat to a hot flash. Haywire temperatures couldn't be good. "Alex, how do we fix this?"

"I'm finding him something to drink to boost him back to normal," Alex said, head basically *in* his backpack. "I know I dumped a Gatorade in here, but Zoe…"

"Tag, how about we sit down?" I suggested. He was fully leaning on me. "There are chairs—"

"Hops, it's really hot in here," Tag whispered. "Can we please go outside?"

"Goddamn it!" Alex cast his backpack aside. "Zoe *did* steal that Gatorade!"

My heart throbbed. *No Gatorade, no Gatorade, no Gatorade.*

"Wait, he has a Capri Sun," I exclaimed, remembering. "I packed it before we left my house. Alex, it's in his backpack."

He snapped his fingers. "That should work!"

From there, we moved quickly. Alex found the juice pouch, stabbed in its straw, and made Tag take a few sips before granting his wish to go outside. "Keep drinking," I said while he helped Tag down from the table and out through the room's large arched window. It wasn't far above the ground; Admissions was on a small hillside.

"It should kick in within ten minutes," Alex said once we were sitting next to him. "Although last time was a different story."

Last time? I wondered and was about to ask, but suddenly there was something more pressing. A lump formed in my throat at the sight of the approaching Campo car. We weren't in its crosshairs yet, but only because it had disappeared behind the auditorium.

Then it would turn the corner and its headlights would find us like an Olympic archer found the bull's-eye.

Thick blood thudded through my ears. I barely heard Alex say we had to go, barely felt him shaking my shoulder. It wasn't until he Alexis Rose-style booped my nose that his hoarse voice registered. "Lily, help me get Tag up!"

But while we successfully got Tag to his feet, it wasn't enough. He stumbled when we tried to make a break for it. "My legs are slush," he said, still stuck in his sluggish cadence. He sank back down in the grass. "I can't move."

"Then we'll stay with you," Alex and I both said.

"No." Tag shuddered with chills. He'd entered another cold sweat. "You guys need to go—*run*." His teeth chattered. "Don't let them catch you."

"Taggart, you're having a hypoglycemic attack," Alex argued. "If you seriously think I'm going to leave you here…"

"Alex, *please*," Tag pleaded. "We can't risk it."

We can't risk it.

My spinning stomach plummeted. Tag had said that to Alex to stop him from chancing a dance with Bunker at the observatory. He was thinking again about the strike in Alex's file, and if he were to get caught again…

"Alex, beat it," I told him. "I've got this."

"What?" Alex gaped at me. "Lily, no."

"Lily, yes," I responded. "We're not going to let you get kicked out of school. Get out of here before you blow it." I hurled Tag's Jester backpack at him. Campo did *not* need to get their hands on it.

Alex caught the bag but shook his head. "He's my best friend. I can't leave him."

"Then don't leave," I snapped. "But at least *hide!*"

"Yeah." Tag shivered again as I gestured to the conference

room. We'd turned off the lights but hadn't bothered to close the window. "Your coffee's getting cold."

"What coffee?" Alex asked blankly.

I stamped my foot. "Now!"

After one last look at his best friend, Alex took the backpacks and darted into the darkness. "You don't know what you're doing, Hops," Tag whispered as I sat back down and wrapped him in my arms, tears pooling in my eyes. "You don't know what's going to happen..."

"No, I don't," I whispered back, watching the dented white Prius blink its headlights before stilting to a stop. My heart rattled in my rib cage. "But I'm ready for it."

AFTER

TWENTY

It went unsaid that I wouldn't be whipping up omelets for breakfast and that we also wouldn't be stopping by the Hub for pancakes. Instead, I sunk to an all-time low, pathetically unwrapping a blueberry Pop-Tart. "Mom..." I started.

"You need to wake up," she said tightly. "No *yawning* while we're in there."

I nodded, not about to argue. Leda Hopper looked like a force to be reckoned with this morning. Gone were her Lululemon leggings and worn flip-flops; instead, she'd dug Banana Republic's finest out of her closet. Skinny black capris with a sleeveless white blouse and a cropped black jacket. Her high heels clicked on the kitchen floor, and she'd even done her hair, blond curls now poker-straight. I couldn't ever remember her seeming so outwardly *sharp*, but then again, why would I? It wasn't every day her daughter had a disciplinary hearing.

My Pop-Tart tasted liked cardboard. Ames had acted fast; it hadn't even been five hours since Gabe and Mr. Harvey had found Tag and me together. "Well, well, well," Gabe had called out, swaggering up the hill with his flashlight. "What do we have here?"

Both he and Harvey had stopped in their tracks when they realized who exactly they had there. "Lily." Harvey sounded fazed for the first time in his career. "Lily Hopper."

I'd burst into tears. "Please help," I said. "Tag needs help. He's having a hypoglycemic attack. I gave him juice but I'm not sure what else..."

Gabe was at Tag's side in seconds, and I suddenly remembered that his sister was diabetic. He'd mentioned it once. "How are you, pal?" he asked.

"That's a complicated question," Tag answered slowly.

"Let's get him up," Gabe said, looking at Harvey. "He needs to go to the infirmary." He paused. "And we should call his housemaster now to update him."

"Very good," Harvey agreed. It seemed like he was letting Gabe take the lead tonight—or at least *pretending* to for training purposes. He gestured at me. "And Lily?"

"I want to go to the infirmary," I blurted, way out of turn. "I'm not leaving him until I know he's going to be okay."

Gabe and Harvey considered, with Harvey ultimately making the decision. They would take me with them, but I had to leave the moment my mother arrived.

She ended up beating us there. "Leda, hello," Harvey said politely, as if not sure how my mom was going to react. She still wore pajama pants but had zipped her North Face fleece up to her throat with her arms folded across her chest.

"Thank you, Roger," she said with a nod before telling me to get my ass in the car and then to get my ass into bed once we got home. I'd curled up under my covers but couldn't go to sleep yet.

Please tell me you're okay, I texted Alex.

Yeah, I'm good, he quickly responded. I eavesdropped on your chat with Campo, then snuck back after you guys left. Now I'm waiting for Taggart.

I let out a deep breath of relief. Alex was safe.

He buzzed in again: Thank you, Lily. It really means a lot to me. What you did.

You're welcome, Alex, I wrote back before surrendering to sleep. I also wanted to wait and hear from Tag, but I was too tired. As soon as my head hit the pillow, I was out cold.

My mom banged on my door two hours later. "Penny is expecting us at 9:00," she said. Bleary-eyed, I reached for my phone to see that it was almost 8:00…and that I had a text from Tag in my notifications. My fumbling fingers couldn't enter my passcode fast enough. I was desperate to know if he was alright.

Stop worrying, I'm fine, he said. The Capri Sun wasn't quite enough to bounce back, so the night nurse gave me some apple juice and monitored me for a little while. Then Mr. Rudnick picked me up and drove me back to the dorm. Fuck, Lily, I'm so sorry. I messed everything up for you.

The corners of my eyes began to sting. Tag was going to be slapped with a second strike. He'd gotten caught in the car with me sophomore year, and now...this. Would Headmaster Bickford kick him out? Only a week before graduation?

Don't be sorry, I typed. It was my choice to stay, and I would do it again. My hearing is in an hour. This is what I'm going to say...

~

"It'll be fine," I told both myself and my mom once we climbed in the car. There wasn't a cloud in the brilliant blue sky, but neither of us wanted to walk to main campus. I buckled my seat belt and noticed Puck on the back stoop, watching as if to wish me luck. "Totally fine."

My mom cut the ignition, closed her eyes, and then looked at me. "Lily, I love you, but you *do* realize you won't be getting out of this without a scratch, right? It doesn't matter that you're a fac brat. If Ames gave certain students special treatment, the school would have no integrity."

"But it's only my first strike," I said.

"It doesn't matter," she replied. "A strike is a strike. Yours may not condemn your privilege to graduate, but all strikes go in student files, and if Georgetown sees that you have one..." She rubbed her temples. "Lily, what were you doing out there?"

A lump formed in my throat, blocking the total truth from spilling out so easily. I wanted to tell her about the Jester's prank, but I couldn't. It suddenly seemed irrelevant. When I thought about last night now, I didn't think about the stolen yearbooks and scavenger hunt clues. Instead, only two people came to mind. "Tag and I have been talking," I said slowly, "and we decided to go on one last adventure together." I swallowed. "I know it was spur-of-the-moment—"

"And stupid," my mom interjected.

"And stupid." I nodded. "But there's only a week left of school, so we said 'tis the damn season and celebrated it."

My mom responded by restarting the car and backing out of our driveway. "Does this mean you're back together?" she asked once the covered bridge was in sight. "Because a little birdie named Bunker seems to believe you are."

Goose bumps riddled the back of my neck. Bunker remembered our impromptu visit? How was that possible? He'd been so hammered.

"He called this morning," my mom continued. "After having breakfast with Mr. Harvey, he called and apologized for not alerting me of your outing last night. He trusted that you would heed his suggestion to return home."

A few heartbeats passed. My mom turned onto the covered bridge, and when the sunlight disappeared from view, I whispered, "I don't think I ever really broke up with him, Mom."

"No," she said softly, reaching across the console for my

hand. "I don't think you really did either." She squeezed my fingers. "But last night, sweetheart…" She trailed off and shook her head. I waited for her to say more, but she didn't. Her focus was now on the road. Students, all sporting their school blazers and colorful backpacks, were on their way to first period. I'd been excused from history for this meeting.

We parked in Admissions' recently repaved lot, and my phone vibrated in my blazer's breast pocket. I fished it out to find a text from Zoe. EVERYONE KNOWS, it said.

My pulse pitched. Already? Everyone knew about the prank *already*? The first bell hadn't even rung yet. Who was in the yearbook office?

Another buzz announced we were in a group chat. Not about the prank, Alex clarified. Everyone knows about you and Tag, Lily. Not his trip to the infirmary or anything, but they know you were caught "hooking up" by Admissions. They know you have hearings this morning.

Naturally, I thought. Naturally, because student gossip traveled at lightning speed around Ames. Faculty gossip too, though most students didn't know it.

"Lily!" My mom waved. She was almost to the building's door while I still stood by the car.

Fuck off, *People* magazine, was the last message I saw before shoving my phone back in my blazer and hurrying after her. Together we entered the airy atrium, and I thought about asking my mom why Mr. Hoffman would've slept here but didn't. She'd been livid when I'd wordlessly returned her keys several hours ago because she'd sure as hell noticed they were missing once Campo had called with the breaking news that I was not asleep in my bed. I suspected she knew that Tag and I'd used her ID to sneak into buildings.

I will tell her the truth and nothing but the truth, I resolved once we started up the atrium's winding staircase. I would tell her absolutely everything, like I always did—everything from being tapped by the Jester to hiding the final clue in student council's conference room.

But first, I had to face the consequences of getting caught right afterward.

The only way to describe Penny Bickford's office was "delightful." It sunnily sprawled across Admissions' third floor with soft spring green walls, all-white furniture, and a vase of freshly cut flowers seemingly on every surface. Floor-to-ceiling windows showcased Ames's stunning ocean views, but I especially loved her tasteful art collection. Several pastel pieces were mine, my favorite being a lakeside landscape from Montana. Josh and my mom had gone on a hike while I'd worked all day on it, and after Penny had unwrapped it on her birthday, she'd kissed my cheek and said it would go perfectly in her office. I remembered my heart filling with such warmth.

Today, though, I couldn't bear to even give the pastel a glance. Headmaster Bickford was already seated at her desk while Dean DeLuca stood near the windowsill. Anthony's father preferred standing to sitting. "Good morning, Leda," Headmaster Bickford said as my mom and I sat in the cushy chairs across from her. She nodded at me. "Lily."

"Good morning, Headmaster," I said feebly, and then no one spoke. We were waiting for one more person.

"*Pardon, pardon!*" Madame Hoffman hurried into the office a few minutes later. "My sophomores are in the language lab this morning, and I needed to get them set up before leaving." She sighed. "There were a few technical difficulties."

"I'll notify ITS later today, Camille," Dean DeLuca said before gesturing for my academic advisor to take the empty chair on my left.

She sat.

But still, nobody said a word. My blueberry Pop-Tart turned in my stomach. Was *I* supposed to kick off this party? Just dive right into my wrongdoing? I had no idea.

My palms had grown clammy by the time Headmaster Bickford folded her hands on her desk and made eye contact with me. "Quite frankly, Lily," she said, her voice level, "I'm shocked that we're sitting here under these circumstances."

All I thought to do was nod.

Dean DeLuca cleared his throat and consulted his iPad. "According to Roger Harvey's report," he said, "you and Taggart

Swell were found together outside Admissions at approximately 5:47 this morning. Is this correct?"

My heart twisted. "Yes."

"And you are aware that students are not allowed outside their dormitories between their curfew and 6:30 a.m.?"

"Rob, Lily doesn't have a dormitory," Madame Hoffman gently reminded him. "She's a faculty child."

"Yes, well," Dean DeLuca said, "faculty children are officially categorized as day students, and unless they have permission to sleep over, day students must be off campus by boarders' curfews." He looked at me. "Lily, since you are a senior, you should've left main campus by 10:30."

I did, I thought. *I always do.*

But this time, I'd come back.

Meanwhile, my mom had the gall to roll her eyes. "My daughter knows the rules, Rob," she said. "Can we skip reviewing the school handbook and cut to the chase?"

"I don't want to be here either, Leda," Dean DeLuca muttered, then put down his iPad and refocused on me. "Lily, you snuck out, right?"

"Well, of course she did," Headmaster Bickford answered before I could. "And I would sincerely appreciate being enlightened as to *why*."

So I told her. I took a deep breath and told her that over the last couple days, Tag and I had talked about having a final hurrah together. "We met up at midnight," I said, "and then took our own campus tour to reminisce about the last four years. All we did was walk around for several hours."

Because at the bare-bones level, that was exactly what we'd done. There had been plenty of stops along the way with an imperative mission to accomplish, but the scavenger hunt was truly a tour. Even though I was omitting the greater story, I wasn't lying.

"It was the wrong decision," I concluded. "Neither of us should've snuck out; we could've saved our walk for daylight instead of darkness."

"Yes, you absolutely could have," Headmaster Bickford said. "You absolutely *should have*." She sighed. "After my many years here, I understand that there's a certain..."

"Je ne sais quoi?" Madame Hoffman suggested.

"*Merci*, Madame," she said. "I understand there is a certain je ne sais quoi about illicit affairs on campus, especially when under the stars, but we have curfews for countless reasons." She paused. "Students' safety being one of them."

"I understand," I said, feeling a tight twinge in my chest. "But I didn't leave him—I *never* would've left him."

"And I believe that's extremely admirable," Dean DeLuca replied. "From what Roger Harvey wrote, you had the chance to save yourself, yet you didn't." His voice softened. "I'm not sure I can say the same for some students."

"Saving myself never even crossed my mind," I said, sitting up straighter in my chair. "I wasn't raised to abandon anyone."

I reached for my mom's hand but made sure to meet everyone's eyes. "Our Ames family has taught me so much over the years, and the importance of always looking out for one another is one of them." I took a breath. "I'm sorry for sneaking out, Headmaster Bickford, but I'm not sorry for staying with him."

I could hear the blood pulsing in my ears, but otherwise it was crickets as Headmaster Bickford exchanged a look with Dean DeLuca. "Lily, darling," she said afterward, "would you please leave us for a few minutes? We have a lot to discuss." She gave me a thin smile. "Why don't you get something to drink?"

"Oh, okay," I said, rising from my chair. "Of course."

She's going to give me a strike, I thought as I chose a seltzer from the marble-countertop kitchenette's stocked refrigerator. My fingers trembled a little when I popped the can's tab and took a long sip. *How could she not?*

I began pacing around the kitchenette and telling myself it wouldn't be the end of the world. Alex had a strike but had still gotten into Columbia back in December. Maybe Georgetown wouldn't care when they saw mine marked on my final transcript. I was a kid, and kids messed up sometimes. This wasn't even that major a mess-up. They had to understand.

"Lil?"

I turned to see my mom standing in the doorway, her face unreadable. "How bad is it?" I hiccuped.

Too much sparkling water too quickly.

My mom leaned against the doorframe. "We need to have

our bags packed by the end of the school day," she said. "If we haven't vacated campus by five, Campo has the right to remove us using plenty of profanity." She sighed. "We'll fly to Montana, and after throwing the rest of our house in a dumpster, Josh will join us. Penny hinted that the three of us should all change our names—"

I laughed so hard that seltzer spewed out my nose. "Seriously, Mom?"

"Yeah, seriously, Lily." She nodded at the office. "Get the hell back in there."

My stomach was churning like the high seas by the time I returned to the hot seat, and I couldn't decide whether to vomit in my lap and risk ruining the chair's pure white fabric or vomit right onto the blue-and-white chinoiserie rug, sending it to a landfill.

Deliberation was suspended when I heard my name. "Lily, you've had an exemplary record," Headmaster Bickford said. "You are one of the most promising young women Ames has seen in a long time, both inside the classroom and outside the classroom." She smiled tenderly. "Except for this hiccup."

As if on cue, I actually hiccuped.

"There's only a week left in school," she continued smoothly, "so we are *not* going to give you a strike—"

"Oh, thank you!" I exclaimed. "Thank you so, so much."

"—but you *will* be disciplined," she finished.

My pulse quickened. Disciplined? What did that mean? Because my mom's comforting hand on my shoulder suggested that it was a bigger deal than Saturday night detention.

"First, you will serve detention tomorrow night," Dean DeLuca said. "7:00 to 10:00 in the science center's lecture hall."

I nodded, bracing myself for more.

"Second, you are no longer allowed to attend the senior prom next week."

"Oh," I said, accidentally aloud. "Oh, okay—wow."

Headmaster Bickford opened her mouth to elaborate, but I didn't truly listen. The senior prom—I couldn't attend the senior prom, a night that I had built up over the years to rival Cinderella's ball. My beautiful soft blue gown was now destined to stay in my closet; I wouldn't be getting my hair and makeup done with Zoe and Pravika, and—shit.

Shit.

I had to tell Daniel I couldn't be his date. Later today, I would have to look into his eyes and say that I'd screwed up and couldn't go. The idea was worse than pulling a prank on him because it involved *speaking* to him. Based on what Tag had told me last night, I hadn't planned on talking to him ever again.

"And finally," Dean DeLuca said, "we are stripping you of your senior dinner privilege and thus your salutatorian duties."

"I'm sorry," Headmaster Bickford added when I didn't

visibly react. "You would've been superb; we know your address would've been wonderful." She rose from her chair. "That will be all, Lily. You may leave."

"Thank you, Headmaster," I said, then shook hands with the Dean of Students. "Thank you, Dean DeLuca."

Madame Hoffman echoed me, but my eyebrows knitted together when my mom stayed seated. "Are you coming?" I asked after my advisor fled for French class.

My mom crossed her legs. "No, I'm not," she said simply. "I'm not finished here."

I'm not finished here.

The words took a second to compute, but then I noticed that Headmaster Bickford and Dean DeLuca had moved into the adjoining conference room. My insides twisted themselves into a knot, knowing they were now prepping for a Zoom call with the Swells in Chicago.

Tag hadn't told me what time his hearing was, but of course they would do us back-to-back. Ames would want everything sorted out before lunch.

Unlike Madame Hoffman, Tag's academic advisor arrived early. "Ah, Leda," he commented. "I wondered if I'd see you."

Mr. Rudnick, Tag's housemaster, sighed and shook his head wearily when he saw my mother, and I did a double take when *Josh* walked into the office. Instead of his usual jeans and assortment of AMES SWIMMING apparel, he was wearing a dark suit. Together, he and my mom looked ready to eviscerate the entire boardroom.

It suddenly struck me that perhaps she hadn't dressed like a shark for my meeting but for someone else's. "You know his parents are lawyers," I said.

"Yes, I'm aware," she said. "Josh and I are *advocates*."

"Because you can never have too many," Josh added, although I saw him glance glaringly at Tag's advisor and house-master. They weren't going to fight for Tag the way Josh and my mom would; they didn't love him like Josh and my mom did.

My heart flared with hope. "Lily!" Headmaster Bickford called from the conference room. "Shouldn't you be getting to your next class?"

I have a free period, I almost said, but my mom nudged me. "Skedaddle."

"Don't let him get kicked out," I whispered. "Please."

"I won't," she said, then looked me dead in the eye. "I am so fucking furious with him, Lily, but I swear I will change my name and move to Montana before I let them kick Tag out of this school."

TWENTY-ONE

I'd put my phone on silent before my hearing, but after leaving Headmaster Bickford's office, I pulled it out of my pocket to find enough texts that made me close my eyes and take a deep breath. Everyone from friends to an acquaintance from my art class last term had messaged to see what the scoop was. *I can't do this,* I thought, feeling the heat rise on the back of my neck. *Not now, not yet.*

Friday was the most popular day for campus tours and prospective interviews, so I could hear chatter from Admissions' lobby, and the atrium was hustling and bustling around me. Three student tour guides gave me long glances as they passed by, and I gulped when one raised an eyebrow. Zoe and Alex and all my awaiting texts were right; everyone did know.

And knowing Tag, he would bypass this chaos by slipping up the back staircase, but there was no chance I was leaving this building without him. *Think, Lily,* I told myself. *Where can you hide for a while?*

I knocked on Mr. Hoffman's door a minute later; it was

already half-open, which I took to mean he wasn't busy. "Come in!" he called, and after looking up from some paperwork, he gave me a gentle smile. His wife had definitely told him about my hearing. "Lily, hello. What can I do for you?"

"Hi," I said quietly, then swallowed. "Would it be okay if I, um, hung out here for a bit?"

Mr. Hoffman nodded. He was a kind and thoughtful man, always dressing up as Santa Claus for the little kids at our neighborhood holiday party. "Of course," he said. "I have a staff meeting soon, but you're welcome to stay"—he stretched to pull a pillow off his armchair—"as long as you'd like."

"Thank you," I said, wondering for the millionth time why he'd slept here last night. But I wouldn't ask that question today. "I really appreciate it."

"Not a problem," he replied, and once he'd closed the door behind him, I reached for his box of tissues. The corners of my eyes stung, prickling with pain before hot tears spilled down my face. My mom—I knew how disappointed she was in me. Four years of nothing but hard work and *this* was how I would graduate. She had been so proud when I told her I was Ames's salutatorian, and now, instead of addressing my classmates at our senior dinner, I would be on the couch at home. Probably with Chinese takeout and marathoning Marvel movies.

Christ.

And Tag, I worried. What was going to happen to him?

When I'd finally wiped away the last of my tears, I unlocked my phone to face my texts. "Can you just not?" I muttered as I deleted almost every frenzied inquiry, because anyone outside my circle wasn't getting any immediate answers. Let alone in writing.

Hey, I hope things went okay, Anthony had texted. I'm sorry if my dad was a dick.

He was harsh, I replied. Just doing his job.

Pravika had sent a series of messages.

OMFG! the first one read. YOU AND TAG? GET IT, LILY!

Veeks, relax, I typed before reading her other messages, then added, It's not what you think.

Because it wasn't. We *had* technically hooked up last night at the boathouse, but it was as if the Jester's prank had pushed us down the rabbit hole to Wonderland. Tag's green eyes had flashed in the moonlight before everything began to spin. "Hopscotch," I remembered him whispering after that first dizzying kiss, the sound of his voice making my body hum. "I don't want this to fall apart. We need to—"

Enough, Lily, I told myself. It was over; it was done. It was nothing but fun and games.

Heart twisting, I deleted what I'd written to Pravika and instead told her what had happened at my hearing before composing a text to Alex and Zoe. Maya too, since I knew Zoe would tell her everything. I couldn't quite pinpoint my hesitation for including Manik, but in the end, I did. He was a Jester's fool, so he deserved to know. No strike, I texted, but detention tomorrow.

Phew! Zoe replied at the same time as Maya said, They took it easy on you!

Ladies, I don't think she's done yet, Alex wrote.

My fingers trembled as I typed, No prom, no senior dinner, no longer salutatorian.

Nobody responded for a while, then a message from Manik appeared. I'm so sorry, Lily. That's awful. I feel awful.

The others echoed him before Maya tried to break the ice. At least you won't have to go to prom with my brother, she said. That's something.

I swallowed. Daniel had texted me, but I hadn't responded yet. Hey, he'd messaged. I don't know how long disciplinary hearings last—never been in one—but call me afterward.

Play it cool today, Alex reminded us. Especially you, Manik.

The Almanacs, I suddenly realized. They were supposed to be distributed this afternoon!

Don't worry, Manik texted. I've got it all figured out. Daniel and I are supposed to meet at the yearbook office at lunch. I'm going to be "running late" to ensure he'll be the one who discovers they're gone.

Once everyone had liked his message, we signed off. I locked my phone, but soon the screen lit up with a private message from Alex: Do you want me to wait with you?

I smiled a little. Alex, you're in class.

Yeah, he said, but I can always go to the bathroom and then just not come back.

No, I thought. Alex could not get in trouble.

Thank you, but I'm okay, I typed. Tag and I need to talk.

Agreed, he replied. I only offered in case you thought a moderator might help.

I laughed. I've missed you, Alex Nguyen.

You too, Lily Hopper, he said. I've missed you too.

~~~~~

I'd texted Tag that I was downstairs, but after an hour, something started gnawing in the pit of my stomach. Second period had ended, and it was now student-teacher consultation…how long was his hearing going to last? Where was he?

Everything in me jolted when my phone finally chimed with answers. I'm in the secret stairwell, Tag had texted. Are you still here?

I'm here! I'm coming, I tapped back, and after scribbling a quick thank-you note to Mr. Hoffman, I burst out of his office and zigzagged my way through the crowded atrium. My heart hammered as I turned down an ancillary hallway and ran straight to the door marked PRIVATE.

Behind it, Tag sat at the bottom of the staircase. "Lily," he breathed and barely had time to stand up before I threw myself into his arms and squeezed him as hard as I could. He hugged me back, one of his wondrously warm hugs that never failed to make me melt.

"Smoosh," I whispered into his chest. "What happened to you?"

"What happened to *me*?" he sighed and pulled back to look at me with gray eyes. "I'd much rather hear what happened to *you*."

I ignored him. "Did you get expelled?"

Tag bit his lip, then shook his head.

"Thank god," I said, releasing all the bottled-up air in my lungs. "My mom swore—"

"I got all but expelled, though," Tag murmured.

My stomach dropped. "What does that mean?"

He raked a hand through his hair. "I didn't get a strike, but in exchange, they took away everything else."

"Me too." I nodded. "Prom, senior dinner, salutatorian—"

"*What?*" Tag's hand tightened on my hip. I hadn't realized it had been resting there. "They stripped you of salutatorian?"

"Yes," I said, quickly adding, "But it's fine, because Alex is next in line and will knock it out of the park."

Tag was silent.

"Will I be seeing you in detention tomorrow night?" I asked.

"No," Tag said, then coughed. "No, seeing as I'll be under house arrest."

My heart rate heightened.

House arrest.

House arrest?!

"I am allowed to attend classes," he continued in a monotone voice, "and eat lunch in the dining hall, but after the bell, I only get an hour to swim before I must report back to my dorm, sign in with Mr. Rudnick, and then spend the rest of the night in my room. Dinner will be delivered." He paused. "Josh negotiated swim practice. Dean DeLuca wasn't going to let me."

"Dean DeLuca's a dick," I muttered, even though we both knew it wasn't true. He really was just doing his job.

Tag laughed a little. "Obviously we can forget about prom and senior dinner, but I'm also not allowed to walk in graduation…"

I gaped, my mouth hanging open like the day's favorite meme.

"…which of course means my parents are now coming to graduation."

"Wait, they originally weren't going to come?" I asked, incredulous.

"No, they had a huge business trip to Hong Kong scheduled," Tag answered. "My sister and her husband were always coming, but you know my parents." He shrugged. "They don't care until suddenly they do."

My eyes welled up. "I strongly dislike your parents."

One corner of Tag's mouth twitched in a smile. "They were useless on the Zoom call," he said. "All my mom could focus on was my hypoglycemic fuckup and whether or not I was okay, and my dad took that as the perfect time to ask why he hasn't received any bills from my therapist recently."

"You have a therapist?"

"I do." He shrugged. "I mean, did—or still do. We haven't

had a session in a while…" He trailed off. "Anyway, your mom scared the shit out of everybody. It was like she was *waiting* to pounce. I expected to be kicked out, and so did Mr. Rudnick and my advisor. They didn't even try to help. But once Josh got my parents to shut up, Leda took over. She not so subtly suggested that Headmaster Bickford strike the strike and let me pay penance instead."

My heart stopped. Freaking *house arrest* had been my mom's idea? What the hell?

"She saved my ass," Tag said with a relieved sigh. "I'm still getting my diploma, and UVA won't hear a word. I owe everything to her."

We stood there in silence for a few moments.

"I know it's our fault," I eventually said, "but I hate this."

"Entirely our fault," Tag said back, "but I hate this too."

More silence.

"Have you talked to Daniel?" he ventured. "Told him about having to abort prom?"

I shook my head. "I'm guessing he already knows it's no longer happening, though, thanks to what *People* magazine has been saying about us."

He avoided my eyes, and I too looked away to silently contemplate our situation. We needed to figure out how to leave this building. It would make or break the prank.

"Manik said he and Daniel are meeting in the yearbook office around lunchtime," I said.

"Okay, good." Tag nodded. "Manik plans to be late, right? So Rivera's alone when he discovers they've disappeared?"

I couldn't help but smile. "Yes, Jester."

"I'm mulling over when to deliver the first clue," Tag said, still half in his head. "It depends on how this first part plays out, then the envelope will hit his mailbox."

"We also need to rethink our alibis," I said, making eye contact with him again. His cloudy gray irises had returned to their natural green. My pulse quickened. "As criminally evil as those two clues about us are, they're looking a little flimsy now that everyone knows we snuck out. Because when it gets out that the Almanacs are missing...they'll wonder..." I winced. "We should assess our options."

Tag gave me a flatlined, almost *bored* look. "Assess our options?"

I suddenly felt the urge to shove him, so I did. He was goofing around, pushing my buttons, and I fell for it every time. "Come on!" I exclaimed when he grinned. "Options, Tag!"

"There are no options, Hopscotch," he said lightly. "There is an *option*."

My stomach somersaulted. Yes, there was, and I knew it was agonizingly waiting for us. Ames was under the impression that Tag and I had been caught hooking up, and we had the chance to run with it. Everyone, including old Bunker Hill, thought we had gotten back together.

How could I be the Jester? Tag would say if questioned. *I was with Lily.*

And I was with Tag, I'd tell others. *How could I have known about the Almanacs?*

I'd never been able to pretend with Tag; it had always been all or nothing with him. But for the Jester's sake, I knew I had to try, no matter how treacherous it already felt and how painful it would be in the end. He might not bleed, but I would.

"Lily." Tag held out his hand. "Do you trust me?"

TWENTY-TWO

Hand in hand, Tag and I sprinted up the hillside's curving stone staircase. Consultation had ended, and there were only a few minutes before third period, so not many students had seen us leave Admissions. There had been a few whistles as we crossed the Circle together, along with an over-the-top catcall, but I was pretty sure that had been Alex on his way to Russian.

Even though we already knew our fates, it felt like we were holding on to each other for dear life. "You're cutting off my circulation," I said as we took the stairs two at a time.

"You're cutting off mine too," Tag replied.

Neither of us loosened our grip.

Because of *all* the classes on our schedules, Tag and I had Latin. *Latin!* It was so painfully farcical that I almost wanted to laugh.

I remembered the bright beam of Bunker's flashlight last night, the way it had captured Tag and me after we'd hidden the Jester's second clue. We had wanted to avoid his cottage at all costs, even army crawling across the grass to stay out of sight!

Yet now here we were, racing for his front door. I gently unwound my fingers from Tag's once we reached the porch. They were so tangled together that it felt like undoing one of those complicated sailing knots Tag had been so good at tying. "Lily—" he started but was interrupted by our phones pinging.

I sighed and pulled out my iPhone to silence it. Bunker always confiscated phones at the beginning of class, storing them in a lacquered cigar humidor, but if one still went off, he held it hostage for the rest of the day.

The Jester's group chat, I figured until I tapped and saw the notification—an email from Ames's student council president. My stomach swished. "Tag," I breathed.

He didn't respond, already skimming his screen.

I glanced down to read mine too.

To: Group_All_Students@ames.edu

From: DRivera@ames.edu

Subject: Almanac Distribution

Hello, Ames,

I am thrilled to announce that today is finally the day! This year's edition of the Ames School Almanac will be available for pickup this afternoon. Come to the auditorium after the bell, where I will be handing them out until dinnertime.

Make sure to bring a Sharpie for signatures!

All best,

Daniel

Tag and I made eye contact, and while I spied a smile playing on his lips, all he did was tilt his head at me. "What?" I asked, heart somersaulting. "What's so funny?"

"He has no idea," he replied. "He has no idea how well he's setting himself up."

I shook my head. "You sound like Alex."

"Yeah, we get that a lot." Tag smirked.

"Alex can be a real douche canoe at times, Tag."

"Well, I guess that makes three of us," he said lightly, then held up his phone. "This email is *absurd*. Could he be more of a narcissist?" He rolled his eyes. "I mean, at least give credit where credit is due. He couldn't give a shout-out to Manik and the yearbook team? Not even half a sentence?"

I scanned the message again, knowing Daniel scheduled most of his presidential emails. He'd probably written this one yesterday because there was no way he was in this buoyant mood right now. Are you seriously ignoring me, Lily? he'd texted again while Tag and I'd been finalizing our game plan in Admissions.

Plus, he couldn't have just sent that email. His phone was currently in a cigar box. "Let's go," I said to Tag in a small voice. "We only have two minutes."

Tag nodded.

"You're not a douche canoe," I added. "I'm sorry."

"No, don't be." He rested a hand on my waist. "We both know I am." He gave me a squeeze so soft that it sent sparks through me. "I'm working on it, though."

I nodded before stepping away from him. Waves of hazy heat pulsed from where he touched me, and it was too much. Affection had always been so natural between us, but now it felt wrong. If no one on campus was watching, I didn't want to keep up this hoax.

This sad, beautiful, tragic hoax of loving each other.

Tag followed me inside once I turned Bunker's doorknob and crossed the cottage's threshold. The front entryway was empty, and so was the living room, but neither of us gave it a second thought. Bunker held Latin in his solarium. "Ah, excellent!" he said when Tag and I entered the all-glass, rounded room. Sunlight streamed through the ceiling, and our teacher had a twinkle in his eye. "We were beginning to worry you'd lost your way."

Tag made a quip, but it went in one ear and out the other. After depositing our phones in the black lacquered box, I realized that there was no place to sit save for what our class called the "chessboard." Another one of Bunker's beloved antiques, the small mahogany table had a marble chessboard inlaid in the center and was only big enough for two people. I closed my eyes for a moment; Tag and I had sat there exclusively for almost three years. It wasn't until we'd broken up that a classmate had silently stolen my spot. She took my chair while I switched to the settee across the room. It was the only time the seven murderous Latin students had ever shuffled seats.

Although now that Tag and I were seemingly back together, my old chair was waiting for me. I chanced a glance over at the settee and indeed saw that Daniel had his original seatmate back. She gave me a friendly half smile before taking a sip of tea, but Daniel's expression was dour when our eyes met.

"Well, well, go ahead and pour yourselves a cup," Bunker said once Tag and I had shucked off our backpacks. He gestured to his tea service table. "We must begin."

Neither of us paid much attention to today's lesson. I'd flipped to a fresh page in my notebook and marked the date using one of my colored pens, but my bullet points were sparse. Tag's page looked identical, but the true tell was his shaking leg. It was one of his tics, which happened whenever he was impatient or full of anticipation…or full of *excitement*.

I didn't want Tag to draw even more attention to himself, so I scribbled something in my notebook before angling it toward him. *Kindly quit the bouncing*, it said.

He picked up his pencil. *TRY AND STOP ME*, he wrote back.

The solution came much too easily. I took a breath and twined my leg around his under the table, quelling the shaking with steadiness. Tag only bounced twice more before his leg relaxed.

But my spine straightened, sensing someone's eyes on me. I didn't need to do a sweep of the solarium to know Daniel was staring. Something in my stomach twinged as I jotted down another message to Tag.

I need to talk to Daniel after class.

He gave me a single nod, knowing it was the right thing to do. Daniel and I'd been study partners forever and prom dates. No matter how much I wanted to, I couldn't just ignore him.

And you should talk to Blair, I added.

Tag's face twisted at the note, and he opened his mouth to say something before realizing he couldn't. We were in class. Instead he dashed off another missive.

WHY SHOULD I TALK TO BLAIR?

Because she asked you to prom, I said.

Tag's reply was swift: *THAT DOESN'T MEAN I SAID YES.*

My heart lurched, and my handwriting became illegible.

You didn't?

"No," Tag murmured softly, shaking his head. "You assumed."

A lump formed in my throat. Yes, I *had* assumed. Last night Tag insisted that he and Blair weren't back together, but she'd still proposed they go to prom...and I hadn't even given him the opportunity to answer. "Oh," I'd said before sweeping the subject under the metaphorical rug, embarrassed that I hadn't heard it from my friends and even *more* embarrassed that I hoped our borrowed time at the boathouse meant something.

I didn't realize Tag had written another note until he tapped his notebook with his pencil. *I DON'T NEED TO TALK TO BLAIR, HOPS, BUT I DO NEED TO TALK TO YOU AND YOU NEED TO TALK TO ME. OKAY?*

My eyes welled up without my permission. He was right; we *did* need to talk. *Really* talk. All the half-told secrets and unfinished truths weren't enough to piece together what had happened between us, and if I wanted anything before graduation, it was closure.

It was clear Tag felt the same way.

We'll talk, I wrote, words inked in fountain pen. *I promise.*

—————

Tag and I did not leave Latin together. When Bunker's clock chimed, he casually packed up his things while I zipped my backpack in record time. "Daniel…" I started to say, but Bunker waved me over before I could get Daniel's attention.

I went to the blackboard as my classmates retrieved their phones from the cigar box. "Yes, Mr. Hill?"

Bunker gave me a look that said, *You need not call me "Mr. Hill."*

"Yes, Bunker?" I tried again.

"I'm sorry to hear about your disciplinary hearing," he said. "From your mother's text, it seems Penny was quite rough on you."

I sighed. "But at least I didn't get a strike."

"No, although I believe a strike would've been less of a punishment," he mused. "Instead, she has stolen all the end-of-year joys you deserve to experience."

"Don't you mean *deserved?*" I asked. "Tag and I didn't follow your advice; I didn't go home last night. We don't *deserve* anything."

Bunker chuckled. "Oh, my dear Lily," he said, "even though you and Taggart discarded my suggestion yesterday and didn't pay a cent of attention to my lecture, you both deserve each and every joy life has to offer." He smiled knowingly. "I suspect one of them was last night."

$$\sim\!\!\sim$$

"Daniel!" I shouted, leaping off Bunker's porch like a flying squirrel. "Hey, Daniel!"

Halfway to the hill's staircase, Daniel turned and paused to wait for me. "Hi, Lily," he said, tucking his hands in his pockets as I sucked in a deep breath to collect myself. "Class was really interesting today, wasn't it?"

My cheeks warmed. His curt tone suggested Bunker wasn't the only one who'd noticed Tag and I were in our own orbit.

Douche canoe, I almost wanted to say.

"I'm sorry," I said instead. "I'm sorry I didn't call you earlier. This morning was extremely overwhelming, and I thought it would be better if we talked in person…"

"Okay." Daniel shrugged when I trailed off. "We're in person now."

"Right." I nodded. "Right."

It was silent for several seconds.

"Lily, I don't want your mom marking me late," Daniel said, checking his watch. "I have a paper due, and based on what went down this morning, it's probably best if you aren't late to your class either."

Bleh, I thought. His voice was laced with condescension, and for once, I couldn't ignore it.

"I can't go to prom with you." I kept my voice level. No matter what, I would be polite. "Part of my punishment is that I'm no longer allowed to go to prom."

Daniel didn't blink.

"I was excited too," I lied. "It would've been great."

"Really?" Daniel cocked his head. "Because I'm not sure about that anymore." He looked away and snorted. "In fact, I highly doubt it."

My brows knitted together. "Excuse me?"

"I liked you, Lily," he said. "I liked you *a lot*—enough to wait for you to get the hell over Swell—but just when I thought we might finally happen, you decide to show your true self."

"Yes, I should've told you sooner," I admitted. "I should've said I only wanted to be friends, Daniel, but I didn't want to hurt you." I stumbled over my words, the back of my neck prickling. "It's just, well, Tag's…"

Daniel rolled his eyes. "It's now more than obvious who Swell is to you, who he's *always* been to you. I'm embarrassed I thought I ever had a shot—humiliated, if I'm being honest."

I didn't say anything.

"But I also feel like I've dodged a serious bullet," he continued. "I didn't figure you as a girl who would sneak out at night. I thought you were different, more focused on the future than the here and now, like me. I thought you were above this place."

All of a sudden, a bonfire blazed in my chest. I wanted to point out that he'd snuck out too but knew he would counter that his breaking the rules was for a noble cause. I knew he would say it was a prefect's *duty* to find his missing freshmen.

So instead, I baited him through gritted teeth. "I did something bad, huh?"

"Yeah," Daniel said. "You did, and this whole circus with Swell aside, it wouldn't reflect well on me if—"

"You are such a douche canoe!" I exploded. "You are the most narcissistic, uptight asshole, Daniel!" My hands went to my hips so I wouldn't clock him in the nose. "I'm the one who snuck out and got caught, yet you're worried about *your* reputation?"

By way of an answer, Daniel's jaw clenched.

Adrenaline coursed through my veins. Any qualms I had about stealing the Almanacs had evaporated. They were gone, and it felt amazing. *You're about to play him*, a voice in my head said. *You're about to play him like a fucking violin...*

TWENTY-THREE

Rather than texting them, I waited to tell Zoe and Pravika the whole Daniel story until lunch. "I am going to destroy him," Maya declared after I finished speaking. She had been discharged from the infirmary an hour ago, her face now full of color. "I'm serious, Lily," she said. "Are we talking crutches?"

Next to Maya, Zoe groaned. "Please don't mention crutches," she said. "Just the idea of them is giving me flashbacks…" She trailed off, remembering Pravika was with us. Pravika, who had no clue that Zoe, Maya, and I had played with the Jester last night. Do we tell her? Zoe had texted earlier, and I'd hesitated a moment before typing back, Definitely.

But not yet, Zoe said.

Not yet, I agreed, because one of the best things about Ames's senior prank was not knowing the person—or *people*—behind it. If we told Pravika, right here, right now, that we were three of the Jester's fools, it would steal some of the magic. Springing the surprise on her afterward would be more fun. I could already imagine the questions she would pepper us with, wanting to know every behind-the-scenes secret.

"Ugh, Zoe," she said, shaking her head. "I still can't believe you twisted your ankle by tripping over your *gym bag*. Why didn't you turn on your light before going to the bathroom?"

Alex had been right: Zoe hadn't broken or sprained her ankle, but she had tweaked it enough to where her skin had bruised light violet overnight. With her fake story circulating, Ames's athletic trainer had conducted an assessment this morning before tightly taping her ankle and wrapping it in a thick ACE bandage so she could walk without trouble.

"I know, Veeks, it was stupid," Zoe sighed at the same time as someone else said, "Ladies, do you mind if we join you?"

The four of us turned to see Tag, Alex, and a couple of their friends holding milkshakes and to-go bags from the Hub. The heavenly smell of diner food wafted over to our table.

"Ooh, boys," Pravika whispered.

"Ew, boys," Maya said and scooted closer to her girlfriend. Zoe laughed and kissed her cheek.

I smirked at Tag. "Only if you pay us in fries."

Smirking back, he pulled out a large cone of French fries from his paper bag. "I figured that'd be your price."

"Why takeout?" I asked after he, Alex, and the other guys had dragged extra chairs over to our table. "Why not eat at the Hub?"

"Because our favorite booth was taken," Alex answered through a massive bite of his grilled cheese. "By Blair."

"Mmm," I said, not needing to hear any more. The schism in their friend group seemed inevitable after Blair had seethed like a snake at Tag during calculus. "Well, I now know why you said *no* to me," she'd harped, to which he simply nodded and said, "Yes, you do."

Meanwhile, Tag had not only gifted me with fries but also with a cheeseburger and a black-and-white milkshake. I pushed away my limp salad and smiled. "Thank you," I said as he unpacked his own lunch. Naturally, it included ten ketchup packets.

"We really came for the five of us to be together," he murmured once the others had fallen into conversation. "Alex and I wanted the team to be in the same place when the news breaks, so Blair stealing our booth was a brilliant excuse for takeout."

I hid my grin by sipping my milkshake, thick and creamy. "Have you heard from Manik?"

"Yes," Tag said. "He was also at the Hub and gave me a thumbs-up. It's really packed, so the wait will explain why he's late to the office." He chuckled. "I'm impressed."

Together we laughed before tuning into the table topic: prom. "You guys need to get your priorities in order and freaking ask someone," Pravika was saying to Tag's friends, which made my heart dip. While my punishment had ended up saving me from a night with Daniel, I still wanted to go. It was prom!

What does he think? I wondered, sneaking a quick glance at Tag. He was chowing down on his chicken tenders. *If it hadn't been taken away from us, would we have gone together?*

We were already dancing with our hands tied.

"Fine, fine, fine," one of his buddies chuckled. "I promise I'll ask someone." He paused. "Pravika, would you like to go to prom with me?"

My friend beamed, and after a round of applause, everyone finished their food...but my stomach soon soured. Our lunch hour was almost over, yet we hadn't gotten any updates from Manik. Why hadn't he texted our group chat? Daniel *had* to have discovered the absent Almanacs by now, right?

Out of the corner of my eye, I watched Tag take out his pump so he could bolus. Alex monitored him too. Their friends didn't give him a second look, knowing it was normal. But they hadn't seen him last night. "All good, Taggart?" Alex asked.

"All good, Alexander," Tag said. He then bumped my knee under the table, silently telling me the same.

I flushed before picking up my phone. My fluttering heart beat faster when I saw that Manik had finally texted.

Prepare yourselves, his message said, and after reading the warning on my phone, Tag unlocked his own and tapped his screen a few times. Something was coming.

Not even a minute later, a chorus of iPhone chimes and vibrating Androids drowned out the voices at our table.

"Another email from my brother," Maya said with a seemingly disinterested sigh. "Probably a reminder to—"

Pravika shrieked. "Oh my god!"

"Holy hell." Alex glanced up from his phone, eyes wide. "Guys, you better read this…"

To: Group_All_Students@ames.edu

From: DRivera@ames.edu

Subject: Almanac Distribution Update

Ames,

Today, as you know, the Almanacs are supposed to be distributed; however, due to unforeseen events, that will not be the case. Editor in chief Manik Patel and I recently discovered the Almanacs to be **missing**. The faculty has been made aware of the situation, and we are working to get to the bottom of it. If you have any information regarding the yearbooks' whereabouts, please email Manik (MPatel@ames.edu) or myself (DRivera@ames.edu).

Thanks,

Daniel

A hush had fallen over the dining hall. Instead of hearing cheerful chatter and the scraping of utensils, I saw students staring at their phones and whispering to one another. "Is this a joke?" a nearby junior asked. "How could the Almanacs be *missing*? This has to be a joke, right?"

Then, as if on cue, our phones pinged again. Only this time, the email wasn't from President Rivera; it was from someone else. Someone *without* an Ames School domain. I shut my eyes and willed myself to keep a straight face before I opened and read Tag's message.

To: Group_All_Students@ames.edu

From: TheJesterXXIII@gmail.com

Subject: Almanac Distribution Update #2

Greetings, Ames,

My oh my, what a puzzle we have here! Missing yearbooks? With only a week left of school? Well, I'd say
that's a mystery that better be solved...
But not without me.
Fear not, I will offer my help soon enough, but for now,
I give you this advice: In troubling times such as these, I
find it best to look to our leaders for hope!

Yours in merriment,
The Jester

I held my breath, hearing nothing but complete and utter silence before some squeaks and shrieks...and then the dining hall erupted into unanimous and uproarious laughter. Our table was soon swarmed. The guys' lacrosse team shook Alex's shoulders and punched his arm. "Dude!" They grinned like they'd won the state finals, even offering him fists to bump. "What the hell?"

"I know, right?" Alex had held up his phone, the Jester's email still onscreen. He was prepared; he knew the school would go after him first. "What the hell is happening? The Almanacs?" He whistled. "Well played, Jester."

Maya faux-furrowed her brows. "Wait, you didn't do it? You're not the Jester?"

"Sadly not." Alex sighed heavily. "And you know it was only my biggest dream in life."

"You'll find a new dream, Alexander," Tag encouraged, ever the loyal sidekick. He was too cool for his own good, so relaxed in his chair with his fingers casually winding themselves in my hair.

I wouldn't suspect him for a second, I thought while trying to ignore the ache in my chest. God, I wanted nothing more than to leave the dining hall and sneak into the student center's secret storage room so Tag could pull my braid loose and *really* tangle his hands in my hair. I wanted to grab hold of his blazer lapels and laugh before—

"I have to go," I said suddenly, even though no one was listening. They were too caught up in accosting Alex. Zoe and Maya were playing their parts well. "I'll see you guys later."

Tag's hand dropped to my shoulder, warm fingertips grazing my neck. "Wait, what?" he said as I shivered. "Where are you going?"

"I'm not sure," I murmured, "but this is too much."

"Okay, then let's go," Tag said, then winked. "I know places."

The collection of clues we'd scattered across Ames flashed through my mind, and I felt my heart twist into a knot. He was the Jester, and I was undeniably a fool for him. "No, no, stay here." I forced a smile. "Alex needs his wingman."

By now, a few of my theater friends had edged in front of the lacrosse guys to question Alex themselves.

"Alright. Okay." Tag nodded slowly. "But I'll see you later, right? Before I have to…" He trailed off, unable to finish the sentence.

Before I have to report to my room, I knew. *For house arrest.*

I still couldn't believe it. House arrest? Seriously? I couldn't remember the last time any student had been put under house arrest. Did the rule even actually exist?

I was going to find out.

———

"Man, was that a *day*," Anthony said on our walk home. The sun was sinking in the sky, rays of light ringing halos around the white clouds. "Do you think Alex expected everything to blow up like that?" He chuckled. "It was chaos."

I hesitated before answering, feeling my mouth turn up at the corners. Anthony—well, perhaps he had suspicions that

Alex had been involved in the prank, but I knew that unlike the rest of the school, he didn't believe Alex was the Jester.

He *knew* Alex wasn't the Jester.

"Did you see Daniel around at all? I heard he's already on the warpath."

I battled back my smirk. Yes, I had seen Daniel; we'd had physics last period, and even though I hated his guts, I'd sat next to him. Neither of us said a word to each other, but I'd caught him surveying Alex across the classroom. Daniel was staring at him with as much intensity as I had when I'd believed he was the Jester.

But naturally, Alex saved himself from any post-class confrontation by going to the bathroom before the bell rang and then simply not coming back. I assumed he'd returned to grab his backpack later.

"I know Alex is the obvious choice," Anthony said as we neared his house, "but he's taking a lot of hits. People need to stop punching him in congratulations. He bruises easily."

I smiled a bit. *Oh, Anthony.*

"Don't worry," I said. "Alex is now safe and sound in his room."

Because after I'd given Tag a short and sweet good-night hug, Alex had been all too eager to follow him inside their dorm.

"I know." Anthony straightened his shoulders. "He asked me to FaceTime during the Bruins-Rangers game later."

"Ooh…" I elbowed him. "*Spicy.*"

Anthony went scarlet.

I laughed, then he laughed too before we said goodbye.

Josh's car was in the driveway when I reached the cottage. "We're in here!" my mom called from the kitchen once I shut the front door behind me, and even though whatever Josh was cooking smelled incredible, my stomach churned. Were we going to talk about my disciplinary hearing?

My mom was attempting to dice bell peppers while Josh monitored multiple pots on the stove. It looked like *a lot* of food. "What's all this?" I asked.

"Dinner," Josh answered, moving to stir something that had started sizzling.

"For a hundred?" I joked. "Are we expecting the whole neighborhood tonight?" I noticed the Tupperware on the countertop, along with the empty YETI cooler on the floor. Josh was not only making dinner for us but also dinner for Tag. I shouldn't have been surprised; Josh had always treated Tag like a younger brother. He took care of him.

"Of course," my mom said after I asked. "Would you want to eat delivered dining hall food?" She looked up from the cutting board and flashed me a half smirk.

Which somehow sent me over the edge.

"Well, it's *your* fault he has to," I said, more sharply than I'd meant.

My mother raised an eyebrow. "Excuse me?"

"It's your fault," I repeated. My heart hammered. "*House arrest*, Mom? In the whole history of Ames, has a house arrest *ever* happened? Did you really need to—"

"Yes, Lily, I did," she interrupted as Josh diplomatically taste-tested what looked like Bolognese sauce. "I *did* need to be that harsh." She put down her knife, having truly butchered the poor pepper. "Penny was going to kick his ass off campus, and no one around that conference table had any objections."

"Except us," Josh jumped in.

My mom nodded. "His parents were hopeless too. They argue for a living, and they didn't even *try* to put up a fight, not even for their son." She sighed. "Everyone was in agreement, so I needed to play another bad cop in order to be the good one." She gave me a long look. "Does 'aut viam inveniam aut facium' ring a bell?"

Her words slowed my heart to a near stop.

Aut viam inveniam aut facium.

I shall either find a way or make one, I thought, closing my eyes to see the words inked on Tag's bicep. There had been no straightforward way to save him from expulsion, so my mom had made one. A merciless one, but still—a way.

"Please say you're not mad at him anymore," I whispered, eyes prickling. "Please say his punishment is enough." My voice wavered. "You can't be angry with him."

My mom picked up her knife to continue brutalizing her vegetables. "Does it look like I am?" she said. "I'm making him at least a week's worth of dinners."

Josh pulled a pan of mac and cheese out of the oven, one that Tag would drizzle ketchup all over. "Oh, you are, are you?" he asked dryly. "We must've gotten our wires crossed." He set the pan on a cooling rack, then gestured to it. "Because I thought *I* was cooking him dinner."

In the cozy kitchen, my mom turned and planted a kiss on the back of Josh's neck. He smiled and blindly reached back to crook an arm around her waist. "No, I'm not *angry* with him anymore," she told me. "I'm still *upset* with him, but I no longer want to set him on fire." She dropped her voice. "Because he never ceases…"

Josh and I exchanged puzzled looks, but when my mom spoke again, my pulse spiked.

"I want to frame it." Her frustration melted into a reluctant but bemused smile. "I want to *frame* that email. One of my students showed it to me."

"Mom," I started, ready to come clean at the same time as Josh said, "Leda, care to share with the class?"

She sighed. "The Almanacs, Josh. The stolen Almanacs? The Jester's prank?"

"Yeah, yeah, Alex Nguyen is a criminal mastermind," he said. "But how does that connect…" His shoulders suddenly straightened, and he whirled around to face me.

I held my hands up in surrender. "Listen, I'm not the Jester." I swallowed hard. "Neither is Alex." My heart pounded. "But we helped him."

Josh sat in shock as my mom and I ate dinner. "I don't want to know," he said before almost immediately changing his mind. "Actually, I want to know."

"These fajitas are amazing, hon," my mom commented at one point, so casually that it was clear she had zero interest in hearing about my involvement in stealing the Almanacs. In fact, she'd told me she didn't. At least not yet. "It's a fantastic prank," she said while Josh delivered Tag's culinary treasure chest, "and I'll admit that half of me is amused—and *impressed*—you played a part." She sighed. "But it ended with you getting caught, Lil." She shook her head. "I'm still very frustrated and disappointed, so I don't want details."

My eyes pooled. It felt foreign not telling her something and stranger still that she didn't want to know.

After dinner, I dumped my backpack in my room and changed into pajamas while my mom sliced us huge hunks of the chocolate chip cheesecake Josh had begrudgingly baked us. "Just promise to practice proper portion control," he'd said. "Don't eat half of it in one night…"

"Should we watch the new *Project Runway* episode?" I asked on the way back downstairs. "Or are you feeling—" The words died on my lips upon entering the living room.

Because Penny Bickford was sitting on our couch, still wearing today's elegant cream pantsuit with her legs crossed like she meant business. "Good evening, Lily," she said.

"Good evening, Headmaster Bickford," I replied, knowing

now was *not* the time to call her "Penny." Something told me she was not here in a grandmotherly capacity.

Where was my mom?

"Your mother has stepped out for a moment," Penny said, reading my mind. "I requested that the three of us speak privately."

"The three of us?" I asked.

"Yes." She nodded. "I would like you to FaceTime Mr. Swell since he is currently housebound."

My stomach sank. Oh—oh, no. Daniel had said he was working with the faculty to find the yearbooks, and because Tag and I'd been caught last night, we were Headmaster Bickford's first lead. "Of course," I said, trying to keep calm. "Just, um, let me grab my phone." I pointed upstairs. "It's in my room."

It was really in my sweatshirt pocket, but I had to warn Tag.

"Pick up, pick up," I muttered a minute later, back in my bedroom. He wasn't answering. "Pick up, goddammit..."

Three tries proved not to be the charm, so I switched to my next best bet. "You're lucky I like you, Lily," Alex said by way of greeting. "I don't hang up on Anthony for anyone."

"Where's Tag?" I asked a bit frantically. "He isn't answering his phone."

"Well, yeah, because he's asleep. He's been knocked out for like two hours."

I glanced at my alarm clock, eyebrows then knitting together. It was almost 9:00. What had Tag done? Gone to sleep at 7:00?

"Honestly, I don't know how you're still standing," Alex said. "With your disciplinary hearing first thing—"

I groaned. *Holy shitballs, how was that only this morning?*

It suddenly felt like weeks ago.

Alex hummed. "Mm-hmm."

"I need you to wake Tag up," I said, pulling myself back together. "It's an emergency. Shake him until he speaks more than gibberish, tell him to put on a shirt, and then to please FaceTime me..."

"Hello, Taggart," Headmaster Bickford said when I returned downstairs and joined her on the couch, close enough that we could both see Tag's face on my phone. He wore a faded and frayed Chicago Cubs T-shirt and sat at his desk with sleep-rumpled dark hair and heavy-lidded eyes. My throat thickened, and I tried to will away the need to be with him right now—the need to bury myself in his warm chest and listen to his heartbeat while he softly kissed my forehead.

"Hello, Headmaster Bickford," he said. "How are you?"

"Ready for a glass of wine," she said bluntly, her headmaster façade falling away and Penny coming to life. "I'm simply going to cut to the chase so I can go home and pour myself one." She sighed. "Did you steal the Almanacs last night?"

A puzzled expression crossed Tag's brow. "Uh, I was with Lily," he said. "Like I told you this morning, she and I were together. We were, um—you know, together." He somehow summoned a blush to further evade the question.

Nerves needled the back of my neck. "It's the Jester's prank," I told Penny. "The Jester took the yearbooks."

"Yes, Lily, I'm aware," she replied. "President Rivera made that quite clear."

"Then why are you asking us?" Tag said. "If you want to know if we saw anyone—"

"I am asking for the obvious reason," Headmaster Bickford interrupted. "The Almanacs were seen in the office yesterday but not today, which means they disappeared sometime within the last twenty-four hours." She looked from Tag to me. "And the only other event of significance within that time frame is your tryst. I wondered if they could be one and the same."

She cleared her throat. "Because to be honest, Taggart, while Mr. Nguyen certainly has an imagination and more than enough enthusiasm, I always thought *you* would make the better Jester."

My heart lurched, but Tag kept a cool face. "Alex isn't the Jester, Headmaster."

"I know," she said as I heard the squeak of the back door. My mom was home. "Though he is considered a likely candidate, so I will be speaking with him tomorrow." She flicked an invisible piece of fluff off her jacket. "Thank you both for your candor." My mom stepped into the room with a bottle of chilled white wine. No matter what the situation was, she knew how to defuse it. Headmaster Bickford smiled gratefully, then advised Tag to get some rest. "You look very tired, dear."

In her heart of hearts, she did have a soft spot for him.

TWENTY-FOUR

The Almanac intrigue was stronger than ever on Saturday. Whispers about the yearbooks' hiding place filled the hallways, and everyone's eyes met during mandatory morning class, trying to decipher whether the Jester was in the room. Alex was officially out of the running, since the entirety of Ames had woken up to an email from him:

To: Group_All_Students@ames.edu

From: ANguyen@ames.edu

Subject: Please stop punching me

Ladies and gentlemen!

While I am extremely flattered that you think me worthy of wearing the jingling jokester's cap, I am NOT the Jester. I know it's a nearly impossible realization to face, but you all must look deeply inside yourselves and come to terms with the truth.

Repeat after me: Alex Nguyen did not touch the
Almanacs!
I will not be taking any questions, concerns, arm punches,
or fist bumps at this time. Please respect my privacy.

Cheers,
Alex

Zoe and I'd agreed that he was good—almost *too* good. *Alex Nguyen did not touch the Almanacs.* Because indeed, he hadn't laid a hand on the yearbooks; instead of helping us move the boxes on Thursday night, he'd held back Maya's hair while she hurled in the bathroom.

Classes concluded at lunchtime, and by that afternoon, Blair Greenberg was the newest nominee. Underclassmen twittered like birds around her Adirondack chair, and surprisingly she wasn't loving it. Pravika, Zoe, Maya, and I were halfway across the Circle, sunning ourselves on beach towels, but we simultaneously sat up when we heard her eruption. "No!" she shouted. "I am not the Jester, so back the hell off!"

"Someone's salty," Zoe commented after Blair burst from her chair, flipped her hair over her shoulder, and then stormed off to her dorm. Zoe smiled teasingly at me.

"Well, there's my brother," Maya said, "on a mission to intercept her."

She pointed to Daniel, who was all but sprinting toward

Blair. He was the only one who hadn't welcomed the weekend, still wearing his Ames blazer, a striped tie, and khakis. My guess was he was sweating bullets under his jacket.

And not just because it was almost eighty degrees.

"Daniel, don't!" Blair barked at him. "Don't you dare!"

"But—" Daniel started, although before he could continue, Blair swerved around him and even flashed him the finger in her wake.

Pravika sucked in a breath. "Okay, she's *definitely* not the Jester."

"Nope," Zoe said. "Just a mad woman."

I bit my pinkie nail.

We went back to soaking up the sun, but before long, my phone buzzed with a text from Alex. Just got out of my meeting with Penny, it said. We talked more about my salutatorian speech than the prank. She also asked how Taggart was doing under lock and key.

What did you say? I wrote back.

That he was just dandy, he said. Because you were visiting him.

My heart twisted and I started rolling up my towel. "I've gotta go," I said to my friends. "Update me if anything interesting happens." I nodded at a nearby circle of sophomores, who were currently theorizing that the Almanacs had somehow been swindled away during the day. Because how *else* would the Jester have gotten into the yearbook office?

My friends exchanged amused, knowing glances.

We're not really back together, I almost said. *It's only an act.*

Although after our "interview" with Penny last night, Tag and I'd fallen asleep on FaceTime together. We'd done that all the time while we were dating. Neither of us ever wanted to be the first to say good night.

Grundy House, or the senior guys' dorm, looked like a converted Georgian manor: faded red brick with a side-gabled roof, four chimneys, and a symmetrical grid of tall, white-framed windows. I bypassed the front entrance and went straight for the first-floor corner room. Rather than transparent window-panes, Tag and Alex's were stained glass, so you couldn't catch much movement inside their inner sanctum. I battled my way through the bushes to find a nondescript wooden stool waiting underneath the window. *How convenient*, I thought, shaking my head before climbing up to knock on the colored glass.

"I'm sorry," Tag wearily called, "but per the order of Ames, I'm trying very hard not to connect with people right now."

"Have you been rewatching *Schitt's Creek*?" I asked when he hoisted up the window, recognizing David's famous line.

"Possibly," he replied, unable to make eye contact. I blushed; he was checking me out in my bikini top and shorts. My friends and I had really committed to getting our vitamin D.

I licked my lips. "Possibly?"

Tag blinked and ran a hand through his hair before our eyes locked. Today's sunshine brought out the green in his irises. "I'm halfway through season four," he admitted.

"I see," I commented as a cat leapt onto the windowsill. Black with white paws, she could only be the beloved but prohibited Stevie. Tag swept her into his arms to protect her from the outside world. "What do you guys do during room inspections?" I asked.

"We have a system," he said and proceeded to explain. I smiled at the part where Stevie was temporarily smuggled out of the room in a laundry bag. "Anyway..." Tag kissed Stevie's head before depositing her back on the floor, "What's up? Has Daniel detonated yet?"

"Not quite," I said. "I just wanted to see how you were doing." My stomach stirred. "And, um, you know, maybe talk?" I pointed to the wide windowsill. "May I sit?"

Tag nodded and backed up a few steps so I had room to arrange myself on the ledge. My flip-flops fell to the ground, and by the time I'd found a comfortable position, he'd perched on the corner of his and Alex's pool table. He took a deep breath. "Where should we start?"

Cheeks still warm, I helplessly shrugged. "I don't know. There's so much."

"Yeah," Tag agreed, rubbing his forehead. "Yeah, there is."

Both of us were quiet for a moment before something struck me. "Alex mentioned you had a hypoglycemic attack last year," I said. "What happened? Where was it? Here?"

"No," he told me. "It wasn't here; it was during spring break." My pulse pitched. *Spring break.*

"Why didn't you tell me?" I asked, because spring break had been in March, and I hadn't broken up with Tag until April. We were still together. Falling apart, definitely, but the thread hadn't snapped. It had never truly snapped.

Tag shook his head. "It wasn't a big deal. Alex was with me."

"But he wasn't the only one," I said, a snakelike suspicion slithering up my spine. There had been a catch in his voice. "Blair was there, wasn't she?"

"Yes," Tag admitted. "She heard I was with Alex in New York and begged us to take the train to Greenwich and come to this party she was throwing." He gave me a look. "Lily, nothing happened."

Blood thumped through my ears. Tag had told me he and Alex had gone out one night, but I never imagined it involving a train ride to Connecticut. I'd assumed it was with one of Alex's many city friends. "If nothing happened," I said slowly, "then why did you hide it from me?"

Tag sighed. "Because I didn't want you to read anything into it. It was just some stupid party. It didn't mean anything, and while I thought about texting you that Blair had invited us, I know she's not your favorite person, so—"

"Blair is *far* from my favorite person," I interrupted, stomach squirming. "Anyone who 'inceptions' people with insecurities and then ruins their relationships…" My eyes watered, thinking about how we might not have broken up if Blair hadn't interfered. She'd successfully pulled Tag toward her while I unknowingly pushed him there myself. I blinked away tears. "I'm not talking about Blair, Tag," I said. "I'm talking about your episode. If it wasn't a big deal, why would telling me be a big deal?"

Tag took a breath. "Because it was *more* than a big deal," he said softly. "It was full-on hypoglycemia, and I ended up in the ER."

My heart lurched. "What?"

"Yeah." He nodded. "Blair's parents were gone, so she let everyone crash at her house—most of her friends were plastered. Alex and I shared the sectional in her basement, and I don't remember it well, but he shook me awake at some point. Apparently I was shivering like I was standing naked in a snowstorm, and my pump was beeping. It turned out my blood glucose was at twenty."

Twenty? I winced. Twenty was too low, *dangerously* low.

"I didn't have my glucagon injection kit," Tag said, talking about his emergency meds. "It was in my suitcase, but Alex and I were out when Blair texted us, and we didn't swing back to his apartment before going to Penn Station." He paused. "I'm such a moron."

I kept quiet, sensing he wasn't finished.

"Alex is so spur-of-the-moment," he continued, "that it sometimes makes me want to be that spontaneous too." He chewed on his lip. "It honestly sucks when I remember that I can't always be like that. It *did* cross my mind to go back for the kit, but racing to catch a last-second train seemed much more thrilling."

"It doesn't sound like Alex to let that fly," I said, hugging my knees to my chest. "He's basically a helicopter parent. Didn't he ask if you had it?"

Tag nodded once, his words unsaid: *I lied.*

"Christ, Tag," I whispered.

"He took care of me the whole way to the hospital," he said. "Blair drove while he sat in the back trying to pour orange juice down my throat. Luckily the ER admitted me right away and force-fed me this disgusting glucose toothpaste before hooking me up to an IV to stabilize my levels." He sighed. "Then Alex went on the rampage. You should've heard him—his voice was shot by morning."

"Well, I'm glad you're okay," I said awkwardly.

Tag slid off the pool table and came to the window. "Lily, I'm sorry I didn't tell you."

"I'm sorry too," I murmured. "I'm sorry I gave you the impression that all I would care about was Blair being there." I took a breath. "It was really nice she drove you to the hospital."

Tag didn't respond; instead, he came closer, wrapped his arms around me, and buried his face in the crook of my neck. His skin was cool against mine, blazing from the sunshine. He smelled like his coconut shampoo with that ever-present hint of chlorine.

Smoosh, I thought as I reached to gently run my fingers through his hair before massaging the back of his neck. My body ached when I felt him press a light kiss to my collarbone. It was all still so easy, so natural, so intoxicating between us.

I hated it.

I loved it.

Only when the sun disappeared behind a cloud did I force myself to escape his embrace. "I have to go," I whispered.

"Stay," he whispered back. "Please stay."

"I can't," I said, shaking my head. "Mr. Harvey's retirement party is tonight."

Tag waited three seconds, then released me. "I have something for him," he said and briefly disappeared into his room to grab something. He handed me an envelope. It was white instead of the Jester's mysterious black, with ROGER written in Tag's famil-iar block-shaped handwriting rather than magazine cutouts. My eyes prickled, knowing that once upon a time, he would've been invited to a party like this. Tag had been welcomed at every faculty neighborhood gathering. I almost opened my mouth to suggest he come before remembering that he couldn't.

"I'll come back," I promised, even though I hadn't moved yet. I felt frozen, still sitting on the windowsill. "I'll be back soon."

"I'll be here," he said.

✦

I whipped up my famous swirled-caramel sheet cake with chocolate fudge frosting. My mom watched me the entire time, but surprisingly it was Josh who'd swiped a spoonful of icing as I'd worked my magic. "It's just that kind of day," he'd said, shrugging when my mom and I had given him puzzled looks. Josh had taught me everything I knew about baking, even though he didn't have a sweet tooth.

The Hoffmans had graciously offered to host Mr. Harvey's party, which had spilled out on the back patio. My mom placed our gift with the others, and before following her outside, I slid Tag's card in between two ribbon-adorned bottles of wine. "You did *not*," Mr. Harvey was saying when I found him. He, Dean DeLuca, Mr. Hoffman, and Josh stood near the firepit. Campo protégé Gabe was also there. They all held Bud Lights.

Meanwhile, Anthony was stuck sipping a Sprite.

"Yes, I swear," Mr. Hoffman said, chuckling. "I spent the night in the atrium."

My ears immediately pricked up. Finally, the reason Mr. Hoffman had been sleeping in Admissions the night of the prank.

But then someone's ringtone went off, a familiar ringtone. "For god's sake," Josh said with a sigh. "Not again."

"What's up?" Dean DeLuca asked.

Josh dug his phone out of his back pocket, and after taking a moment to collect himself, he accepted the call. "Hey, Manik," he said. "The house isn't on fire, is it?"

Everyone nearby kept quiet; I suspected they wanted to overhear as much of this conversation as I did. Why was Manik calling Josh?

"Well, you go ahead and tell Daniel that I haven't changed

my mind," Josh said. "When he and I texted this afternoon, I told him they weren't necessary. We conducted them two weeks ago, right on schedule." He paused to listen to whatever Manik was saying. "I understand their rooms are probably certified disaster zones," Josh patiently continued as my pulse quickened. "But, Manik, I always cut the boys a break this time of year. They're busy studying for exams and packing to go home. It's fine if loose-leaf paper and laundry litter their floors. It'll all get cleaned up eventually. We don't need to sidetrack them with a round of room inspections…"

Room inspections. I not only balked but also wanted to laugh. Daniel was pushing for room inspections so he could tear them apart, hoping to find the yearbooks hidden in someone's closet or stowed under their bed. He now suspected the freshmen boys.

I couldn't stay at the party past dinnertime. "No special treatment," my mom had said. "If Ames gave certain students special treatment, the schools would have no integrity."

I understood. I truly understood.

Although, Madame Hoffman didn't let me leave for detention without a paper plate weighed down by a large selection of desserts. "I've overseen detention before, *ma chérie*," she said. "Your stomach *will* start rumbling."

Ironically, Bunker was supervising this evening of ennui, checking names off a list and confiscating phones at the science lecture hall's entrance. "Lily." He nodded at me when I placed mine in the cardboard box. "I expect your homework is finished, so I hope you brought something to entertain yourself…"

My fellow delinquents were mostly underclassmen; I watched them glumly unzip their backpacks and unload textbooks upon textbooks and binders upon binders. Their laptops too, even though I knew there was no Wi-Fi in detention. *This might be in your best interest*, the teacher's pet in me wanted to say. *You have no choice but to study for finals.*

The large lecture hall was so quiet that I nearly jumped when someone took the seat next to me. "Hey, tiger," a familiar voice said, and I turned to see Alex smirking at me as he got comfortable in his swivel chair. "How're we feeling tonight?"

"Absolutely euphoric," I deadpanned, then asked, "What are you doing here?"

Alex shrugged. He was now focused on pulling the plastic wrap off my plate of goodies. I glanced over at the hall's doors to see that Bunker had shut them; we were now officially cut off from humanity.

"Do you even have detention?" I whispered.

"Yes," he muffled through a mouthful of red velvet cupcake. "It's not strictly in writing, but Bunker said it was possible his list was mistaken."

I rolled my eyes. "Alex, get real."

"Oh, this is my favorite." He ignored me, breaking off a piece of swirled-caramel cake. "You made this for the holiday party sophomore year."

"Shh!" a junior hissed before I could respond. He sat two rows ahead of us, Microsoft Word on his computer screen. "I'm trying to write a paper!"

"Then you're sitting in the wrong sector." Alex gestured across the room, where a cluster of students sat typing like they were being timed. "The laptop club is over there."

"You're a terrible person sometimes," I told him after the underclassman relocated.

"So what?" Alex said. "It's not like I need his vote or anything."

I was quiet for a moment, then murmured, "Alex, the election was ages ago. I know how much you wanted to be king of the school, but—"

"I wanted to be the *president*, Lily," he muttered. "I wanted to be the president so I could make Ames a better place. Rivera only wanted it for his precious résumé, so he could get into Harvard." He snorted. "I won't challenge you to name all the improvements he's made, because we both know..."

The rest of what he said was gibberish, thanks to the lemon bar he'd shoved in his mouth. I assumed it had something to do with Daniel accomplishing virtually nothing as student council president. He had done his duty, but nothing more.

Little did he know that the "more" was upon him.

I said so to Alex, who smiled slyly.

"Yeah, Daniel. Look what you made me do."

I booped him on the nose. "Karma."

Alex chuckled and reached for my figure drawing sketchbook. "What's new in here?"

"Meh, not a lot," I answered as he started flipping through it. "You know I prefer landscapes."

"Yeah, but you're so good at people too..." He trailed off, landing on a certain page. My heart twisted while he stared at it, and I cringed when he glanced up at me. "You still have this?" he asked quietly.

"Obviously," I tried to joke but instead heard myself whisper and waver.

Alex looked down at the sketch again. It was a drawing of Tag, a very old one from freshman year. We weren't even friends when I'd done it. I remembered Pravika, Zoe, and I had been doing homework in the library, and we'd spotted Tag in one of the reading rooms. "Lily, look!" Both my friends had grinned. "Look who's over there."

With them, my secret crush had been anything but a secret.

"Fine," Zoe had said after I refused to go talk to him. "Then I dare you to go *draw* him."

My stomach dropped. "What?"

"You heard me." Zoe nodded at the sketchbook tucked under my arm. "Draw him."

Pravika gave me a little push, and for some reason, I let myself be pushed. I'd walked into the reading room, and before my legs melted like two candlesticks, I went straight up to Tag's mahogany study table. "Hey, Tag," I'd said, and when he looked up from his book, his face was bathed in the warm lamplight.

"Hey, Lily," he said with a smile. "How are you?"

I'd ignored his question, immediately breaking into a ramble. "I have an assignment for art class," I said. "We're drawing people, so I need to draw someone, and I was wondering if I could draw you."

"Draw me?" Tag comically quirked an eyebrow. "Like one of your Spanish girls?"

"Okay, it's *French* girls," I'd sighed, unaware at the time that he'd purposely misquoted *Titanic* so I'd relax. "The line is 'draw me like one of your French girls.'"

"Do you want me to pose?" he asked once I was seated across from him, sketchbook open to a fresh page and charcoal pencil in hand. His evergreen eyes caught mine, and I blushed under their glimmer.

"No." I shook my head. "Just be…" I searched for a better word than "normal." I didn't want him to be normal. "Just be at peace," I said quietly. "Okay?"

Tag's lips curved into a slow smile. "I can do that."

When he went back to reading a worn copy of *Dune,* I began to draw. For the next couple of hours, there was complete silence between us—a silence that felt strangely comfortable and would eventually grow so lovingly familiar. "It's almost scary," Pravika once said. "How you guys can understand each other without saying a word."

The sketch made me ache. The way Tag rested his head in one hand while he read, dark hair disheveled and his fifteen-year-old facial features gentle. While his eyes focused on the page, his right hand had absentmindedly reached across the table—as if hoping to find someone else's. "I hugged my sketchbook on the way home that night," I now murmured to Alex, remembering how my heart had swelled. "I'd never been more in love with a drawing."

Alex responded by rubbing his temples. "You went to see him today."

I nodded. "Yes, and we talked about—"

"I *know* what you talked about," he interjected. "He gave me the recap while we had spaghetti Bolognese for dinner." He sighed. "I should've been there. You guys aren't talking about what you need to; I clearly need to guide the discussion."

"And what exactly would that be?" I asked with a pounding in my chest. "What is this oh-so-fascinating topic that must be addressed?"

The expression on Alex's face shifted from exasperation to extreme pain. I waited for him to say something. "Do you remember..." he said slowly. "What I said the night of the prank? About Taggart wanting a girlfriend?"

My mind flashed back to the three of us—the A team—trekking toward the sculpture sanctuary. Tag had been leading the way and out of earshot when Alex claimed Tag gushing about his cat translated to him secretly wanting a girlfriend.

"Sure," I said. "You said he wanted a girlfriend but that Blair didn't count as one, and then you made this bizarre metaphor about her being a box of Band-Aids."

"*Bizarre?*" Alex wrinkled his nose. "It's not bizarre; it's brilliant."

"*Brilliant?*" I sighed. "Alex, I have no idea what you mean."

Alex lowered his voice. "You dropped his heart, Lily," he said. "You dropped it and *shattered* it. And I tried to pick up the pieces and put them back into his chest, but one is missing and the others won't work without it."

I felt a sharp pang in my ribs, an epiphany dawning on me. "Oh," I breathed.

"Again and again, he goes back to Blair because he's missing the most important piece of sparkling glass," Alex continued. "He keeps patching up the dark hole with the same bandage because he believes you are lost and that he's never going to find you."

My eyes welled up with tears. I tried wiping them away, but it didn't work. "Alex…"

"He desperately wants to find you, Lily."

"He doesn't *need* to find me." I quietly started to cry, right there in detention. All this time! All this time, Tag had loved me, and I hadn't let myself believe it. "I'm here. I *promise* I'm here. Yes, I hid for a while, but I'm not lost. I'm found, and I've always been his. You know that, Alex."

"Of course," Alex said matter-of-factly. "I mean, I know

everything." He paused. "But he doesn't, Lily. He thinks you're pretending for the press."

"Which was his ridiculous idea!" I whisper-exclaimed. People were looking at me now, but I didn't care—it was too late to care. "I'm *not* pretending."

Alex put his hand on my back. "You should try telling him that."

"Okay, well, this is me trying," I said with a hammering heart, but before I could defiantly burst out of my chair, Alex's hand moved to my shoulder and gripped it tightly to keep me seated.

"Miss Hopper, you're currently detained."

I groaned and shook him off. "And we have no one to bail us out."

"You mean *you* have no one to bail you out," Alex said, casually standing up. "I am free to come and go as I please, since I do not actually have detention."

"God, I hate you," I said, laughing.

Alex shook his head. "I don't believe you."

"Why not?" I asked.

"Because," he said, "you've got Tag's favorite smile on your face."

The wind whipped and whispered to me once I'd rushed down the science center's marble steps after detention. *Don't let him,* it said, the words coursing through me like the ocean's current. *Don't let him count you out.*

For the last several hours, all I could think about was my conversation with Alex. He was right; Tag's and my communication skills were terrible. We had to stop skirting around the truth, no matter how scary it was. I couldn't let another night pass without telling him.

Ames's student music festival had been tonight, but the stage was abandoned by the time I blazed through the Circle. People still filled the Adirondack chairs and hammocks, though. I spotted girls in plaid miniskirts, baggy jeans, plastic chokers, and long hair twisted up into double buns. This year's theme had been a throwback to the nineties.

My lungs were writhing in pain once I made it to the three willow trees that cornered Grundy House. Their branches blew in the breeze, toward Alex and Tag's window. Light streamed through the stained glass, and I could hear Dave Matthews and multiple voices trying to talk *over* Dave Matthews. Just because Tag couldn't have outside visitors didn't mean his housemates couldn't come to call. My guess was they'd ditched the music festival in favor of hanging here tonight.

But nothing would wreck my plans. I exhaled, then sucked in a deep breath before leaving the trees and darting through the bushes to the wooden step stool. "Password?" Alex shouted after I knocked on the window. The other guys chuckled.

"Guys, shut up," I heard Tag say, his voice sounding so close. "It's Lily."

Blood now pulsing in my ears, I was suddenly at a loss for an opening line when the enormous window squeaked upward, so I trusted the first thought that came to mind: I grabbed both sides of Tag's face and pulled him toward me. It wasn't until our lips were mere inches away from each other that I caught the scent of spicy cologne. Familiar, I realized, but not intimately familiar.

Not *Tag*-familiar.

My heart dropped in horror as Alex pleaded, "Please don't kiss the messenger."

Stifling a scream, I pushed him away so hard that he fell back into his room to reveal Tag and two friends, all staring at me. Tag not only stood shirtless in old paint-splattered khaki shorts, but he also sported the classic Stetson he'd bought in Montana and a pair of gold boots that could've only been a gag gift from Alex. They looked more Wonder Woman than Wild West, but that was neither here nor there—shivers went up my spine. "I like 'cowboy,'" I remembered him saying the night of the prank. "Cowboys are loyal."

Stevie meowed me back to the moment, slinking across the room to weave through Tag's legs. I blinked to see the boys still gawking at me, as if *I* were the one wearing a Halloween costume. "Okay," I said slowly. "We're going to forget this *ever* happened." I paused, gathering courage. "But we're also going to do it *again*."

I tilted my head at Tag, fighting a laugh. He looked absurd. "And this time, someone else is going to answer the knock."

All four boys nodded, and the second Alex closed the window, they sprang into action. I waited three heartbeats, then raised my fist to tap the glass. The person on the other side wasted no time in opening the window.

"Hey there, cowboy," I said once we were face-to-face.

"Howdy," Tag said back, and I felt my heart still when he laughed. It was like time had stopped. He now looked even more outrageous in an inside-out T-shirt, but at the same time, he'd never been more handsome—his broad swimmer's shoulders, those eyes like emeralds, and the way his hair fell across his forehead.

Everything in me melted. Taggart Swell, Taggart Swell, Taggart Swell! I wanted to shout his name from the center of the Circle. Because I loved him. I loved him from my head to my toes, fully and faithfully—and dare I say it, *forever*.

But none of that came out of my mouth. I was too spell-bound to speak.

After a few moments, Tag cleared his throat. "What are you doing here?" he asked, nervousness rippling through his voice.

With that same ripple, I answered, "Making it count."

Tag kissed my cheek. Just a simple, sweet, delicate kiss, but it was enough—enough to twist my heartstrings. I wanted to kiss him. I so very badly wanted to kiss him.

His warm breath brushed my lips. "Hops?"

I almost nodded.

I almost nodded and leaned in and kissed him until my lungs fluttered for the final time. I almost did. After all, there was nothing holding us back.

Except.

"I know we still have a lot to talk about," I murmured, turning so that he cupped my face in his hand, "but I need to tell you something."

Tag nodded. "Okay."

"I'm not pretending," I said. "I know everything has changed, but at the same time, nothing has—at least for me." I swallowed hard. "I'm in love with you, Tag. Truly and totally and still falling in love with you."

With the faint curve of a smile, Tag pulled me into his arms and onto the windowsill. And he held me; he held me until our heartbeats synchronized. "We do have stuff to talk about," he eventually said. "I have a lot of questions, but…" He took a breath. "I'm not pretending either. Not even close." He pressed his forehead to mine. "I'm in love with you too. I love you and only you, Hopscotch. You're it. No matter what's happened…" His voice caught. "You've always been the one."

My eyes pooled and tears soon slid down my cheeks. Tag wiped them away, his thumbprint an invisible tattoo on my skin. "It's all my fault," I whispered. "We wasted so much time."

"But something tells me the greatest is yet to come," he said, then cradled me closer and murmured in my ear, "and that we'll make it count."

TWENTY-FIVE

My mom and I ate breakfast at the Hub on Monday morning. She was tired but hoping to get wired, since this was the last week of classes. Seniors were celebrating; our plan was to graduate on Saturday and leave campus as soon as possible for grad parties, but the underclassmen would stay behind and endure several days of exams. I knew my mom was mentally prepping for intense consultation meetings along with a few nightly course review sessions. "This is unacceptable," Josh said when he stopped by our table to confiscate the Red Bull my mom had just popped. "It's not even eight, Leda."

She groaned. "Caffeine, Josh. I *need* caffeine."

"Then I'll get you some coffee."

"I hate coffee."

Josh folded his arms across his chest, brows furrowing. "Really? You do? Because in all the years I've known you, I don't recall you *ever* mentioning—"

"Okay, tea," she cut in impatiently. "Black tea with a splash of milk."

A smile curled on Josh's lips before he bent down to kiss the top of my mom's head. "Any sugar?"

My mom answered by grabbing his sleeve and pulling him in for a real kiss. A handful of guys whooped and whistled from their corner booth while Pravika shouted, "Please get married!"

Already goin' to the chapel! I thought to myself, suddenly wishing they would announce the big news to Ames. It didn't matter if I was graduating, if this was "my year." I wanted my mom and Josh to openly celebrate their engagement. Nothing would make me happier.

Although at present, I was pretty happy.

Really happy.

"Hey!" I called to seemingly no one in particular when I arrived at the auditorium for our morning school meeting. It was the final one of the year, meaning it was the final one of my Ames career.

"Hello there!" Tag called back. He was standing with Alex under one of the building's white columns, but then he stepped out of the shade and into the sunshine and smiled.

My stomach somersaulted. If I had wings, I would spread them wide and soar over to him. But instead, wedges weighed me down to the ground, so I could only move so fast. Tag, though, had a much easier time closing the distance between us in his desert boots. Flowers grew in my chest when he swept me up his arms and spun me around before blissfully kissing me. We had Alex and an audience, but I barely noticed. *Hello, love,* I thought as I laughed against his lips and kissed him back. *I've missed you.*

Our relationship had blossomed again, even after all of yesterday's heartbreaking honesty. Alex had made himself scarce so Tag and I could talk about everything. I'd perched on his windowsill while he'd dragged his desk chair across the room to sit with me. Stevie had tried to snuggle up with him, but he handed her to me so he could pull my dangling legs onto his lap. His hands on my bare skin made my mind go hazy. Tag's affection—*Christ.* I had to blink several times to collect myself, and only after did we make eye contact. "What happened, Hopscotch?" he asked. "What happened to us? I know bits and pieces came out when we were at the boathouse, but I want to put the puzzle together." He traced a slow circle on my knee. "Why did we end?"

My pulse quickened. I'd suspected the question was inevitable, but it was still so daunting that I waited several heartbeats before responding. "I felt you pulling away," I said softly.

Tag sighed. "But I felt you pushing me away."

"I think both our perspectives are truthful," I told him. "Although I can only speak from mine, just like you can speak from only yours."

Tag offered me his hand, and I threaded our fingers together. A silent signal that said neither of us was going anywhere. "Keep going," he said. "I'm listening."

I nodded. "You became super popular when you started

setting swimming records, which made me so proud." I took a breath. "But your new popularity made me feel so insecure, Tag. Girls were suddenly around all the time. At first, they were like buzzing bees, just annoying, but soon it escalated to flirting with you right in front of me. I felt so awkward standing there. You didn't flirt back, but you're *you*—so charming and genuine—that it kind of felt like you *were* flirting. You didn't dissuade any attention. And then..." A lump formed in my throat. "And then came *Blair*."

"Lily, wait—" Tag tried, but I shook my head.

"Blair messed with my mind," I forged onward. "Those other girls were *nothing* compared to her. She pretended to befriend me so she could begin to befriend *us*, and then she cooled her fake friendship with me to heat something real up with you. I can pinpoint each and every..." My voice cracked. "You talked about her constantly; you studied with her more and more. I know I sound like a beyond possessive girlfriend, but that's how anxious she made me. I worried, Tag. I worried so much. I knew she liked you, and the way things were going, I worried it was only a matter of time until you realized you liked her too." My insides twisted. "That's when pushing you away came into play. I became so crippled with self-doubt that I knew I could never be a worthy opponent to Blair. I pushed you away to ease the pressure, and when that didn't work, I broke up with you." I winced. "We're human, so we all have our insecurities, but I'm not an insecure *person*. Blair turned me into one, and as much as I love you, I knew I needed to end things to go back to being *myself*."

After I stopped speaking, Tag was quiet and contemplative. We sat in silence and listened to the seaside wind whip for what felt like hours. He got up and draped a blanket around my shivering shoulders before he found his voice. "No, you aren't an insecure person," he agreed as my heart thudded. "All your friends and family know that…including me." He grimaced. "Which is why it never dawned on me that those girls hanging around might've bothered you. I admit I got caught up in the attention; I liked it a lot, especially after you grew distant. But it was *never* my intention to pull away from you, to hurt you like that." He took his hand off my knee to rake it through his hair. "God, Lily, I close my eyes now and see I'm the biggest asshole. I'm sorry, I should've realized—I won't ever forgive myself for not realizing how you felt."

"It would've been easier if I'd *told* you how I felt," I said. "Our communication skills went down the drain."

"And then someone turned on the garbage disposal and obliterated them," Tag muttered before locking eyes with me. "Blair—Lily, I *never* thought about Blair that way until after we split. She was an unexpected friend, that's all. You've called me clueless before, and you're right—I am. Honestly, I had no idea that she had an ulterior motive while we studied for statistics or when she wrote that stupid newspaper interview. I was *yours*, Hops. Yours to the point where, even if you weren't in the room, I could still feel you all over me." His voice dropped. "You will *always* be all over me."

I didn't respond, eyes stinging and heart swollen. I felt the same way.

"Blair and I dated." He exhaled. "She came on to me quickly, and I didn't slow anything down because I needed a distraction from missing you. Man, did I *miss* you." He smiled sadly. "She knew that too. Blair isn't as comfortable and confident as everyone thinks. Your name found its way into our fights and caused several of our meltdowns." He shrugged. "Along with a whole host of other issues."

"Then why did you keep getting back together?" I asked after wondering for so long. "If there were so many problems?"

Tag thought for a moment. "Because she was my friend," he said. "Believe it or not, we do have some stuff in common. A shared hatred of math homework for one, but she also has extremely checked-out parents, so we bonded over that…" He trailed off. "She's the one who suggested I see a therapist. You know, the therapist my father mentioned during my hearing."

My eyebrows knitted together. "Seriously?"

"Yeah." He nodded. "It was during an argument, so she didn't suggest it in the most sensitive manner, but she did." His lips twitched. "Dr. Perzi had some interesting hot takes. She said another reason I probably went in circles with Blair was because I should've been alone for a while after we broke up, but I was unhappy being single and wanted someone, and while that someone was you, you didn't seem like you wanted or needed anyone."

"Because I didn't," I told him. "I didn't want or need *anyone*;
I wanted, needed, and *burned* for you."

Tag gave me a look. "Did you just quote *Bridgerton?*"

I gave him a look back. "Did you just admit to watching
Bridgerton?"

He flushed. "You know Alex controls the remote."

I shook my head and giggled—really, truly *giggled*. Tag soon
started chuckling, and then sweet tears of laughter streamed
down our cheeks. "You are—" I started but dropped off when
Tag burst from his chair and made a mad dash across his room
to his bookcase. His trifecta of cameras sat on the top shelf.

"The light," he said, selecting the antique camera that he
coveted. "Lily, look—the light is lovely."

Golden hour? I wondered, because that was Tag's favorite,
but when I turned, I saw the sun had nearly slipped from the
sky. Instead, the world was now rose-tinted with flashes of
fluorescent blue. "Not sunset..." I murmured.

"No, not sunset." Tag rejoined me at the window. "We're
beyond that." He grinned, then raised the camera with me in its
crosshairs. "This is the afterglow."

～～～

There was no assigned seating for school meetings, but it went
without saying that seniors sat in the first several rows and freshmen toward the back. I found Pravika and Zoe in our usual

section, the third row on the far left. Sometimes Maya sat with us, but I guessed she was with her artist friends. "What are you doing here?" I asked, surprised when I noticed Tag talking to Zoe.

"Being a kind and considerate boyfriend," he said, gesturing for me to take the empty seat between his and Zoe's. He sat down and took my hand to kiss the inside of my wrist.

Sweet shivers ran up my arm. "Attentive too," I noted.

He winked. "Always."

"Back together and brutal," Zoe said and shook her head before turning away and pulling Pravika into a conversation.

"Where's Alex?" I quickly whispered.

"Home court." Tag pointed to the center sector, where Alex laughed with his and Tag's circle of friends. "We agreed not to sit together," he said. "Apparently Rivera still has an eye on him, and if he were to see us *literally* right next to each other, I suspect…"

"He'll jump on you," I finished, because something told me Headmaster Bickford clearing Tag's name from the Jester's scheme meant nothing to Daniel. The only person he ever believed was himself.

"Exactly." Tag nodded. "Whereas if he spots me with you, the only logical explanation is that I'm—"

"A kind and considerate boyfriend," I parroted.

Tag lifted the armrest so he could snake his arm around my waist. "Don't forget *attentive*," he murmured, breath warm against my neck.

"Maybe you two should leave," Zoe suggested when I blushed. "Go get it on downstairs or something?"

The house lights blinked a couple minutes later, and Dean DeLuca walked across the stage toward the steadfast mahogany podium. He congratulated us on reaching the homestretch, but no one was really paying attention. It felt like all the air was being sucked out of the auditorium as Anthony's father reviewed this week's schedule. Daniel was due to speak next, and everyone was anticipating what he had to say about the missing yearbooks.

It'd been three days, after all. No prank had ever lasted three days.

"Happy Monday, Ames," President Rivera said once the Dean of Students had passed the baton off to him, then paused to collect himself. He didn't look so hot this morning; everything about him looked *wrinkled*. His blazer, his khakis, his dark hair. "I want to take this opportunity to talk about the Almanacs." He sighed. "Unfortunately, they have not yet been recovered..."

Out of the corner of my eye, I saw Tag carefully fish his phone out of his pants pocket and dim its brightness after unlocking it. "What are you doing?" I whispered.

"Preparing to pull the trigger," he replied, opening his Gmail.

Daniel cleared his throat. "I am directly addressing you, Jester." His eyes scanned the auditorium's middle rows and predictably landed on Alex. He didn't flinch. "While your thievery was funny at first, I now implore you to return the Almanacs. They ensure every year ends on a high note; you don't want to be responsible for souring this one, do you?" His voice croaked. "*Please* return them."

In response, Tag tapped his screen.

"Nobody is ever on their phone during meetings," I muttered.

"One person is," he muttered back.

"Oh my god!" Blair Greenberg exclaimed after three seconds, waving her iPhone in the air. "The Jester!"

Tag flashed me a smirk before handing over his phone.

To: Group_All_Students@ames.edu

From: TheJesterXXIII@gmail.com

Subject: School Meeting

President Rivera,

You beseech me to "return" the Almanacs?

If so, I must politely decline. Simply returning them was never in the cards. Per my last communiqué, I said I would *help* solve the mystery. Not solve it myself.

Ames, what say you? Is it high time I offer my assistance?

Yours in merriment,

The Jester

"*Yes!*" resounded through the auditorium in varying tones. Some shrieked and shouted, while others were overcome with laughter. Tag's thumbs flew across his screen, dashing off another message.

As you wish, it read.

And then I watched him delete the Jester's email account.

～

Ames was abuzz the rest of the day, no longer entirely fixated on who the Jester was but wondering what kind of help they would soon provide. "Maybe a map of some sort?" Pravika posed when she, Zoe, and I went to Provisions for lunch. Somehow Zoe kept a straight face, but I almost choked on my sandwich; she was so close to the truth.

Tag, when are you hiding the first clue? Maya texted our chat later. After class?

Nah, he texted back. I'm swimming, then back under house arrest.

None of his fools responded.

Don't worry, he assured us. I have a plan.

Which involves...? I wrote but didn't receive an answer until Tag and I lingered by Bunker's house after Latin. Daniel had rushed out of the solarium as soon as class had concluded.

"Which involves you dispatching the clue," Tag said. "Okay?"

"Me!" My spine straightened. "You want *me* to hide it? Why me?"

"Because it needs to be you, and you're the only one of you." His mouth twitched in amusement as he pulled something out of his blazer's breast pocket: a familiar black envelope with **CLUE ●NE** in random magazine letters. I noticed the oversize O resembled *Vogue*'s iconic all-caps typeface. My mom had picked up the latest issue on her errands yesterday.

"Here and there," I remembered Tag saying when I'd asked where he'd gotten magazines to create the scavenger hunt's clues.

"I thought Alex would do it," I said, stomach stirring even though all this mission involved was slipping the envelope into Daniel's mailbox. He routinely checked it on his way to the library after dinner. It was supposed to be easy, but when I looked up at the gray sky, I reconsidered. The weather was going to turn, which meant instead of hanging out in the Circle tonight, everyone would take refuge in the student center.

Tag nodded when I said as much. "That's why Alex isn't in charge of the clue," he said. "He's quarterbacking the diversion that'll ensure no one will see you disguised as USPS."

My brows knitted together. "What's the diversion?"

"He's asking Anthony to prom."

"Stop it!" I gasped. "He's promposing?"

"Yes, and apparently it involves striking up the jazz band."

I groaned. Anthony loved jazz. "But I don't want to miss that…"

I tried to maintain my confidence during the last couple classes and as I unfolded my umbrella after the final bell. It looked like the entire student body was migrating toward Hubbard Hall. My stomach lurched when I saw Daniel, but thankfully Maya was all but dragging him into the Hub. "Let's get milkshakes!" I heard her say. "Because you need to *chill*, Dan."

There were students in the mail room, so I anxiously awaited their departure in a nearby alcove. Pravika was among them, slowly sifting through her mail by a trash can. I watched her scan a graded assignment, then crumple it up and toss it into the garbage.

Let's go, I thought. *Let's go, let's go, let's go!*

Eventually the sound of a saxophone turned people's heads. Mine also wanted to turn, but I couldn't let myself get distracted. Even when the band's trumpet, double bass, and drums joined in, I stayed focused on making my move. The mail room mass exodus finally happened when someone shouted, "Look, Alex Nguyen's on top of the piano!"

Then I heard him start singing.

Because of course Alex could sing.

Pulse now racing, I ran to Daniel's mailbox. My hands shook a little as I unzipped my backpack and pulled out the hilariously mysterious first clue. But before sliding it into the wrought iron mailbox, I found myself studying the envelope again. The "E" looked like one of *People's* block letters. The colors were black and blue, back from Ryan Reynolds's Sexiest Man Alive issue. My mom and I loved Ryan Reynolds.

Is this ours? I wondered, head now spinning. *Is this our copy?*

Tucked in my skirt's waistline, my phone suddenly vibrated. It sent my heart rate so high up in the sky that I swore and slipped the clue through the mailbox's slot before sprinting through the standing ovation Alex and Anthony were now getting toward the restrooms.

"Mom, hey," I answered once the stall door slammed behind me. "What's up?"

She ignored my question to instead ask her own. "Are you still on campus?"

"Uh-huh," I said. "I'm in the student center. Alex just—"

"Would you mind coming by my classroom?" she asked. "We need to talk."

Talk? I thought. What did we need to talk about? I hadn't done anything wrong. Well, I mean, anything wrong besides getting involved in the prank, but she knew that already. Her tone didn't make things easier to read either. She didn't sound upset, but "calm" wasn't an accurate adjective either.

My mom sighed. "What we need to talk about, dearest daughter, is what Tag has done with our entire archive of magazines."

TWENTY-SIX

My footsteps echoed against the English building's parquet floor, and I climbed the stairs as slowly as possible, thinking about our magazines. I remembered the impromptu dinner party my mom had hosted last week. I'd noticed the lack of "reading material" on our coffee table but had been so thrown by the Jester's bid that I hadn't thought too hard about their disappearance.

Tag asked her, I realized. *He asked her if he could have them.*

But had she known he was the Jester at the time?

I didn't think so.

I wiped my feet on her classroom's doormat—HI, WELCOME TO CHILI'S! it read—before turning the knob and pushing into the room. My mom sat at her corner desk with her laptop, review packets already distributed around the big oak table. "Hi," I said, gingerly taking a seat as if I were a student on the first day of class. "I'm here."

She closed her laptop and joined me at the table. "I only have forty-five minutes before my pre-dinner sophomore study session," she said. "Let's cut the bullshit."

"I'm sorry." I knotted my fingers together. "It's my fault there's bullshit between us."

My mom laughed. "Oh no, Lil, stop," she said. "I've just always wanted to use that line." She took my hand so she could untangle my nervous fingers. "Relax. We're touching base."

I nodded and then watched her stretch across the table to grab something from her pile of study materials. My pulse quickened. It was our newest *Vogue*. Taylor Swift was giving off Gatsby vibes with her 1920s flapper look.

"Tag stopped by several weeks ago," my mom said casually, "asking if he could have our magazines for a project." She gave me a look. "Please tell me he won't be needing more."

I shook my head. "What you gave him was sufficient."

"Okay, thank god." She gave me a relieved smile but soon let it slip away so she could arch an inquisitive eyebrow. "Would you care to elaborate on said project?"

"You want to hear about the prank?" I asked, sitting up straighter in my seat. Because ever since she'd said she was too disappointed in me to want details, I had been *waiting* for her to change her mind.

"Yes," she answered. "I know you helped our Jester steal the Almanacs—"

"Along with Alex, Zoe, Maya, and Manik. They were also tapped."

My mom blinked. "Yet you and Tag were the only ones caught," she commented, then announced that she needed a drink. She got up to grab a Red Bull from the mini fridge hidden under her desk. I highly suspected she wished it were whiskey. "Okay, so the six of you pull this absurdly hilarious heist," she resumed. "But there's obviously a second act happening now, so how do the magazines come into play?" She kept eye contact with me. "Clue me in, Lil."

I couldn't help it; I burst into laughter. *Clue me in.*

She couldn't have teed this up any better.

"What?" my mom asked. "What's so funny?"

"You," I said through giggles. "You're funny. Because the magazines—Mom, Tag used the magazines to create *clues.* Scavenger hunt clues! We stole the Almanacs and then scattered all these clues across campus. Tag crafted them using individual letters he cut out of the magazines. They look like—"

"Creepy ransom notes," my mom concluded. There was a hint of a smile as she shook her head. "I will never cease to be charmed by his cleverness."

"Each clue is a riddle," I added. "There are seven total, and the last one leads to the Almanacs. They took a while to hide, and there were, um, complications. The biggest one being…" I trailed off because she already knew.

The biggest one being Tag's hypoglycemic attack.

My mom sipped her Red Bull. "Did you memorize the clues?"

I stuck my tongue out at her. Naturally I knew the clues by heart; I was an actress. Memorization was one of my sharpest skills.

"Alright, well, take me through the night," she said.

So I did. I told her about sneaking out to meet the Jester and the other fools at midnight, full of excitement. But by the time I'd reached our depleted numbers and Tag downplaying his symptoms, my voice began to waver. "The final clue is in Admissions," I said. "It was just Tag, Alex, and me by then. We tried to run when we saw Mr. Harvey's headlights, but Tag couldn't move." I swallowed. "I forced Alex to hide, Mom. I know he was as guilty as Tag and me, but I didn't want him to get caught. He put up a fight, not wanting to leave Tag, but I made him." I grimaced. "And that's it. Mr. Harvey busted us."

My mom had stayed incredibly stoic during my story, but now she exhaled so deeply it was like she'd been holding her breath the whole time. "Christ, I have so much to say," she said. "So much to say, but it won't be in chronological order."

"It's a lot," I offered.

She touched my cheek. "I spoke with Tag after his disciplinary hearing, but I need you to know that having a good time *never* trumps safety. He never should've ignored his signs, and when they came to light, you should've stopped and called me. I think I'd probably passed out to a podcast by the time you snuck back home, but for the life of me, I don't understand why you didn't come upstairs for help." She shook her head. "It's not like either of you."

A lump formed in my throat. "I know," I said. "It's not us, Mom—and I'm sorry. I'm so sorry. I just think we both felt a shit-ton of pressure to pull off this prank and were so anxious about it that both our judgments failed spectacularly."

She rose from her chair. "Spectacularly, huh?"

I stood too. "Yes."

My mom opened her arms and I fell into them, vision blurring as she held me tightly. Her hugs sometimes made me wish I'd never grow up. I loved her warmth and the ever-familiar scent of her rosewater perfume and eucalyptus soap. I loved the way her curls tickled my face. I loved everything about her. "You paid a high price," she whispered, "but damn am I in awe of you."

"Thank you," I whispered back, and when she pulled away, she smiled and tucked a lock of my hair behind my ear before clapping her hands together.

"Now, when does Daniel get his first clue?"

⌒

"Alex says Anthony found our golf cart," Tag said on FaceTime that night. "After doing a neighborhood loop, he ran along the beach and spotted it in the dunes. Since we'd left the keys in the cupholder, he drove it back to B and G and left it outside the garage. I guess the guys didn't think anything of it."

"Wow." I let out a slow whistle. "Thank god for Anthony."

"Seriously," Tag agreed. "Dear Saint Anthony."

We laughed. I'd told him about my talk with my mom,

and he shared his too. "It was right after my hearing," he said. "She took my sleeve, dragged me into Penny's little library, and before I could even blink, she'd kicked off her heels and was pacing the room and whisper-scolding me…"

"Do you think Daniel has the clue?" I asked a couple minutes later.

"My gut tells me he does," Tag answered. "Especially since so many teachers are returning our final assignments this week. I wouldn't be surprised if he's checking his mail multiple times a day." His pragmatism shifted to sarcasm. "But alas, if only we knew someone who could find out for sure. Who do we know that has experience in the reconnaissance field?"

I snorted. "No experts."

"Did I say expert?" He smirked. "I don't believe I specified a skill level."

I smirked back. "Well, in that case, I know just the person for the job!"

He's still awake, Manik reported at 11:00. He's watching Curb, and I'm stuck listening to it because the door between our rooms is open, and he lost his headphones.

What's Curb? Zoe asked as everyone else disliked Manik's message.

"Bleh, I didn't like *Curb Your Enthusiasm*," my mom commented. We were nestled in her bed with peppermint tea; I'd convinced her to forgo burning the midnight oil in favor of watching *Pride & Prejudice*. Although we'd seen it so many times that we could mouth Lizzy's lines while my mom also played *Wordscapes* and I texted the team.

"Okay, but you love *Seinfeld*," I pointed out. "Isn't Larry David behind both?"

"Yes, but *nothing* can beat *Seinfeld*," she replied. "I mean, come on, Elaine's dancing—"

I sprang out of bed so I could imitate Elaine's famous cringe-inducing dance. "*Like a full-body dry heave set to music*," George Costanza would say.

My mom laughed and started tickling me once I'd flung myself back on her mattress. It was only when Mr. Darcy helped Lizzy into her carriage that we froze. "The hand flex!" we squealed.

He's going to sleep, Manik texted. I repeat: He's going to sleep!

Which means you should be "going to sleep," Tag responded.

Manik sent a thumbs-up emoji. After that, the chat was silent. I could picture Tag and Alex playing pool in their room to pass the time. Even after a cup of tea and a trip downstairs to stress eat some chocolate pudding, my muscles remained tense. It's pouring outside, I messaged Tag at 11:45 when we still hadn't heard from Manik. Maybe he'll try tomorrow?

Because Daniel should've embarked on his quest by now. Clue One told him to collect Clue Two at midnight, and the observatory was at least a fifteen-minute walk from his dorm. Plus, he was now the one who had to handle Ames's streetlamps, nocturnal dorm activity, and the formidable Campo squad.

Tag quickly buzzed in with a reply, but before I could read it, a new group chat message popped up from Manik. He's gone! it read. He closed our door, but I heard him sneak out the window and down the fire escape (sounded like he slipped).

OMFG, Zoe said at the same time as Maya wrote, LMAO!!! King of my heart, Alex said.

And Tag: Let the games begin.

⟋

I couldn't decide whether to stay up and wait for Daniel. My mom's bedroom windows overlooked the front lawn, but there was no barometer for when he'd arrive for Clue Six. Tag and I hadn't gotten to my house until 4:00 a.m., and there'd been innumerable obstacles along the way. What troubles would Daniel encounter? The rain certainly wouldn't help the cause. "I hope he has an umbrella!" was the last thing my mom said before switching off her bedside lamp and snuggling into her pillow.

Did I pull an all-nighter?

Tag and I texted for a while, joking about Daniel's current location—*Still trying to hop the telescope balcony's gate!*—but Alex confiscated his phone around 1:30. Taggart has run out of screen time, the last text read. Good night.

"Lily, go to sleep," my mom mumbled after I slid out of bed and accidentally stepped on a squeaky floorboard. It was 2:45.

"I'm getting a snack," I whispered.

A beat passed before she flipped on her lamp. "What kind of snack?"

I brought the whole bowl of chocolate pudding back upstairs. "Has he come to commit his federal crime yet?" my mom asked through a big spoonful.

"Federal crime?"

She gave me a look. "It's illegal to read other people's mail."

I shook my head and together we finished off the pudding. Josh would be horrified when he saw the empty bowl in the sink tomorrow.

"Okay, this is pointless," my mom said an hour after we'd gotten back under the covers. "If we're going to do this, we're going to do this *right*."

Two minutes later, we were in official stakeout mode at her window. I'd grabbed both cushions from her love seat for us to sit on, and she'd lowered her blinds just enough so that Daniel wouldn't spot us spying on him. My mom patted me on the back for having the good sense to leave the outdoor lights on, and while we waited, I told her about Daniel refusing to help Tag last spring and also blaming me for nearly ruining his reputation. "He thinks he dodged a bullet," I said. "Because if we'd been dating, my oh-so-scandalous lifestyle wouldn't reflect well on him—*him!*"

My mom snorted. "He's all yours, Harvard."

The rain stopped at 3:30.

"Do you think he got caught?" I rubbed my eyes. "Are Gabe and Mr. Harvey—"

"Look!" She snatched my arm, and I gasped when I saw Daniel Rivera *finally* approaching our cottage. The wet pavement glistened, but he did not. The student council president was a walking puddle, his hair plastered to his forehead and clothes absolutely drenched by the storm. "I think he's carrying at least ten extra pounds," my mom observed as we watched him drip-drop his way to our mailbox.

"At least," I agreed. Daniel's steps were slow, stilted, and not particularly sneaky. It was safe to say he was exhausted from battling the rain and oceans winds all night.

Oh, and his adventure might've been a little tiresome too.

I watched him unlatch the mailbox and turn on his phone flashlight once the next clue did not immediately present itself. My pulse pitched excitedly when he extracted the envelope. "Mr. President! Mr. President!" I narrated. "To an emergency cabinet meeting you are sent!"

"Its agenda contains quite the hook." My mom matched my theatricality. "What happened to Ames's beloved yearbook?"

I smirked. How was he going to take this?

The answer was "not well."

We giggled like little girls when Daniel crumpled up the clue and threw it across the lawn before rethinking such a strategy. "I was worried that he would show everyone the clues," I whispered as Daniel squelched over the wet grass. "But I don't think he will. The Jester has not only made the school laugh, but he has also made a laugh of its *president*." My lips twisted into a smile. "Daniel won't—"

"*Meow.*"

"Oh my god," I breathed. "Puck's out there."

Our cat was circling Daniel, his meowing getting louder and louder with each suspicious step. "No, no, go away," Daniel hissed. "Get the hell out of here!"

My mom dashed over to her bedroom's overhead light switch. We exchanged evil grins. "Ready?" she asked.

I saluted her. "Set."

"Go!" we exclaimed, and once she flicked the switch, her bright lights streamed through her blinds and scared the shit out of Daniel. Was somebody awake?!

You better run, Rivera, I thought while he sprinted up the street. *You have that final clue to find...*

To: Group_All_Students@ames.edu

From: DRivera@ames.edu

Subject: URGENT ALMANAC UPDATE

Everyone,

It is my pleasure to announce that the Almanacs have

been safely recovered! I found them before breakfast this morning, and I promise someone will have eyes on them until their long-awaited distribution this afternoon. I wouldn't put it past the Jester to cheat us again.

All best,
Daniel

TWENTY-SEVEN

All of Ames rushed off to the auditorium after classes, but I called a summit first. Alex, Zoe, Maya, Manik, and I met at King's Court, where our fateful dance with the Jester had begun. The ivy-covered chapel gleamed in the sunlight, and birds chirped as my fellow schemers and I gathered around Kingsley Ames's bronze statue. *Still unimpressed?* I thought, amused upon seeing the statue's scowl. *Even though we did it?*

I wasn't one for speeches, so I simply pulled out the flask I'd borrowed from my mom. Alex hooted as I unfastened and raised it. "To the Jester," I said, smiling.

"To the Jester!" my friends echoed.

"And to us," I added. "For he assembled one fantastic band of fools."

"And to us!"

"Cheers." I grinned and took a sip before presenting the flask to Alex. He smirked, assuming it was Tag's Diet Coke. But everyone sprung backward when a light liquid came squirting out of his mouth.

"Lily Hopper!" he whisper-exclaimed. "Is this what I think it is? Is this *champagne*?"

"Nonalcoholic champagne," I corrected. "We must keep our wits about us, must we not?"

Alex chuckled, and once our circle had taken celebratory swigs, we set off for the auditorium. Zoe and Maya left us in the dust, racing away together, and Manik also broke into a run to see how distribution was going. "The editor really should be the one to hand them out," Alex said. "Or at least *help*."

"You never know; the opportunity could present itself," I replied. "Bequeathing three hundred yearbooks in the blazing sun on maybe two hours of sleep?" I shrugged. "Daniel might be desperate for some assistance."

Alex was quiet for a moment. "I wish Taggart were here."

"Me too," I whispered, a bittersweet pang in my chest. Tag had decided to skip his swim today, but that meant he had to report directly to his room after class.

The Almanac line twisted and turned across the auditorium's flagstone terrace. It was so long that it dropped off the curb and continued along the street. "We need to play a game to pass the time," Alex said once we reached the end of the road. "I can't just stand—oh, thank god!"

I followed his gaze to find Anthony approximately a thousand people ahead of us. He was waving. "You go," I told Alex. "I'll wait."

Alex gave me a look. "Are you sure?"

"Yeah." I nodded. "People will give you a pass since you're his prom date, but they won't take kindly to me cutting."

"Ah, the proper etiquette for butting in line..." He winked. "Please pardon me for never giving it a thought."

I smiled and shook my head when he joined Anthony; from what I could see, no one gave him any trouble. If anything, they flocked around him.

Never has there been a more apt school mascot, I thought, *than the seagull.*

Somehow, I passed over an hour in line. Pravika found me and we chatted for a while, although I couldn't stop staring at her hefty yearbook. The cover was beautiful, light blue with an inlaid gold foiled campus map and THE ALMANAC printed overtop in red. "You can look through it if you want," she offered, but I didn't want any spoilers.

It felt like a triumph when I finally made it to the terrace. I looked up from my newly downloaded *Wordscapes* app to see an elaborate balloon archway. When I rose to my tiptoes, my heart warmed. Manik was at the table, grinning while he gifted the result of months and months of hard work to students. *Yes!* I silently cheered. *Yes, Manik!*

But unfortunately, it was Daniel who handed me my copy. I wondered if anyone had commented on the heavy blue-gray bags under his eyes. "Thank you," I said before politely asking if I could also have Tag's Almanac.

Daniel paused, checking my name off his master list. "You want Swell's book?"

I shrugged. "He can't exactly get it himself."

"And whose fault is that?" Daniel muttered as he shoved Tag's Almanac into my arms. "Be sure to give him my best."

"Will do, Mr. President." I stepped out of line after watching Daniel roll his eyes, but before successfully fleeing the terrace, I felt a hand on my shoulder.

A familiar hand.

"I know it was you," Daniel said when I turned.

"Excuse me?" I asked, pretending my pulse hadn't just jumped.

"I know it was you," he repeated, voice even icier. "You're the—"

"Daniel!" someone shouted.

"Yeah?" he said, overtly irritated.

Blair Greenberg appeared. "Prom?" she asked.

Daniel couldn't nod fast enough.

"Great." She flipped her hair over her shoulder. "My dress is—"

"Hey, Blair!" I blurted before I could stop myself, but she raised an eyebrow when I didn't say anything more. My heart hammered. What did I want to say?

That I don't hold it against you, I thought. Yes, I had originally blamed Blair for my breakup with Tag, but truthfully, it came down to me. Blair was not responsible. Her feelings for Tag had psyched me out, but she still had a *right* to them. We both had the right to crush on Tag, a wholeheartedly equal right. She had chosen to shoot her shot when it looked like Tag and I were drifting apart, and while their relationship hadn't been healthy, it hadn't caused the ruin of mine.

Blair snapped her gum. "Lily?"

"Congratulations on valedictorian," I said quickly. "I can't wait for your speech."

"Thank you." Blair smiled back, a genuine grin. Something told me she knew. "After multiple drafts, I think it's going to be great."

I grinned back. "That's awesome."

And that was that.

"You were saying?" I prompted Daniel once Blair had gone.

He glared at me. "Lily, I didn't get to sleep until five in the morning."

I pretended not to follow. "How is your insomnia my fault?"

"Because you're the Jester! Swell helped you steal the Almanacs on Thursday and then last night you sent me on a twisted scavenger hunt—"

"Wait, a scavenger hunt?" I laughed. This was the performance of my career. "You had to go on a *scavenger hunt* to get them back?" I wrinkled my nose. "Sounds a little childish."

"Yeah, believe me, it was," Daniel said. "But only you could've done it."

"Why?" I challenged. "Because I'm a fac brat?"

His sneer slipped off his face.

"My mom keeps a close eye on her keys, Daniel," I said. "I also don't abuse living on campus." I put a loving hand on my heart. "I make the most of it."

Then I spun on my heel to take my leave.

"Swell!" Daniel called after me. "Swell—"

"Demanded FedEx sort out shipping, remember?" I called back, holding up my Almanac for emphasis. "Swell saved your ass!"

Students had fanned out on the Circle and Crescent to dig into their Almanacs, but I hurried over to Grundy House's willow trees. "Excellent," I whispered when I saw that my secret stash was still safe under the swaying branches. Quickly and quietly, I grabbed everything and snuck over to Tag and Alex's window. My stomach swirled with magic as I set down his yearbook and then placed his surprise champagne on top of it. I'd written *Long Live The Jester!* in whimsical letters along the bottleneck.

And, for the finishing touch, I reverently added Tag's jingling green-yellow-and-purple Jester's hat. Something told me Daniel wouldn't want it as a keepsake, so I'd snuck into the storage room once the pyramid of Almanac boxes had been dismantled and moved back to the yearbook office. Daniel had chucked the hat into a dusty corner, but still—there it was, waiting for me. Next year's Jester would have to buy his own; this was Tag's trophy.

"Hey," Tag said after I'd crept back to the trees and called him. "Promise me you're not still standing in that life-sucking line."

I smiled. "How do you know it's life-sucking?"

"Prior knowledge," he said. "Previous experience."

"Well, perhaps you should open your window…" I shifted from one foot to the other, ready to remember this moment. "And see for yourself."

TWENTY-EIGHT

Alex was not impressed with my prom attire. "Lily, you couldn't have dressed up even *a little?*" He gestured to my worn J. Crew shorts, Tag's favorite Dave Matthews Band T-shirt, and my striped espadrilles. "I mean…"

"Why does it matter?" I asked as I snapped a photo of Zoe and Maya. My friend's white jumpsuit was to die for, and Maya looked amazing in her deep turquoise dress. "I'm behind the scenes today." I looked up from the camera lens. "Who cares?"

"*I* care," Alex said. "It's not professional. You look like we booked you as our photographer only fifteen minutes ago."

"You literally did," I reminded him, cradling Tag's Nikon close. There were several school photographers roaming around the Circle for Ames's prom processional, but my oh-so-vain friends wanted a personal one. I was available, after all, and Tag had more than one camera to spare. He'd given me a refresher tutorial before letting me sling the Nikon's bag over my shoulder and report for duty.

The sun was still up since it was only 4:00. After the photo shoot, the seniors and any underclassmen dates would board their awaiting motorcoach and drive an hour and a half into Boston. For as long as I could remember, the prom had been held at a fancy hotel there. "We'll go have tea sometime," Penny had told me earlier, knowing I was bummed about missing tonight. "They do a wonderful afternoon tea..."

"For fuck's sake!" I shouted when my group suddenly scattered. "I can't take pictures of you if you're all in different—"

"*Language*," someone said, and I turned to see two arm-in-arm faculty chaperones smirking at me. My mom stole the show in her dress, a one-shouldered black gown that made her look like she'd time traveled here from the Roaring Twenties. It was tea-length and covered with intricate swirls of silver beads, which flawlessly matched the art deco diamond on *that* finger. "Please announce everything already," I'd begged her and Josh the other night. "It'll make my year if you announce it!"

People had been congratulating them nonstop.

"Are you sure you'll be alright tonight?" my mom asked after I took a few shots of them. She affectionately smoothed Josh's hair. "Because remember, Mrs. DeLuca said you're welcome for dinner."

"I'll be fine," I said. "I'm going to test a new fish taco recipe—"

Josh mimed a chef's kiss.

"—and then I'll probably FaceTime with Tag while watching Netflix."

My mom nodded. "I left my keys in case you need anything."

"Thanks," I said with a lump in my throat.

"Oh, Lily." She wrapped her arms around me. "I'm sorry you have to miss this; I know how much you were looking forward to it."

"But on the bright side," Josh said, "you won't have to suffer through a three-hour round trip, eat an uninspired meal, hope the DJ is decent, and stop students from sneaking off together."

I rolled my eyes. "Why did you volunteer to chaperone again?"

He straightened his bow tie. "I didn't. A chaperone promposed to me."

The three of us laughed, and I hugged them goodbye (and wished Josh good luck) before backing away to let a group of girls gush over my mom's engagement ring.

I hadn't taken a picture of Pravika and her date yet, so I started scanning the crowd for her, but before spying her sunset orange dress, I spotted another pair of chaperones. Bespectacled Mr. Rudnick stood talking to Penny Bickford at the edge of the Circle. My pulse quickened, and as soon as they parted, I made for the maple tree. Penny's silver-blond hair was pulled back in a classic chignon, and I knew tonight's pantsuit had to be Chanel. "Lily, darling," she said. "Hello—"

"He's alone!" I blurted.

Penny blinked. "Pardon?"

"Tag," I said, out of breath for absolutely no reason. "Mr.

Rudnick is his housemaster, and since he's chaperoning, Tag is all alone in Grundy."

"Oh," Penny said. "Oh my."

"Yeah!"

"Well, that is an oversight on our part," Penny said after a moment. "An *extreme* oversight." She glanced at the motorcoaches, which students were now boarding, before warmly touching my cheek. "We will be back at midnight."

"I know." I nodded. "But Tag…"

Penny smiled. "Midnight," she repeated. "He'll be alone until midnight."

My heart suddenly spun. *Alone doesn't just mean "alone,"* I realized. *It also means "unsupervised."*

I grinned as Penny left for her bus, tapping out what I knew was an all-faculty email on her phone. Not only was she letting them know Tag was unsupervised, but she was also giving him *authorization* to be unsupervised. Headmaster Bickford's word trumped all.

Midnight, I told myself. *We have until midnight.*

———

I called Tag once I'd crossed the covered bridge. "Hey," he answered. "I was about to text you a screenshot from this email Headmaster Bickford cc'd me on—"

Blood pounding in my ears, I let the words fall right out of my mouth. Just like he had freshman year. "Tag Swell?" I said. "Lily Hopper here. How are you?" I didn't give him time to answer. "I'm fine, even though I hate history. The debate today was awful, wasn't it? I was too quiet, way too quiet. But you were incredible, really incredible. Anyway, I was wondering—" I closed my eyes. "Would you like to go to prom with me?"

Tag was silent for a beat...then two, then three. "Yes," he said after five seconds. "That would be nice."

I grinned.

"Did I really mention that debate?" he asked. "When I invited you to formal?"

"Yeah." I laughed. "You really did."

He groaned. "God, why did you say yes?"

"Because I'd been waiting the whole year to hear your voice on the phone."

Again, Tag was quiet.

"I'll pick you up at 6:30," I said before hanging up on him and breaking into a run.

I had so much to do.

***

My prom dress was beautiful, but I couldn't find the enthusiasm to take it off its hanger and finally slip into it for real. I knew exactly why.

Daniel.

I had bought the light blue gown after he'd promposed to me, so I'd imagined taking pictures with him while wearing it and dancing together while wearing it. Why would I ever wear it with Tag? Maybe someday I wouldn't think of Daniel when I looked at the dress, but that day was definitely not today.

And besides, I had something so much better. My lungs fluttered like frantic butterfly wings as I dug through my closet, and I let out a long sigh when I found the cocktail dress still hanging in its dry cleaner's bag.

"Hello there," I said after ripping away the plastic. "Please still fit."

I had to suck in my breath when doing up the zipper; the hemline was a couple inches too short, but other than that, it looked perfect. I loved the deep shade of gold, the jacquard fabric's textured but delicate floral pattern, and the sweetheart neckline with crisscrossing spaghetti straps. "You're a daydream," my mom had said when we'd found it at Nordstrom together. "Tag's going to lose his shit when he sees you."

And I suppose he *had* lost his shit three years ago—tripping over a stray rock on our driveway—but when I pulled up to Grundy House later and saw him waiting out front, I almost forgot to put my golf cart in park before getting out to greet him.

That's my man, I thought.

"Nice dress!" he called as I wobbled in my mom's silver strappy sandals. His arms slid around my waist. "Hops, you look..."

"Like a daydream," I said after kissing him. "You look like a daydream, Tag."

He laughed, and it only made him more handsome. His dark brown hair was tamed for the moment with product, his green eyes shined, and instead of the traditional black tuxedo, Tag had opted for a white dinner jacket. I swooned like a Bond girl. "Trust me, I'm no 007," he said. "Since I believe it's *you* who has supplied our sweet ride." He took my hand and escorted me to the golf cart. "Where are we going?"

Thanks to a test drive earlier, I knew the woodland trails were wide enough to accommodate our golf cart. It was a tight fit in some spots, pine branches brushing up against us and wheels bumping over the uneven terrain, but I squeezed the steering wheel in excitement. Tag didn't know our destination; in fact, I'd blindfolded him with a scarf before we had left his dorm. "This smells like you," he'd said, "so I'm not *actually* complaining, but how long must I be shrouded in mystery?"

"Okay!" I now announced, slowing the golf cart to a stop and shifting it into park. "We're here!" I stepped down to the ground and hurried around the hood so I could help Tag out of his seat. "Are you ready?"

He nodded eagerly, but after I untied the scarf and he blinked, his face dropped. "I knew we were in the woods," he murmured, "but I thought you were taking the shortcut to the ropes course." His throat bobbed. "Not bringing us to the sculpture sanctuary." He gestured to the plank walkway, which I'd lined with paper luminaries. The sun hadn't set yet, but it was dark enough under the trees. "I never thought you'd want to come back here."

"Well, you thought wrong," I told him. "I don't care about Blair, Tag. I care about *you*. I know you love this place; you've always loved it." My cheeks warmed. "You even made a wish here sophomore year. We blew off watching the pre-prom and came here, and you tossed a penny in the fountain and wished to take me to prom. And while we're not on a bus to Boston, I pulled a lot of strings to make it come true." I gestured to the lighted path. "So if you don't mind?"

"I don't." Tag shook his head. "Not one bit."

I exhaled but then swiftly inhaled when he playfully threw me over his shoulder. He didn't put me down until we'd reached the sanctuary itself. Buildings and Grounds had agreed to turn on the little landscape lights, which were apparently installed underneath the deck's benches, as well as spotlights for all the artwork. I'd strung twinkly lights around the bubbling fountain and set a dinner table for two. Mrs. DeLuca had lent me the linens and created a flower arrangement for a centerpiece. And after a few swipes and taps on my phone, Spotify started drifting through my Bluetooth speaker. Music to add to the mood.

"This is happiness," Tag said reverently. "Happiness, all because of you."

My heart twinged. There was serious Tag and goofy Tag and thoughtful Tag and dorky Tag. However, there was also sweet Tag. I'd missed him. "Are you hungry?" I asked. There hadn't been time to cook a full-course meal, so Chinese takeout it was. We shared the various cartons that had been kept warm in Josh's YETI, but I'd ordered an extra fried rice so Tag could have his own. "Tell me when it's over," I said, covering my eyes while he squirted ketchup all over the poor rice. "It's disgusting."

"It's a religion," he countered.

After dinner, Tag used his pump to bolus, and we speculated if Alex would pull a muscle on the dance floor before popping a bottle of bubbly. Nonalcoholic, of course.

Tag started humming once we'd at least had two flutes each, even tapping the table in tune. "Why not, *junge Dame?*" he asked when I shook my head. "We have the music." He pointed at my speaker, then circled his finger around the hexagonal deck. "And this is a pretty good makeshift gazebo. It's got benches and everything."

I rolled my eyes. "Herr Swell, I am not reprising that role. It was two years ago. We were *sixteen*."

He shrugged.

"Fine!" I exclaimed. "Fine, you queue it up while I take off these torturous shoes…"

Two minutes later, Tag and I had been transported back to *The Sound of Music.* We both remembered the lyrics to "Sixteen Going on Seventeen," but we decided to skip the instrumental version so we could simply sing along and dance. Our choreography was a travesty. Rolf chased Liesl around the deck's benches before zapping her waist and running the other way while Liesl decided to launch herself on his back and rake her hands through his hair.

And the song was halfway through its second run by the time their kiss ended.

Tag was flushed when we broke apart, and my heart wanted to twirl out of my chest. He turned back to our table and picked up the fake champagne. "Do you want another glass?"

"Yes," I breathed. "I do, but can we pour it somewhere else?"

We brought the bottle but not the glasses. Tag kept his hand on my knee as I drove us through the faculty neighborhood and haphazardly parked the golf cart in my driveway before we raced each other to the beach. I unbuckled my mom's heels while Tag suspended the insulin delivery on his pump before wrapping the cannula cord around the device and stowing it in his shoe for safekeeping. "Ready?"

The pearlescent moon gleamed with glittering constellations circling the sky. "Thank you," I said when Tag offered me the champagne. It might be nonalcoholic, but the drink still sent a special warmth through me. I could feel the fizz in my veins. Tag took a sip as we navigated our way through the sand toward tonight's tide. The sea swirled, and we laughed while kicking up wet sand and running away before the cold water could catch us. "Shitballs!" I exclaimed when I dropped the bottle, so I also dropped down before it could tip over and spill what liquid was left. I wanted us to drink it all and then put it next to our Chicago Marathon bottle on my bookcase.

Tag's shoulder brushed mine when he collapsed next to me, and he had to shout over the incoming roar of the Atlantic. "What a stupid place to sit!"

I grinned. "Oh, but what a pretty place to fall!"

And then I fell backward and let the seawater wash over me. The ocean was so icy that my lungs shrieked with pain, but as quickly as the water came in, it left. I glanced at Tag; our eyes met in the moonlight, and we held each other's gaze. Another wave had yet to crash, but I suddenly felt like I was going to sink and drown and die. "What a pretty place to fall," he echoed after a moment, and that was it—I rolled on top of him, took his gorgeous face in my dripping hands, and kissed his salty lips before the ocean overtook us again. This time, I didn't feel the cold cut through me, just Tag hooking his arm around me so we didn't get separated.

If we were going to wind up shipwrecked somewhere, it needed to be the same island.

We didn't last more than five minutes before our teeth started chattering.

With my mom and Josh at the prom, there was only one faint glimmer in my house—the fairy lights in my bedroom. Tag and I were caked in sand, but we didn't stop to hose off at the back spigot. We were too drunk on each other. "Towels," Tag mumbled as we stumbled up the stairs in the dark, my legs locked around his waist and his strong hands splayed across my shoulder blades. "We should at least get towels."

I kissed along his jawline. "They're in the bathroom."

"Really?" he asked, mouth on my collarbone. "The bathroom?"

"Yeah." I nodded. "The bathroom."

"Huh, never would've guessed."

We went straight to my room. Tag gently set me on the floor once he'd untangled his fingers from my mermaid hair. His too was disheveled, sticking up in all different directions. Our soaked clothes had become second skins since leaving the beach, now sealed to our bodies. Tag smiled and kissed me, this one sending a crackling current through my body. I knew he felt it too, because suddenly we were hurrying to undress each other. He peeled off his tux jacket while I feverishly unknotted his bow tie before going to work on his shirt's buttons. "Take it off," I breathed. "Please." I turned so he could undo my dress, my chest now heaving. "You should've seen the dance I did earlier."

After he fiddled with the zipper and slipped the dress over my head, I twirled back around, beaming. "Ta-da!"

Tag stared at me. Green eyes wide and head angled just so, like he was in awe. My pulse wavered, but I tried to play it cool.

"What?" I raised a suggestive eyebrow. "You've seen me like this before."

He silently shook his head.

I unclasped my strapless bra. "Yes, Tag, I'm pretty sure—"

"Lily."

My heart stopped when he said my name. All I could do was look at him too, shirtless in his dripping boxers. *This is different,* I realized with a deep ache. *After a year of so much secret pining, this is totally different.*

We moved toward each other again, but it wasn't long before I gently pushed him away. It took almost everything in me. He'd been kissing my neck, and my hands had been tugging his hair. "Where are you—don't—wait." He couldn't speak in full sentences. "Hold—Hops—on—"

"Relax, I'm getting something," I told him, then flicked his shoulder. "Something that wasn't on the Jester's packing list."

The tips of Tag's ears reddened, remembering our *almost* during the prank. I laughed and pulled open my top dresser drawer to find the small box of condoms. After first sleeping with Tag (and an honest discussion about it), my mom had left them in my room with a Post-it note attached. *Only with someone you love, Lily!*

To me, Taggart Swell was the only someone to love.

"What?" I asked after climbing into bed with him. He'd suspended his insulin again and was looking at me in amusement as he set his pump on my nightstand. I grinned. "What is it? Do I have seaweed in my hair?"

Tag kissed both my dimples. "Yes," he whispered, taking the sealed wrapper from me. "You do, actually."

I giggled into his neck. "Spare me *The Little Mermaid* lines."

"What about a song?" he suggested, sitting up and ripping open the condom. I drew slow stars around the freckles on his back. The seaweed could stay. "Wasn't it your childhood dream to play Ariel onstage?"

I didn't have an answer. Nothing witty or even partly clever came to mind, especially when he turned back and grinned at me.

That grin. God, that mischievous grin.

"I'm so happy we're here," he said a minute later, our limbs entwined under my covers. "I know it wasn't easy, but..." He held my gaze. "Aut viam inveniam aut facium."

"Find a way or make one," I agreed, and then we kissed before finding a rhythm that made me crest like an ocean wave.

TWENTY-NINE

"We can't fall asleep," I whispered.

"We won't fall asleep," Tag whispered back, even though his eyes were closed, and I could feel his heartbeat slowing as his fingertips grazed my ribs. "We have something to do."

"I know," I said, heart slightly sinking. "We have to get you back."

Because according to my retro alarm clock, it was 11:15. Josh was probably gritting his teeth on the prom bus. *Only forty-five more minutes!* I imagined my mom chanting in his ear.

I switched on my bedside lamp to see Tag yawn. "No, no," he said. "I meant we have something to do *before* that." He raked a hand through his hair. "This might be my last chance." He kissed my shoulder before getting out of bed, and while admiring the view, I saw his shoulders sag. "Shit, my clothes." He sighed and gestured at the sopping mess on the floor. "I don't think it's even possible to put on that tux."

"Well," I said brightly, "if you give me a little more intel regarding this secret mission of ours, you won't need to try…"

We left my house looking like we were off to meet the Jester at King's Court. I wore a dark sweatshirt and pulled up its hood to hide the hickeys that were blooming on my neck while Tag had buttoned up the Scotch-plaid flannel he'd let me borrow on prank night. It also hadn't taken me long to find a pair of black sweats he'd left behind in my closet last year. Tag drove the golf cart while I swatted his sleeve after we soared over the faculty neighborhood's speed bump. "What were you *thinking*?" I teased. "This is a residential area! Children are at play!"

He chuckled and cut the cart's ignition once we reached Hubbard Hall, and after a grand flourish of my mom's faculty ID, we snuck inside and made for the mail room. I watched Tag unlock his mailbox, shaking my head when he reached in and emerged with what looked like a single playing card. It had been taped to the mailbox's roof. "I wanted to be ready at a moment's notice," he explained.

"Sound logic." I nodded. "Here we are at exactly that."

Tag grinned. "This ritual is extremely sacred," he told me. "Every Jester taps their successor by slipping them *this*." He flashed me a joker card. "I never really wondered who tapped me."

I gave him a look. "Really?"

He shrugged. "Really."

"It doesn't feel appropriate for me to be here, though," I said. "I'm not the Jester."

"No, but you're still in the deck," Tag countered, then casually nodded his chin to the left. I caught his drift and shook my head when I unlocked my mailbox to find a different card. He laughed. "Hey, Bunker called you our crown jewel!"

I carefully slid the queen into my back pocket. Anyone else would say it was silly, but I believed it was also poetic. Tag and I had been broken, and these cards had brought us back together. "But I'm not a queen," I told him. "No matter what Bunker thinks, I'm definitely not. I'm just Lily." I took his hand. "I'm just Hopscotch."

Tag let out a long sigh. "I feel that," he said. "Because I don't want to be the joker anymore—on special occasions, maybe, but I'm so ready for someone else to be the Jester. I've gotta go back to being Tag."

I winked. "Who shall it be then?"

"That *is* the question..." he mused. "Although we both know there's only one answer."

And with that, he marched forward and tucked the joker card into Anthony DeLuca's mailbox. The first fac brat Jester—I was already proud of him. *No body, no crime,* I thought before we vanished from the mail room like ghosts.

The stars still shimmered outside, so Tag and I decided to walk the rest of the way to his dorm. He wanted to hold my hand but couldn't grasp it; I kept five steps between us, walking backward and smiling at him. "Come on," he said, reaching for me. "Come here."

I responded by melodramatically extending my arm, our fingers still not touching.

He groaned. "Hops!"

Even irked, his voice was everything.

"How about tag?" I grinned, but since I loved him, I dropped the teasing and stopped to wait...or so he *thought*. I had an end game. "You're it!" I exclaimed when he held out his hand, and I quickly kissed him before darting off up the street.

I knew he would follow.

He caught me from behind within ten seconds, snaking an arm around my waist and pulling me close. Sweet and spellbinding shivers went through me. "Yes," he murmured, lips brushing my ear. "You are."

ACKNOWLEDGMENTS

Okay, this book took a village to write and almost a decade to untangle *how* to write, so please, kindly give me a few minutes...

We'll start with the creative genius in the room: Taylor Swift. You will never read this, but I wish you would. I grew up singing along to your songs, and I still do—but now I also ardently admire and am inspired by you. If I have writer's block, you help smash it to bits. (Legally) incorporating your work into mine has been mind-boggling fun!

Thank you to my fabulous agent, Eva Scalzo. You are not only the most caring and considerate agent but also the most caring and considerate friend. When I needed my hand held last year, you squeezed it tightly. Thank you for answering all my texts and giving me such thoughtful life advice. It was an honor to sprinkle pieces of you throughout WHAM.

To Annie Berger, my editor: I can't believe we've been together for three books! As always, thank you for your guidance and insight; I have learned so much from you and look forward to our next collaboration. Although I apologize in advance for the extraneous detail and flashback action that I'm sure will be present in my first draft.

Everyone at Sourcebooks! Thea Voutiritsas, Madison Nankervis, Gabbi Calabrese, Laura Boren, and my cover artist Josephine Rais. It has been a pleasure working with you and bringing Lily's story to life. A special shout-out to Steph Bohrer for such an awesome cover reveal!

I am beyond grateful to my beta readers: Kelly Townsend, for staying up until all hours of the night reading. Never stop sending me stream-of-consciousness texts! Sarah DePietro, you are still my most trusted creative consultant (and a godmother too wonderful for words). And Kismet Jamison, thank you for reading a half-finished Word doc and encouraging me to keep going. You have no idea how much I needed that boost.

Micheal Perzi, for being one kick-ass woman! While our dynamic duo-ship was far too short, I enjoyed every conversation and consider you a mentor to this day. I wish you nothing but the best.

Thank you to my family at Barnes & Noble. I know I talk nonstop about the good, the bad, and the ugly of my writing and that I'm too stringent about shelving, but thank you for embracing it! Your support means the world to me. Paul Byrne, you are one of the kindest people I know, and I am incredibly fortunate to have you in my corner.

To Anthony Brambilla, for your art direction and spending hours on my website (I still can't believe I got away with only paying you in Chinese food). Thank you for the clowning around, the sight-sorting smackdowns, and for being my friend. #Yentas

Michael Atkins, I remember you hanging out in my dorm room while I drafted my novice manuscript. In some ways, it feels like yesterday, but as you love reminding me, it was actually a millennium ago. I smile at the hyperbole, thankful that you remain one of my closest confidants.

And Dan Heintz, for the *last time*, I did not name Daniel after you! Will you please believe me now that I've put it in writing? But fine, sure, okay, thank you for Tag's tattoo (and for loving my sister the way that you do).

Forever thanks to Madison Darby Palmer; there is no one I am more grateful to be friends with than you. I really did know after that tie-dye afternoon that our friendship would be a lifelong marathon, not a simple sprint. You are the Alex to my Tag, the Tag to my Alex. XO, K.

Christopher: Howdy, partner! Navy blue might be the best color, but I am so happy to be in the lavender haze with you (open a new tab and look it up). You see me, hear me, and support me—and man, do you make me laugh. I strive to do the same for you, recharge hugs and all.

My family. Ross and Mary Lou Webber, thank you for hosting several writing retreats! Long weekends in Haddonfield did wonders for my work, and watching the Olympics together will always have a special place in my heart. As one of eighteen grandchildren, I felt spoiled having my grandparents all to myself.

Timmy and Tommy Tibble, my siblings: I loved childhood with you, but I might love adulting with you even more. You are both clever, confident, and exceptional human beings. It's a privilege to watch you each make your way in the world, even if you still rib me every chance you get!

Thank you, Mom, for always encouraging me to return to this book's premise. You are its unrivaled champion, and after so many walks on the canal and the beach, here we are—holding it in our hands. None of this would've been possible without your love and support. I pitched Leda and Lily's relationship as Lorelai and Rory, but in every one of their scenes, I imagined Jen and Kaethe.

Dad, the original Jester. You lived such a life and were a masterful storyteller; it is no wonder we asked you to "tell us about the time you stole the yearbooks!" at the dinner table so often. It pains me that you cannot read this book, but I take comfort in the fact that I shared its first iteration with you. I remember you laughing and telling me I had something, and to this day, I know how proud you are of me.

Lastly, to the St. George's School Class of 1982: I'm sorry you didn't get answers until your tenth reunion, but in the end, wasn't it worth it?

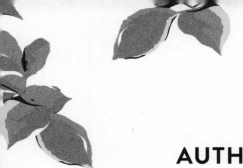

AUTHOR BIO

K. L. Walther was born and raised in the rolling hills of Bucks County, Pennsylvania, surrounded by family, dogs, and books. Her childhood was spent traveling the northeastern seaboard to play ice hockey. She attended a boarding school in New Jersey and went on to earn a BA in English from the University of Virginia. She is happiest on the beach with a book, cheering for the New York Rangers, or enjoying a rom-com while digging into a big bowl of popcorn and M&Ms. Find her on Instagram @klwalther9 or visit her at klwalther.com.

FIREreads

⑤ #getbooklit

Your hub for the hottest young adult books!

Visit us online and sign up for our
newsletter at FIREreads.com

 @sourcebooksfire

 sourcebooksfire

 firereads.tumblr.com